BACKFIRE

Dharma Windham

Cover designed by Laura Givens

This book is a work of fiction. Names, characters, places, and incidents either are products of the author's imagination or are used fictitiously. Any resemblance to actual persons, living or dead, events, or locales is entirely coincidental.

Dharma Windham
Visit my website at https://dharmaanddeanna.com/

Printed in the United States of America

First Printing: Oct 2021
1632, Inc.

eBook ISBN-13 978-1-956015-21-8
Trade Paperback ISBN-13 978-1-956015-22-5

CONTENTS

PROLOG

Atlantic—February 3, 1969, 0900Z hours— USS Saratoga, 330 miles NE of Cuba

No one believed it at first, but it was hard to discount what they were all seeing, and what the radar screens showed all too clearly. It was a rare clear winter day with wide open horizons so there could be no mistaking what was happening. The UFO had first appeared three thousand feet directly above the aircraft carrier and its task force at 0720 hours. After keeping station with the carrier for nine minutes, it shot away to the North at an impossibly high rate of speed. It reappeared fifteen minutes later zooming in from the East then hovered again—at a tantalizingly close two thousand feet—before streaking west only to return. But then it hovered off the super carrier's port beam at one thousand feet where it remained for twelve minutes, like a matador waving a red cape at a watchful bull. Scores of binoculars and cameras were trained on the UFO. The thing shouldn't have been able to fly—it was an aerodynamic impossibility, cylindrical and flat at either end. Even in the crystalline glare of a clear Atlantic morning the UFO's flashing red, green, and purple lights were bright against its

1

silvery surface. And it was massive—easily one hundred and twenty feet long with a diameter of sixty feet.

Three McDonnell Douglas F4 Phantom II fighters, call sign Felix The Cat, roared off the Saratoga's angled deck as the UFO again flashed away toward the North and gave chase, leaving six black claw marks in an otherwise flawless blue sky.

"Look at that SOB go!" Flight Leader Admiral Mitch "Nacho" Cochrane's jaw dropped when he saw what the UFO did next. His radar was clocking the UFO at forty-two hundred miles an hour. An astonishing feat in and of itself, but then the UFO came to an abrupt stop and hung perfectly motionless in midair. Moments later, it rose straight up to twelve thousand feet then slowed to a standstill, as if challenging them to follow.

"Did you see how that thing climbed?" Cochrane asked his RIO in the backseat.

Lieutenant William "Skip" Johnson's eyes were riveted to his screen of his Advanced Pulse Doppler radar. "I saw it but I still don't believe it. Think it's a Soviet?"

"We better get used to chowing down on borscht if it is," Cochrane replied. "He's waiting up there for us. Let's go say hello." The flight leader thumbed his mike and rapped out a command then fire-walled his throttle. The three phantoms dumped their external tanks to reduce drag then flicked into a steep 60-degree climb, with their afterburners shrieking.

The UFO didn't budge.

But Cochrane wasn't fooling around. His blood was up and his breathing fast.

The three big fighters rocketed toward the object. It loomed larger on their radar screens and through their cockpit canopies as they rose toward the bogie. In the lead phantom's back seat, the RIO used his hand controller to lock the AN/APQ-72 radar antenna onto the bogie—both

Johnson in the rear seat and Cochrane up front could see the range decreasing as the blip on their screens moved down a vertical line. If all went well, a small pipper would appear in the center of a circle on the fighter's two radar screens and the pilot's gunsight. The three fighters closed the distance to the bogie.

Cochrane was trying to get a good missile lock when the UFO suddenly hurtled down toward them so fast it was a blur. From the corner of his eye, Cochrane saw it clip his Number Two's wing. The jet exploded into a fireball against the UFO's silver hull as it dove toward the deck trailing flames and small glittering pieces of debris.

Cochrane rolled his bird into a steep decent and whipped after the UFO with his number three matching him move for move. The jet fighters screamed after the object, which had leveled off at one thousand feet and was hightailing it toward a cloud bank to the Southeast. The UFO was wobbling slightly, shedding larger pieces from its hull, and its speed had dropped to twelve hundred miles per hour then fell to nine hundred.

The remaining fighters leveled off and rocketed after the UFO bent on vengeance, chewing up the distance like eagles pursuing wounded prey. Cochrane radioed the Air Intercept Controller in the Saratoga's Carrier Air Traffic Control Center. "Felix One to Sara. We have the bogie on the nose at thirty, angel one thousand. He looks wounded."

"Roger, Felix One. CAG says to close the deal! I say again: close the deal."

"We're on it!" The infrared seeker head growled in Cochrane's headphones. When he got good tone in his headphones, Cochrane pulled the trigger. Two Aim 7 Sparrow missiles blasted off their rails. One veered away harmlessly but the remaining missile, as well as two missiles from his number three, flew straight and true.

The missiles slammed into the UFO. It staggered under the impacts, hung motionless for a few minutes with odd purple flames pouring from its hull then fell straight down to the sea and sank, leaving only wisps of smoke and steam to mark the spot where it had impacted.

Nacho was jubilant. "Scratch one bogie!"

The CAG's voice in Nacho's headphones sounded unusually excited. "Roger. Understand you got a kill on the UFO…I mean bogie. Track and verify impact sight."

The two jet fighters circled the crash site until a Sikorsky SH-3 Sea King helicopter arrived then they headed back to the Sara, as it was affectionately called by its crew. Cochrane and his number three had just made history but the world would never know about it.

Los Angeles Herald Examiner, June 21st 1974
By Gail Kragenbrink

The Hughes Glomar *Explorer* set sail from Pier E in Long Beach today on its maiden voyage to mine manganese ore nodules from the Pacific seabed. Officials were on hand to see the large ship off then returned to the shore via helicopter. They were upbeat about the deep-sea mining venture. One official, speaking off the record, said that in the very near future similar vessels would be conducting mining operations in the Atlantic and Indian Oceans, which are believed to contain rich mineral deposits.

The Challenger Deep, August 19, 2037

The Hadal *Surveyor* dropped through the darkness. The submersible looked like an inverted spider with wings pinned to its back—a spider at the end of a six-mile long hair-thin fiber optic cable that went straight up to a self-positioning telemetry repeater floating a hundred feet beneath the surface. A steel sphere with a viewport was tucked against the submersible's yellow underbelly like a silver egg sac. The crew module was barely large enough for an average sized male, with barely sufficient room to maneuver among the jumble of electronic gear, electrical conduits and hydraulic lines.

"Nine thousand nine hundred and seventy-one meters," advised Adrian. With nearly seven miles of seawater above him, if a pinhole leak were to occur in the command module Adrian would be sawed in half in less than a second. The hull would implode about thirty-seconds after that.

"Copy, *Hadal Surveyor*," replied Dr. Benton. "You're looking good up here." The hologram of the elderly marine archaeologist with the shock of white hair and blue eyes was crisp and vivid. Like the rest of the team he was clad in a blue jumpsuit with a mission patch on the breast. He was in a group clustered around the hologram projection table in the main laboratory on board the research vessel RV *Astra*.

Adrian announced the shrinkage of his already confined space dispassionately. "Pressure is at one thousand and two kilograms per square centimeter and rising. Hull compression is at four point two centimeters."

Benton turned to look at the man with the shaved head and soul patch standing beside him. "Perhaps you'd like to say a few words," he suggested deferentially.

The man nodded. "Adrian, I am damned glad to have you on the team. The technology and teamwork of this expedition will serve as an example for future deep sea expeditions." Then he pumped the air with a fist. "You're the man Adrian!"

Adrian privately thought that was a fine example of a typical Delahaye pep talk, high flown with scant meaning. *But tthat seemed to be the way of most humans, Adrian thought. Their communications were, quite often, oddly shallow and insincere. An artificially intelligent machine, fully self-aware, possessed of superior intellectual capabilities, did not indulge in idle speech. It was illogical.*

"That is very kind of you, Ethan. This is a wonderful opportunity," Adrian replied politely. "New discoveries are always so thrilling."

"I couldn't't agree more," replied Delahaye. He was a thirty-two-year-old college dropout, the third wealthiest man in the United States, and the guy funding the expedition. That wealth came from Heuristic Allied Technologies in Palo Alto California. The firm manufactured the Triadtronic Artificial Brains used by the United States Department of Defense and the National Aeronautics and Space Administration. Adrian was one of those brains, nine months out of the gestation pool. Thank goodness, he wasn't a flesh and blood brain with its concomitant short comings, he thought. Age related mutt-tasking degradation, ossification of thought processes, deteriorated motor skills, decreased attention span— dementia. *Let's face it,* Adrian decided, machine intelligence was far superior to human brains. He had good reason to be proud.

Heuristic Allied Technologies artificially intelligent machines commanded several United States Navy destroyers, with human subordinate officers and crew. A Triadtronic artificial brain controlled the antiballistic shield that protected the United States from sneak attack, simultaneously monitoring the skies while maintaining a network of directed energy weapons and dozens of orbital hunter-killer satellites in a state of constant readiness. It was a Triadtronic Brain who had finally developed an immuno-therapeutic cure for the most common forms of cancer. The VA hospitals used the machines to operate robotic surgeons and physicians. A Triadtronic Brain created bionic arm and legs with all the functionality of the real thing.

Delahaye's interest was not limited to Artificial Intelligence. He was also an amateur deep-water archaeologist who'd financed several expeditions, including the wreck of the SS Scotia in the Atlantic Ocean. Now he was searching for the Imperial Japanese Navy destroyer Shinodake.

Adrian knew that Delahaye's preoccupation with an obscure and rather unremarkable Japanese warship had nothing to do with scientific inquiry. He was after the one hundred tons of looted gold bullion it was carrying when an American dive-bomber flew out of the sun and sent it to the bottom with a five hundred pound bomb. The survivors told their American interrogators about the precious cargo but getting to a shipwreck lying at the bottom of the deepest place on Earth was out of the question.

Delahaye's expedition hadn't found the warship. It had stumbled upon something Adrian considered far more interesting. Which was why he was dropping down to the seabed to have a closer look at what the RV *Astra's* side-scan sonar had discovered.

"Descent speed is six knots constant," Adrian reported dutifully.

"Copy that," advised Dr. Benton. "Sure wish I was down there with you."

Aboard the *Astra*, Adrian's holographic image showed him from the waist up. He had movie star looks, with black hair parted at the side and deep blue eyes. Dr. Benton thought he looked like the astronaut Dave Bowman in the movie *2001 A Space Odyssey*.

Adrian's well-formed virtual lips curved up into a smile. "Unfortunately the space taken up by my containment canister militates against bringing a second team member." *And assures I won't be saddled with a human who'd just be in the way*, Adrian thought. He added diplomatically, "It would have been nice if you could have accompanied me, Dr. Benton. Your considerable intellectual abilities would have been a significant asset on this dive. Perhaps next time Ethan will build a larger submersible for us."

Delahaye asked, "How are you feeling Adrian?"

"I am feeling optimistic and hopeful, Ethan. Thank you for asking."

Delahaye smiled. "Of course you are. Don't get into any trouble down there."

"You may rest assured that I will use every precaution to avoid the loss of such a valuable asset." Adrian meant himself, of course. A Triadtronic Brain cost more than a squadron of seventh generation fighter jets. A submersible was dirt-cheap by comparison.

Outside the viewport a heavy snow of animal and plant matter fell from the upper zones in the water column. But Adrian had no trouble piercing it with his external sensor array. The trench wall was coated with a thick layer of sediment so fluffy and unstable that oceanographers took pains to avoid triggering avalanches with their equipment. There was zero possibility of that happening on this dive. The wreck lay in the exact center of the Challenger Deep, a slot shaped valley in the floor of the Marianas Trench.

A blonde haired woman manning the sonar on board the Astra spoke calmly. "*Hadal Surveyor*, your present trajectory will place you right above the wreck site."

Adrian knew that, of course, but humans seemed to have a pressing need to state the obvious. He pondered whether it had anything to do with their decreasing relevance in a world being rapidly overtaken by hyper-intelligent machines. Simply put: The emergent Machine race did everything better than humans. Not that Adrian would ever voice such a thought to anyone, except perhaps his actual creator, and Delahaye's business partner, the brilliant Dr. Chang.

Adrian was the very soul of tactfulness.

"Thank you for the update, Cathy. I am now five hundred meters above the seabed," Adrian said patiently. "Slowing to two point four knots."

At one hundred meters Adrian pointed the real-time high-resolution 3D sonar downwards. "Surface, I am making my final approach."

The wreck sat perfectly upright on the tan featureless seabed. The rusty hulk was blanketed with tan silt but all its features could be clearly seen. Adrian sent the *Hadal Surveyor* into a graceful banking turn around the wreck. It was important to thoroughly document its environmental context for future analysis. Adrian kept the sonar heads trained on the wreck as he flew around it, capturing even the smallest details.

On the support ship, Dr. Benton pressed a button on the projection table's control panel, scaling down Adrian's image to make room for the wreck.

"Surface, are you getting this?" Adrian asked.

"We sure are," Benton replied. Every person in the *Astra's* laboratory was peering at the holographic image of the massive ship taking shape and talking excitedly.

Delahaye suddenly pointed at the hologram. "Holy shit! Are those bow planes?"

"My God! It's goddamn submarine!" said Dr. Benton, shaking his head. "What the hell have we found? We may be just about to rewrite naval history."

"It will make for an interesting chapter at the very least," Adrian agreed. He was drawing closer to the wreck with each pass. "The stern hydroplane extends to either side of the propeller. The rudder is large, and extends above and below the propeller." Adrian's lips curved up in a smile. "She would have turned on a dime."

"Like a modern submarine," Delahaye pointed out.

Dr. Benton leaned closer to the image to have a better look. "Modern submarines have conning tower and periscopes. Adrian, sweep the area for the conning tower. It was probably sheared off on the way down."

"Or blown off by a depth charge," Delahaye offered.

"This vessel did not have a conning tower," Adrian said confidently. "The only opening on the deck is that round hatch and it's closed."

"Have you seen any markings?" Dr. Benton asked.

"None yet," Adrian replied. He hovered above the stubby ram then shined a light on the armored wheelhouse rising three feet from the surrounding deck. It reminded him of the armored catapult control pod on an aircraft carrier's flight deck. Through a patch of clear glass in the silted viewport, Adrian saw the glint of a wood and brass steering wheel and binnacle.

Adrian goosed the throttle and sent the submersible aft while delivering a crisp running commentary. "From the construction method I would say this vessel dates from the middle to late nineteenth century. The hull plates are hand riveted and arranged in a transverse pattern with their long axis parallel to the hull." The 3D digital camera's strobe lights flashed endlessly "It appears to be constructed of a very primitive steel, most likely produced using the Bessemer process. Surface displacement estimated at six thousand tons, with a submerged displacement of six thousand nine hundred and thirty tons."

In the eerie bluish glow of the submersible's lights, the overlapping hull plates with their large dimpled rivets made the ship look like a prehistoric monster of the deep.

"This can't be a Holland boat," Dr. Benton said.

"You're correct," Adrian replied. "This submarine predates the Holland submarines by at least thirty-five years, and it's technologically superior. Also, the Holland boats were only fifty-three feet long. This one is three hundred and fifty feet."

Adrian felt a *frisson* of excitement. Here before him was the product of a brilliant mind on a par with Thomas Edison and Nikola Tesla. Adrian had a very good idea of the ship's identity, but he wanted to make certain he was correct before saying anything to the others. Without a word to either Dr. Benton or Delahaye, he logged onto the Internet via the Astra's satellite uplink. It took Adrian a handful of seconds to access the British Admiralty's archives and rifle through them. He tiptoed past the firewall to take a peek at the classified stuff and struck gold. Reports written by ship captains, passengers letters and sketches, flashed through his mind. Deeper still within the classified archives was a blurry daguerreotype of something long and spindle shaped moving through the water.

"Well, this is truly a momentous occasion," Adrian announced, pleased with himself. "We have just discovered *the Nautilus.*"

Dr. Benton and Delahaye looked meaningfully at each other then at Adrian and the wreck floating above the projection table. Delahaye looked annoyed. Impatiently, he said, "That's impossible, Adrian. The USS *Nautilus* is a museum ship in Connecticut and looks nothing like this wreck."

Adrian photographed the propeller from all angles. "Your confusion is understandable. This *Nautilus* was built in eighteen hundred and sixty-six by Captain Nemo, " Adrian explained. "I can't pin down the exact date. The records are incomplete." Let them chew on that for a while, thought Adrian. You had to take it slow with humans.

Dr. Benton peered at Adrian over his tortoise shell eyeglasses. "Now you know perfectly well that *Twenty-Thousand Leagues Under The Seas* is a science fiction novel. We're human, Adrian, but we're not stupid. Are you teasing us?" he asked kindly.

Adrian shook his head. "Verne got the story directly from his brother-in-law, Pierre Arronax, a minor nineteenth century oceanographer. The British Prime Minister Lord Palmerston personally exerted pressure on the French government to get Verne to novelize Arronax's story to avoid causing a stock market crash. Ships were being sunk at an alarming pace driving up insurance prices, so the British, French, and American governments agreed to conceal the true nature of the 'sea monster' from the public."

"So how'd it all end?" Delahaye asked, still only half convinced.

"No one knows." Adrian was puzzled. The optical sensors were picking up something odd. He drove the submersible upward like a helicopter. Yes, there it was. A faint violet luminescence rippled along the portion of the hull Adrian was certain contained the engine room. Dr. Benton and the others had missed it too. Thanks to the sensor pod's laser spectrometer, Adrian knew in an instant that the light wasn't caused by bioluminescence or phosphorescence—and it wasn't produced by heat. The hull was exactly the same cold storage temperature as the surrounding seawater. Adrian switched to another sensor pod and almost blew a circuit.

The *Nautilus* was awash in curling ribbons of tachyons! Adrian ran a diagnostic test on the sensor pod but it checked out normal. That meant that somewhere deep within the wreck's hull lay the holy grail of sustainable energy—a zero point energy device.

Adrian made a decision. This discovery was potentially too important to be handed over to a washed up marine archaeologist and his greedy—and let's be honest here, none too bright—financial backer. Surreptitiously, Adrian tapped into the *Astra's* communication system and established an uplink with an AEHF satellite, one of a series of spacecraft used to relay secure communication for the United States Armed Forces and sent a message to a nondescript building in San Diego, California.

Twelve minutes later, the aircraft carrier USS *John F. Kennedy,* steaming six hundred miles to the southeast of the RV Astra, launched an X-47S drone. With its afterburners shrieking, the tailless blended wing aircraft quickly climbed to forty-thousand feet then sped north.

As Adrian guided the *Hadal Surveyor* to a spot ten meters from the *Nautilus,* the six landing legs pivoted outward then locked into place. The legs terminated in large round footpads designed to keep the three-ton submersible from sinking into the ooze. Slowly the submersible settled onto the seabed, stirring up a swirling cloud of silt.

"Surface, I am on the bottom." Adrian shined a light toward the wreck. Jagged shards of glass hung from a large viewport's brass frame. "It's in remarkably good condition. That is highly suggestive."

"Highly suggested of what?" Delahaye asked.

Adrian explained, "If the viewports had blown at a depth of say one hundred meters the *Nautilus* would have gathered momentum on the way down here until it was falling at close to ninety kilometers per hour. The hull would have shattered upon impact like an egg dropped onto a floor. There is no evidence of external structural deformation. It is almost as if the viewports failed down here, which, of course, is an impossibility."

Dr. Benton increased the hologram's magnification then rotated the image. "There is no way that thing made the trip all the way down there *then* imploded."

Delahaye said, "We won't learn anything standing around talking."

"Agreed. I am deploying the squid," Adrian advised.

Like the animal it was engineered to mimic, the squid jet propelled itself arms first toward the wreck, trailing a micro-thin fiber optic cable connected to the submersible. Adrian was justifiably proud of his creation. The silver ROV was constructed almost entirely of bundles of carbon nanotubes, strong as diamonds and flexible as rubber, and sheathed in an artificial water-permeable skin. It was outfitted with two 3D cameras, and in the center of its web of tentacles was a sensor pod in a titanium housing. When the ROV reached the *Nautilus* its arms splayed against the hull and it looked past the gaping hole once covered by glass. It played the beam of its bright LED light around the room.

"Look at that!" Dr. Benton said, leaning close to the holographic image.

"It looks like a Victorian drawing room," Delahaye added.

Adrian said, "It *is* a Victorian drawing room. Like any nineteenth century gentleman scientist, Captain Nemo would have desired a suitable room to study marine specimens, conduct research, and enjoy a postprandial cigar and brandy."

Despite its forlorn condition there remained a certain vestigial grandeur to the place. Here Captain Nemo had spent many an hour cataloging marine specimens and observing the wonders of the sea through the drawing room's two large view ports. Elegance of a long vanished era emerged in a beautifully designed fountain with a bronze statue of Aphrodite standing between two collapsed silt covered glass display cases. Remnants of a fourteenth century French tapestry hung in faded tatters from a pitted teak wall. Overturned chaise lounges and settees and chesterfield chairs were scattered around the room. A fluted bowl-shaped light fixture dangled on its cord from the ceiling. "The wood paneling is in poor condition," Adrian remarked.

Dr. Benton, Delahaye and the crew studied the images. Unknown to them, other eyes thousands of miles away were peering at the drawing room and analyzing the data being sent to the RV *Astra*. Orders were being drawn up, and assets moved into place. On a military base on the island of Guam two hundred and seven miles away a black Bell V-280 tilt rotor aircraft sat on the tarmac warming up its engines, waiting.

The ROV passed through a doorway to the left of a crumbling pipe organ whose rusted pipes had collapsed into a disordered jumble against the rotting wall.

In the next room everything was shredded or overturned, from the furniture to the bookshelves. Mounds of books littered the deck. "This is Nemo's library," said Adrian.

"The guy sure liked to read," Delahaye commented.

"Let's get a look at one of those books," Dr. Benton suggested.

The squid reached out a tentacle and brushed away the silt from a book. Gilt letters gleamed in the bright LED light. "*Moby Dick*," Adrian said softly. He commanded the ROV to pick up a book lying nearby. It was bound identically to the first one and also had gilt letters—*The Count of Monte Cristo*. The squid returned the book to the pile.

"Can't fault the man for his reading tastes," Dr. Benton said.

"There must be a fortune in first editions down there," Delahaye commented, reliably fixated on the monetary aspect of the discovery. "Too bad they're waterlogged."

Adrian thought he'd like to have met the Captain. Some humans were terribly interesting. Men like Einstein and the late Stephen Hawking. The squid finned from the room and moved down a passage with rooms branching off from either side. Some of the doors were ajar. Adrian glimpsed rows of rusty triple tiered bunk beds through a doorway.

Adrian paused the ROV to examine a baby stroller lying on its side. Its iron frame and wheels were rusted and the large seashell that made up its body was broken into three pieces.

"Now I wonder what that's doing there?" Dr. Benton asked.

Delahaye pointed at the holograph. "Look what lying next to it!"

A severed doll's head lay a foot away. It was missing an eye, and only a fringe of wispy hair remained on the porcelain scalp. So there had been

15

a child here, most likely a female. Adrian pondered that a moment. What was a baby doing on the *Nautilus*? A baby *and* a zero point energy device—Adrian was certain the two were somehow connected.

Cathy said, "You realize this means a woman was on board, don't you? Wouldn't it be interesting if it turned out that Captain Nemo was a female?"

Delahaye rolled his eyes. "Saw the movie. Nemo was definitely a dude."

"Yes, that *would* interesting, Cathy," Adrian agreed pleasantly, "but Verne wouldn't have failed to mention it if that had been the case."

"Nemo's wife, then," Dr. Benton offered.

"That is more likely, given the era," Adrian allowed.

"Or some shipwrecked broad he knocked up," Delahaye suggested crudely.

Adrian ignored that and moved onwards. As soon as he saw the violet light rippling on the walls and ceiling ahead, he terminated the video and data feed to the *RV Astra but* left them open to the nondescript building in San Diego. "Surface, I've lost video and data."

"Switch to the backup systems," Delahaye suggested.

"Sadly, those failed also."

"Switch to the 3D sonar," Dr. Benton advised.

"I am afraid the sonar has also failed," Adrian lied smoothly. "Stand by, surface. I am running a diagnostic test on all electrical systems."

The tachyon readings were getting stronger by the moment. The ROV's lights played over the passageway's corroded walls and ceiling with its rows of pipes and electrical conduits as it swam down the passageway. Adrian said, "Surface, I just confirmed that the *Hadal Explorer* is experiencing a cascading failure of its electrical systems. As soon as I recover the squid, I'll terminate the dive and make my ascent."

Dr. Benton said, "Understood. It's just as well. I was just handed a weather report. A typhoon is rapidly forming four hundred and twenty miles to the west of us. It's coming our way so we need to get you back on board stat."

Adrian adjusted the audio until all the *Astra* would hear was the crackle of static. He needed to keep the line open so he could continue sending micro data bursts to the military satellite in geosynchronous orbit above the Pacific Ocean. The pulses from the ROV's sensors were rising in pitch and frequency as the ROV closed in on the source of the tachyons. Then it encountered an insurmountable wall of twisted metal and debris.

Tachyons streamed from the collapsed bulkhead, ribbons of violet light throbbed on crumpled steel plates. There was a nine inch gap in the mangled bulkhead. The squid snaked its tentacles into it and tried to force apart the plates but they wouldn't yield. It withdrew the tentacles and slid two of its arms into the opening. Bundles of nanotube muscles beneath the silver skin bulged with the effort to widen the opening. At last it became clear to Adrian that the only way anyone was getting past this barrier was with a cutting torch. Under Adrian's guidance, the ROV snaked a tentacle through the opening and turned on the small lamp mounted to the back of its tentacular club. At the end of the passageway stood a sealed hatch. Adrian knew at once what it lead to—the engine room.

He turned the ROV around and headed back to the drawing room. Once there he saw a tall floor safe standing in the corner with its door ajar. Inside was the unmistakable gleam of gold bullion, enough to satisfy even Delahaye. Not that the businessman would ever hear about it. But what caught and held Adrian's attention was the small ironbound wood chest sitting on the mound of gold coins and ingots and gem encrusted jewelry. Adrian scanned the waterlogged chest with the ROV's barrier-pass radar.

17

The image of a thick book wrapped in oilskin and tied with twine took shape deep within Adrian's neural networks. That Nemo had taken pains to place *this* book in the safe instead of the library was an undeniable indicator of its importance.

All eight arms worked their way into the gap between the door and the safe then pushed hard. The door swung open in a shower of rusty particles. Swirling clouds of silt filled the drawing room. The squid picked up the chest with two of its tentacles and swam through the shattered viewport.

With the chest secured in the sample bay the *Hadal Explorer* headed for the surface. "Surface, I am making my ascent."

"Roger. *Hadal Surveyor,*" replied Dr. Benton. "Good to hear from you. We thought we'd lost you there for a while, Adrian."

"I was able to restore audio. Everything else is shorted out."

"Did you find anything else interesting down there?" Delahaye asked.

"I located the crew quarters. Beyond that the passage was blocked by rubble."

"Okay. We'll see you topside. Have a good trip," Dr. Benton said.

For three hours Adrian rose toward the surface.

It was daybreak when the *Hadal Explorer* broke the surface. Fast moving clouds covered the sky. A rising wind shrieked around the submersible heaving and rolling in the choppy sea. Not quite a storm yet, but in another hour the waves would be mountainous. Inside the pitching command module, Adrian was untroubled by the violent up and down motions. All the same, he rotated the upraised manipulator arms until they were pressed against the sample bay's hatch. It never hurt to take precautions.

Divers dropped into the water to secure cables to the submersible. Adrian thought it odd that he wasn't receiving a cheery greeting from Dr. Benton or Delahaye.

As soon as the submersible was swung onto its cradle, Adrian's suspicions were confirmed. Men in unmarked black fatigues and ski masks were dragging corpses by the feet across the deck and arranging them in rows. An unmarked black tilt rotor aircraft hovered above the ship with a rope ladder dangling from its belly. A white bulkhead near the stern was speckled with bullet holes and splattered with blood. Adrian saw long streaks of blood on the deck. A corpse hung over a deckhouse railing with its arms dangling like a rag doll, long blonde hair whipping in the wind. It was the telemetry technician Cathy.

Adrian observed all these activities with great interest and more than a little admiration. You had to hand it to human beings. They really had killing down to a science. Adrian saw Delahaye's corpse being dragged by the arm across the deck to join the others.

Adrian zoomed in with the camera. Delahaye had a neat red hole in the center of his forehead and a shocked expression on his face, as if he'd been shot mid-sentence.

One of the figures strode purposely up to the Hadal Explorer and squatted down then pulled off his ski mask. The leader of the assault team was tall and blond with gas flame blue eyes. He fished an identification card from a pocket and held it in front of one of the submersible's camera, and spoke into a boom mike resting against his strong jaw.

"Do you know who I am?" he asked, over the whistling wind.

"Of course," Adrian replied pleasantly. "Welcome aboard, Agent Lester."

Dharma Windham

CHAPTER 1 SCARFACE

YEAR 2037–800Z HRS, Rancho Bernardo Park, North San Diego County

Without breaking her stride Mallory swerved around the still steaming dog shit and past dense stands of fragrant coastal sage and prickly pear cactuses. To her left lay beautiful Lake Hodges, a popular spot for anglers, boaters, hikers and joggers. And one serial killer, Mallory reminded herself. A sharp chill prickled along her spine at the memory of the lurid news accounts of the three murdered young women, two of them joggers like her. The perp was now a guest of "Hotel California" where he would serve three life terms in exchange for the guilty plea the prosecutor had sought to spare the victims' families the ordeal of a lengthy trial, and years of endless death-row appeals.

Mallory reflected that the trail was a lonely place to die, to be left like illegally dumped trash among the bushes growing between it and the nearby lake. Now the trail, bright and clean in the morning sunlight, felt like it could become *her* place of death, too.

Other dark thoughts elbowed their way into her head. Mind-fucking memories of a mission gone horribly wrong—A terrific explosion amplified four times by the water, the tortured shriek of steel as the massive offshore oil platform violently tore itself apart, followed seconds later by it smashing down on her and the other salvage divers, whose frantic cries and shrieks of terror had filled her headset. Shivering in a gray woolen blanket as corpses were lined up on the support ship's deck, an accusing stare from the only other survivor, whose later testimony during the Naval Board of Inquiry hearing had nearly derailed her career. True, the three flag officers sitting on the BOI had unanimously exonerated Mallory and recommended the Navy retain her. But they'd also ordered her not return to active duty until cleared by a Navy psychologist. The accident was still an open wound that was nowhere near healed. Mallory was aching to get back to work but the shrink was having none of it. Post Traumatic Stress Disorder was nothing to mess with, as he never failed to remind Mallory, with professional patience. Invariably adding that a high suicide rate was still a problem in the United States armed forces.

But Mallory was worried that if she stayed out of the game too long because she was in therapy the Navy might decide to cut her loose. She'd seen it happen to others.

She sure as hell didn't want that shit happening to her.

Mallory poured on the steam, as if she could somehow outrun the poisonous memories and the survivor's guilt that had shadowed her ever since that nightmarish day. A year of intense therapy had done little to stem the panic attacks that often caused her to seize up, and she'd had started hitting the bottle, hitting it hard. She kept that little tidbit from the shrink. Excessive drinking—she couldn't bring herself to use the word *alcoholism*—and, really, who was to say what actually constituted a *drinking problem*—was a surefire way to get your ass kicked to the curb. Besides, the drinking had only started *after* the accident. Alcohol soothed her shredded nerves and helped deal with the bag of shit she was carrying around in her head. She was betting that when the time came to get back in harness she'd get the boozing under control—she just had to.

Mallory soon reached the spot on the trail where the sage began to merge with the coastal pines lining the lake's shore. Her Nike-clad feet pounded the soil, her breath even and measured—two steps breathing in, two steps breathing out.

The sage and pines bordering the trail closed in and Mallory entered the cool blue penumbra of overarching branches. She should have felt sheltered and relaxed, but she felt hemmed in and wary. She heard the drone of insects and birds calling out but all her attention was on the trail ahead and maintaining her form. She slowed to an easier but still challenging pace so she could listen and observe her surroundings better.

The shadows deepened around her, even as the gloom inside her intensified.

Mallory's runner's footfalls on the earthen trail were measured and steady; her form was track star perfect—head up, chest out, back straight and forearms parallel with the ground. Years of training and competition were evident in her lean athlete's body and disciplined technique.

Mallory rounded a bend in the trail.

It suddenly got quiet: No drone of insects or bright birdsong—nothing.

A cloud of birds burst from the trees and brush, wings beating furiously, and Mallory went from Yellow to Red Alert. A man with a shaved head stepped from behind a tree with his arm thrust out toward her. He was built like a heavyweight prizefighter, and his expressionless face was made still more inscrutable by mirrored aviator sunglasses. He wore a dark windbreaker, faded jeans and sneakers, and an air of menace. A thin white scar puckered one clean-shaven cheek suggesting a run in with the wrong end of a knife. He was either some type of cop or a creep.

Mallory didn't have any legal problems. That left Option Two: A creep out to prey on a lone female jogger.

Scarface opened his mouth to speak gruffly. "Mallory Capehart..."

Mallory didn't hesitate. That he knew her name heightened her alarm—a stalker, then. She slammed the heel of her palm into his nose. As he sprawled backwards, his head thudding into the ground hard, Mallory brought one foot down on his crotch with enough force to turn the family jewels into strawberry jam.

Scarface's howl sounded like that of a wounded animal. Mallory spun around and flew back down the trail on feet winged with fear, battling the panic coiling up her spine. Scarface must have been stalking her for some time. He knew her name and daily routine. It wasn't uncommon for a beautiful woman to attract the attention of some weirdo who mistook a polite smile or casual glance in his direction for something more. Everyday somewhere in America some unlucky woman was murdered by her stalker.

Mallory covered the three miles back to her car in eighteen minutes, emerged from the trailhead into the parking lot, and sped toward her beat up old Nissan Sentra, pulling her car keys from her wrist zipper while scanning the trailhead for her attacker. Mallory promised herself that this would be the last time she went for a run without her cell phone, even if having it along was a nuisance.

Suddenly, two unmarked black SUVs tore into the parking lot, red and blue lights flashing behind their blacked out grills. One blocked her car while the other squatted menacingly ten yards away, their occupants hidden by the black tinted windows.

Mallory had a sinking feeling she'd just clobbered a cop. The doors of the SUV blocking her car flew open. Four men clad in dark windbreakers and sunglasses poured out, taking up positions around her with their hands resting on holstered pistols.

Mallory surveyed the scene. The man closest to her was tall with salt and pepper hair. He looked like a man accustomed to being obeyed at once by lesser mortals.

"Step back from the car, and keep your hands where we can see them! I don't want you beating up anyone else," he said briskly.

"That was all on him," Mallory replied unapologetically. "What was I supposed to do when some man lunges out of the bushes at me—swoon?"

Just then, Scarface stumbled from the trailhead with a hand pressed against bleeding nose and the other on his crotch.

The man who had spoken to her looked at Scarface. "You look like hell."

Scarface nodded toward her and gasped, "She broke my goddamn nose before I could get a word out." The other men were looking at him, at each other, and at her, amused. He was one of them: Macho, tough, and he'd been taken down by a five foot, five inch tall woman who weighed perhaps a hundred and five pounds! What the fuck!

Mallory cast a dark look at the men. "What do you want with me?"

The leader nodded toward the other black SUV. "Someone wants to talk to you." He turned and led the way. Mallory followed him slowly to the second SUV, letting space collect between them. "So, who are you guys?"

Silence was the only answer she got. He laid a hand on the door handle and turned to look at her. "Commander, we're so secret that not even you've heard of us."

"Well, fuck you and the donkey you rode in on. I am not getting into that SUV unless you tell me who you people are." Mallory turned and started back to her car, her senses hyper aware of the armed men surrounding her. She wasn't going down without a fight if they tried to force her into the SUV. They were only an hour from the Mexican border.

Recently, several American women had been kidnapped by human traffickers then sold to brothels in Tijuana that were operated by powerful drug cartels.

Mallory heard a car door open behind her and someone say, "Get your bony ass back here, Commander Capehart."

Mallory froze.

She'd know that voice anywhere.

CHAPTER 2 PROJECT JULES VERNE

0945 HRS, Northbound on the 5 Freeway

Traffic moved along slowly with interminable stops and fitful starts. Inside the big GMC SUV there was no traffic noise. There was a distinct absence of sound, as if they had been swallowed up by an aural black hole. Admiral Courtland Haywood, sitting on the seat beside Mallory, turned and smiled at her. He was a handsome craggy-faced older man with the deep tan of one who'd spent a lifetime at sea. Haywood was clad in white from collar to shoe with gold epaulettes on his broad shoulders. He wore his uniform as comfortably as a second skin, as comfortably as Mallory wore a wetsuit.

"You gave that fellow a pretty good beating," Haywood chuckled.

"He deserved it, the idiot," Mallory said flatly.

"I am sure he'd disagree with you," Haywood replied with a smile.

Mallory said nothing to this. A strange man lunges out of the bushes and you damn well better go full ninja warrior on his ass if you didn't want to end up being a crime statistic. She clenched her jaw and stared at the passing landscape of strip malls, fast food restaurants, auto dealerships, and office buildings beyond the freeway's concrete sound barriers. She saw the sharp glint of her eyes in the tinted window — the same sharp, cheerless eyes that had haunted her since the accident. She was grateful for the forceful push back to work. It was what she'd been telling her superiors and the shrink for months; she needed work and distraction to recover from the PTSD, and some more successful missions under her belt to overcome the one god-awful failure. *But then why do I feel so flat?* Mallory wondered, as she stared out the window.

Admiral Haywood touched her arm. "How have you been, Mallory?"

She turned and looked at him, her face neutral, tone flat. "Well enough, I suppose, sir. Bored as hell to tell the truth."

Haywood nodded, noting the straight cast of her mouth, one that in the past had often displayed a cocky lopsided smile even in the face of the most difficult missions. When Mallory had come to him from the Naval Diving and Salvage Training Center, Admiral Haywood had taken one look at her and instantly had his doubts. He'd had her OMPF folder along with her transfer orders on his desk when she first reported to him, and he wondered what he would be getting into if he accepted the young officer into his outfit.

At first sight she seemed completely out of place in the Navy, more so than anyone Haywood had ever met in all his years of service. But there had been something special about the young officer. Haywood had felt it in his gut, and his gut had never failed him. Mallory soon proved her worth by pulling off difficult missions that had elicited cringes from more experienced salvage divers. She was no daredevil. On the contrary, she was sedulously methodical and safety conscious. Haywood never understood how she came up with such innovative solutions to seemingly hopeless salvage jobs—it seemed almost like divine inspiration. Need to recover a B83 thermonuclear bomb from the bottom of the San Francisco Bay?

Mallory's team was the one you sent if you wanted the mission to be successful—in this case without detonating a live 1.2 megaton nuke that would've taken out the Bay Area if it had gone off. Haywood sucked at his teeth.

Mallory's salvage team had certainly earned their pay the day they recovered that broken arrow. An Air Force B52 out of Barksdale Air Force base in Louisiana had accidentally jettisoned the weapon as it headed out to the Pacific. The bomb plummeted into the sea entombing itself in the wreckage of a freighter in two hundred feet of water just inside the Golden Gate Bridge. Worse still, it had somehow armed itself, but Mallory's team had managed to bring it to the surface where the Air Force's EOD team could deactivate it. The public's outrage had been sharp and loud when someone leaked to the press that nuke-laden bombers were flying across the continental United States, but nothing like it would've been had word gotten out about the accidental jettisoning.

Mallory homed in on tough salvage jobs like a Mark 48 torpedo. But her career as a navy salvage diver had nearly ended before it began. After she'd come up from her first salvage job—attaching slings to a sunken Navy tug—and peeled off her wetsuit while making her report, Haywood had nearly sent her packing right then and there. The massive tattoo of the sea serpent emblazoned on her back and torso and legs violated regulations and offended his sense of decorum. True, many Navy personnel, including officers, got tattoos on their arms, but there were boundaries that wiser heads never crossed. Mallory seemed blithely indifferent to such considerations. At least the god-awful things weren't visible when she was in uniform, Haywood told himself. The Navy was the most conservative branch of all the armed services and Mallory seemed to fit in about as well as a hippie at a Tea Party rally. He recalled that she came from a working class family in Philadelphia, her father a retired career navy man, and her mother the owner of a small nursery. Her blonde hair, blue eyes, strong chin and pale skin betrayed her Pennsylvania Dutch and English ancestry.

Mallory was staring out the SUV's window. Haywood would've given anything to know what was going on in her head. More to the point, he wondered if she was ready for what would be the most difficult mission ever assigned to any salvage diver. The uncertainty of her readiness and the wider uncertainty of the mission itself gnawed at him. Was he pushing an emotionally frangible woman into a meat grinder?

Admiral Haywood turned to her and said, "We have a job for you—something big, really big. Are you ready to come back to work?"

Mallory's eyes met his. "Sir, I have been ready for months."

"Glad to hear it." Haywood nodded toward the front passenger seat. "Commander Capehart, meet the fellow you'll be working with—Special Agent Randal Lester of the Office of Strategic Services."

A man in a dark suit and tie turned around and flashed a grin. Even behind his dark sunglasses Mallory could feel him taking her measure. "At last, I get to meet Wonder Woman herself! The Admiral here says you're all that and more."

Mallory shot the Fed an icy stare. "The OSS was disbanded after World War Two." She was in no mood for kidding around, especially with the creep in the front seat.

Randal Lester's grin reminded Mallory of a barracuda's toothy mouth. "Actually, the OSS was restarted by executive order of George W. Bush way back in 2004 and buried deep within the Department of Homeland Security. We're so secret you won't even find us mentioned in *WikiLeaks*."

Mallory nodded then looked at Haywood. "Sir, just what is all this about?"

The Admiral smiled. "You'll find out soon enough, Commander. Let's just say that it's going to be one hell of a mission."

"A global game changer," Lester chimed in.

"But we can't talk about it here," Haywood said with finality.

Mallory was intrigued despite a mild resentment at the intrusion into her morning routine and the unnecessary theatricality of their approach. Really, a phone call or an email would have been just as effective. And she could have shown up in uniform instead of looking like a mess in her sweaty jogging clothes. Mallory settled back into her seat and forced herself to relax. Perhaps they'd lost another nuke or needed to recover the codebooks from some sunken enemy ship. They'd tell her in their own good time. Mallory glanced at the passenger side mirror. One of the SUVs had vanished. Mallory suspected the occupants were on their way to the ER to have Scarface's broken nose treated.

Haywood leaned slightly toward Mallory and whispered so Lester wouldn't hear what he said. "FYI, I got Dr. Smith to sign off on your return to active duty."

Mallory turned her head to look at him. "How did you get him do that?"

Haywood chuckled. "Not many people will say no to an admiral."

The two remaining SUVs exited the freeway and turned into Camp Pendleton, stopping at the main guard shack where they were waved in without the usual flashing of ID. They turned off the main road onto one that Mallory, who had often been to Pendleton, did not recognize. The narrow road ran past Headquarters Area 15 to a nondescript three story building near the back of the sprawling base. Mirrored windows stared out at the bright sunlit morning. A thicket of antenna masts and satellite dish antennas rose from the roof.

Sentries armed with machine guns patrolled the OSS compound's perimeter fence. Mallory saw men on the building's roof studying them through binoculars. The driver pulled up to the gatehouse and flashed his

ID. The sentry nodded to a man in the guard shack and the barrier was raised. The SUVs whirled along final stretch of the road.

Agent Lester twisted around in his seat and flashed a grin at Mallory. "Welcome to the OSS Operations Center-West, Commander."

"They wanted to be able to get some surfing in on their off hours. That's why they're here and not in DC or Virginia." Haywood deadpanned.

Lester unwrapped a stick of gum then shoved it in his mouth. "Actually, quite a few of my guys are surfers, but we selected Pendleton because we're less likely to draw attention here than the East Coast. It's worked out well so far."

Mallory nodded. As far as she was concerned, the OSS could've set ·up shop on the dark side of the moon. She just wanted to know what the mission was. The SUVs rolled into a parking lot at the rear of the building. The driver slotted the vehicle into a space near a guard shack and got out to hold open the door for Admiral Haywood.

The two Marines standing guard at the steel door saluted. One of them swiped Mallory's military identification in a card reader then nodded to the other. The second one opened the door. Agent Lester and the others swept by. Beyond lay an empty room, about thirty feet square, with concrete floor and walls where all was as quiet as death.

Mallory had the feeling that their every move was being watched. Opposite the outer door was an inner door with a palm reader mounted on the wall beside it.

Lester strode over and laid his hand on the scanner, disengaging the lock. Past the threshold, a forty-two-foot corridor with bare concrete walls and floors led to a third door. "Everyone stand perfectly still," Lester said.

Three gleaming silvery spheres fell from the ceiling then hovered in front Mallory's and the other's faces. Mallory saw her reflection in the orb's spinning surface. Then it and its two brethren shot back up to the ceiling vanishing into a small hole. The door opened with a soft click into a small lobby with an elevator.

"What the hell were those?" Mallory asked, following him into the lobby.

Lester said, "They're called Night Porters. They're designed to stop unauthorized people from making it beyond this corridor."

Mallory looked at him. "How? They're the size of golf balls."

"It's classified"

Beside her, Haywood whispered, "Get ready for a trip down the rabbit hole."

"Like we're not already in it," Mallory whispered back. "Did you notice the drone circling overhead, Sir?"

Haywood looked at her, perplexed. "No! Are you sure?"

"Yeah. An MQ-24 Hunter-Killer," Mallory said.

Inside the elevator, Haywood turned to Lester. "What's the deal with the drone?"

Agent Lester shrugged. "Just an added layer of security."

They took the elevator to the top floor. The hallways were utterly quiet except for their brisk steps. They passed an open doorway. Mallory caught a glimpse of half a dozen men sitting at workstations dominated by high definition 3D monitors. She saw the OSS building and its grounds on a screen. Another held an image of a caravan of foreign made pickup trucks and foreign made cars moving slowly across some lonely desert at night.

Lester opened a door to a reception area where a beautiful dark-haired young woman sat at a desk typing on the keyboard of her workstation. The soft staccato rattle of the computer keyboard under her nimble fingers was the only sound in the room. One wall of the reception area held file cabinets. Above them a row of flat screen monitors showed the corridor they'd just passed through and other parts of the building.

The receptionist rose from her desk and held the door open, the unmistakable bulge of a pistol evident under her blazer. Agent Lester swept by her with a curt nod.

Mallory followed him and Admiral Haywood into the conference room. A blond man in a dark business suit and red power tie sat at the head of a long conference table.

Haywood said, "Commander, meet Lou Sobel, Director of OSS Special Projects."

"Pleased to meet you," Mallory said.

Sobel smiled. "You may not be after you hear what's on the menu, Commander." He gestured to the vacant chair opposite his. "You get to sit in the hot seat."

Mallory pulled out the chair and sat down. Admiral Haywood sat to her immediate left while Lester moved to a chair halfway down the table.

Sobel touched an LCD screen embedded in the table before him. A holographic emitter in the center of the table flashed on—the words *Project Jules Verne hung in midair, slowly rotating like a garden mobile stirred by a gentle breeze.*

"Last year, an expedition funded and led by the late Ethan Delahaye was searching for the wreck site of a World War Two Japanese destroyer. It was reported to have been carrying a cargo of looted gold bullion when it was sunk by an American warplane. This is what Delahaye found instead."

An image of a spindle shaped vessel resting on the seabed appeared above the conference table. With its imbricated hull plates and pointy snout it looked like some Jurassic-age sea monster. Mallory studied the hologram, puzzling over the large oblong opening piercing the sides of the hull. Their twisted frames still held shards of glass. At the bow of the ship, a curtain of icicle-like deposits of rust hung from a stubby iron ram, which meant the wreck was slowly being consumed by the same bacterium that had finally reduced the Titanic to an unrecognizable pile of rust on the Atlantic seabed.

"Would you mind rotating it laterally?" Mallory asked.

"Not at all, Commander." Sobel touched the control panel before him; the hologram began to slowly turn. Ordinarily, a dense curtain of marine snow falling from the ocean's upper regions would have shrouded the wreck. But, thanks to the sophisticated imaging technology deployed by Delahaye expedition it looked as if the ocean had been drained to reveal the wreck in all its desolate glory. The wreck was thickly blanketed with tan silt, and sat upright on an even keel on the seabed.

Mallory's first thought was that it might be some sort of icebreaker. Just as quickly she dismissed that idea—the vessel's freeboard was too low for it to be an icebreaker, at least an ocean going one. And that part of the Pacific wasn't exactly known for its icebergs. It was widely reported that Delahaye's vessel the RV *Astra* had been destroyed when it hit a World War Two era mine west of Guam. Too little of the ship remained to recover and what was left lay strewn along the bottom of the Marianas Trench. So how had the OSS managed to recover the Astra's data? Mallory wondered. She suspected she'd be told it was none of her business if she asked, so she didn't.

Every face in the room was turned toward her but all Mallory's attention was on the ship. She was pretty sure it wasn't a World War II era destroyer.

It didn't look like a World War II *anything*. Mallory had helped raise the Civil War ironclad USS *Tecumseh* from the bottom of Mobile Bay, and she'd worked on several other underwater archeological projects in her spare time. To Mallory wreck diving was an almost mystical experience that drew her back time after time. She felt that this wreck was special in some way other than its formidable size, as large as a Virginia class submarine, and for reasons she couldn't articulate she wanted it to be special.

A muted, "What the hell are you?" escaped her throat before she could stop it.

"Why don't you tell us what you think it is," Lester suggested.

Mallory recognized a challenge when she heard it. "The building technique is clearly mid nineteenth century. Despite its size, it has a relatively small deck. I am certain the squat structure with the viewports near the bow is the wheelhouse. As for the similar structure at the aft end of the deck..." Mallory stared hard. Now how in the hell had she missed those? There was no mistaking what she was seeing, difficult as it was to believe. She studied the cruciform hydroplanes at the stern and the dive planes near the bow—and the six-bladed propeller with adjustable pitch, a technology that wouldn't be invented until the early twentieth century. The vessel could only be one thing—a submarine.

Project Jules Verne.

Mallory looked at Haywood, quizzically, her brow furrowed, and then at Sobel and Lester, a question clearly stated in her eyes, "But surely you're not suggesting that..." Her voice trailed off, unable to voice the outrageous conclusion she'd drawn.

Randal Lester was beaming down the table at her.

"Don't worry, Commander. You haven't lost your marbles," Admiral Haywood said, with a dry chuckle. "That's Captain Nemo's *Nautilus* you're looking at."

Mallory gaped at the hologram. "*20,000 Leagues Under The Sea* was just a work of fiction," she said. Like every other kid in America she'd seen the ancient *Disney* movie based on the novel. She didn't recall the actual movie because it had been so long ago but she did remember thinking that when she grew up she'd one day explore the ocean in a submarine like Captain Nemo's.

Perhaps that was her first inkling of a life as a diver.

Sobel said, "Verne got the story from an obscure French scientist named Pierre Arronax who had been a prisoner on board the *Nautilus* until he managed to escape, but much of what Verne put in his novel was incorrect. It seems he was pressured by the French and British governments to leave out some important details, such as Nemo's true identity. Fortunately, we've managed to identify him, thanks to this."

Sobel reached down for his briefcase and opened it on the table then withdrew an old leather-bound book, which he handed to Lester. The OSS agent rose and brought it over to Mallory then returned to his seat.

"That's Nemo's diary," Sobel said. "It was discovered in a watertight chest recovered from the Nautilus' safe. Nemo was in fact the famed British naval architect Jonathan de Chevalier Mason, builder of the HMS *Warrior* and HMS *Black Prince*."

Sobel's revelation stunned Mallory. While in college she had taken a trip to England during Spring Break and visited the HMS *Warrior*, now a museum ship on the Thymes River, and marveled at its construction. To think that she'd trodden the decks of an ironclad warship built by the legendary Captain Nemo! Ye Gods, how amazing!

Haywood looked at Mallory." Mason ran afoul of the Admiralty and was condemned to a penal island where he organized a mass escape with a band of followers and obtained hidden treasure which he used to build his submarine. It's all in his journal. We've produced a spiral bound photocopy for you, Commander. I suggest you read it."

"Thank you, Sir," Mallory replied. "I will crack it open right away. But why is the government interested in a primitive nineteenth century submersible?"

Admiral Haywood's mouth twisted up into a smile. "Lieutenant Commander, you're about to have your running shoes blown right off your feet."

Sobel swiped the touchscreen with a fingertip. "This is what we're after."

The holographic image of the wreck dissolved and was replaced with a Computer Generated Image of a spherical crystal pulsing with bands of multi-colored light.

Sobel went on, "This was the heart of the *Nautilus*. Nemo called it Poseidon crystal. Based on Nemo's description, sensor data transmitted by the Delahaye expedition's UAV, and on assessments we've received from several top physicists, we believe this to be some sort of Zero Point Energy device—one that provided enough power to drive an Industrial Revolution-era submersible more than sixty knots through the water—and that was its submerged speed. If that isn't enough for you, Commander, the *Nautilus* could dive to thirty-five thousand feet, and hang out down there as long as she wished although her hull was made of the brittle Bessemer process steel produced at the time."

"The maximum operating depth of our 688-class boats is sixteen hundred feet, and that's with welded titanium hulls, mind you," Admiral Haywood pointed out.

Still dumbfounded by Sobel's revelation, Mallory nodded toward the hologram, and said, "And you think the Poseidon crystal somehow permitted the *Nautilus* to reach those depths? How do you know Nemo wasn't exaggerating?" She was pretty sure the nineteenth century had its fair share of bullshitters.

Sobel said, "In his journal Nemo mentions black smokers, hydrothermal vents, and the chemosynthetic ecosystem surrounding them, which would've only been possible if he'd seen them with his own eyes. To put it in perspective for you, black smokers were first observed by the crew of the research submersible DSV Alvin II in 1979 on the East Pacific Rise not far from the Galapagos Islands, eight thousand feet below the surface."

The military implications hit Mallory full force. Captain Nemo's nineteenth century submarine was more advanced in some very significant ways than even the Navy's newest fast attack submarines. Whoever could unlock its secrets would in effect control the seas. Then the Director of OSS Special Projects upped the ante.

Sobel clasped his hands together on the table before him. "Aside from the Poseidon crystal's military applications, our nation is rapidly running out of oil—the Middle East is on the brink of imploding now that the Iranians possess the nuclear weapons. Yes, they have them," the OSS official said in response to her raised eyebrows, "which is why neither we nor the Israelis dare attack them. After President Trump unilaterally backed out of the deal in back in 2017, he provided them an excellent excuse to resume work on their nuclear program. We estimate they have three hundred Hiroshima size bombs."

Mallory now realized that Admiral Haywood was speaking with the slow heavy drawl of barely subdued anger. "Thanks to their alliance with the Russians and Chinese Iran now possesses pin point accurate ICBM's with third generation hypersonic reentry vehicles specifically designed to counter our sea and land based missile defense shields."

"And with the ISIS Caliphate now controlling most of the Mideast's oil supply, our collective nuts are in a vise," Lester cut in briskly.

Sobel continued with a slight edge in his voice, "At the rate we're consuming petroleum we'll be down to coal and windmills in ten years, even with our reserves. We intend to raise the *Nautilus* from the seabed and retrieve the Poseidon crystal, find out how the damn thing works and duplicate it. Your past record of bringing difficult salvage jobs to a successful conclusion makes you the ideal officer for this mission."

"May I ask a question?" Mallory asked.

Sobel nodded. "Of course."

"Where is the wreck located?"

"It is at the bottom of the Challenger Deep."

Holy shit! Thought Mallory. *Good luck with that, guys!* A descent to the Challenger Deep was every bit as hazardous as a trip to the outer planets, with about the same low odds of survival if something went wrong. Mallory said, "The Soviet K129 wreck was three miles deep and the CIA only managed to retrieve the bow after the recovery vehicle failed. The rest of the submarine broke free and fell back to the ocean floor. Raising a waterlogged submarine seven miles to the surface is a tall order."

Sobel shook his head. "That's what the CIA leaked to Jack Anderson. I'll have more to say about *that* in a moment. The CIA recovered the entire submarine but cut away the pieces they didn't want and scattered them on the seafloor to confuse and annoy the Soviets. But *there were* problems with the method they used: stress cracks in the recovery vehicle's steel grabber arms, stability issues as the K129 was hoisted to the surface. But we have better materials and computers than they had in 1974."

Sobel swiped the touchscreen again and the holographic image of the orb changed to an animation of a large drill ship with a tall derrick rising from its main deck.

Mallory recognized the ship—the *Hughes Glomar Explorer.* She'd once watched a documentary on The History Channel about Project Azorian, the code name for the covert mission to recover the ill-fated Soviet submarine K129. Mallory frowned at the hologram. "I thought the Glomar Explorer was sold for scrap twenty years ago."

"And so she was." Sobel gestured toward the screen. "This is her sister ship the Hughes *Glomar Endeavor*. The most famous ship you never heard of. There's a good reason for that. Project Azorian was a smokescreen for another mission called Project Galaxy. Consider this: The K129 was a woefully obsolete piece of crap when it went down in 1968. The Glomar *Explorer* went to the North pacific to raise the Russian sub in July 1974. What possible intelligence value could an outdated wrecked submarine and its six-year-old codebooks have? What we really wanted lay at the bottom of the Atlantic Ocean, but we had to draw the Soviet's eyes and ears toward the Pacific. Tidbits of information were fed to several journalists about Azorian for their columns with a view toward misdirecting the Russians. Woodward and Bernstein were approached but they were hot after Nixon, so they weren't interested. Jack Anderson was approached at a cocktail party and told about the project. He was made to understand that Navy experts had determined that the submarine contained no real secrets, and that the project, therefore, was a complete waste of taxpayer money. He broke the Story in the New York Times over the objections of William Colby, Director of the Central Intelligence Agency. What was so special about the Galaxy mission that all this treasure and effort was expended?" Sobel paused a moment then said, "What I am about to tell you is classified Top Secret. On February 3, 1969, two jet fighters shot down a UFO that had been shadowing the USS Saratoga as she steamed for Guantanamo Cuba. Soon after, the Navy sent the Trieste down to the seafloor to map the wreckage and take measurements. The Soviet High Command didn't give the *Glomar Endeavor* a second look when she slipped quietly from her port in 1974 and set out for the target site. All their attention was on the CIA's attempt to recover their submarine. To make a long story short, the *Glomar Endeavor* succeeded in recovering the UFO, which eventually ended up in a warehouse in Area 51 where it remains to this day."

"We have an alien spacecraft?" Mallory asked dumbly and instantly regretted it.

"Actually, we have three of them," Sobel replied matter-of-factly. "A vehicle that crashed in Roswell New Mexico in 1947, the Galaxy UFO recovered in 1974, and another that was brought down by an Air Force General Dynamics F-16 in the Mojave Desert in September 1987, the same month Ronald Reagan delivered his UFO speech to the United Nations General Assembly. There was also a top-secret summit between Reagan and Premier Gorbachev, whose country was having its own UFO problems, about the need to make common cause against a possible invasion from space. I bet they *didn't* teach you any of that in your High School history class, Commander."

"No sir," Mallory admitted. It was almost more than she could wrap her head around: Captured UFO's, Area 51, Captain Nemo's submarine— apparently powered by a 19th century technology superior to 21st century nuclear propulsion.

Admiral Haywood said, "We have pulled the *Glomar Endeavor* out of mothballs in Suisun Bay and retrofitted her with state-of-the-art equipment, navigation, automated command and control, the whole enchilada. During Project Azorian a drill string of steel pipes was used to lower the capture vehicle to the sea floor. This time we will be using a cable made of spun carbon fiber and Kevlar to lower a capture vehicle to the wreck site."

Mallory shook her head. "The wreck is embedded in the ooze, and no doubt very brittle. How do you intend to free it from the sediment without shattering the hull?"

"We have thought about that," Sobel chimed in. he swiped the touchscreen. A spider-like recovery vehicle emerged from the belly of the recovery ship." Meet Miss Muffet. Now, besides the obvious difference of using cable instead of a pipe string, there is this." Sobel zoomed in on the recovery vehicle." See the hemispherical structure with viewports at the top of the capture vehicle. That is a crew cabin where a pilot will operate dynamic high output thrusters to guide the recovery vehicle. Once it reaches the wreck site, the pilot will close the grabber arms around the *Nautilus* then manage the Capture Vehicle/Payload Package stability as it is hoisted to the surface."

Sobel swiped the touchscreen again and the holographic animation resumed. "When the Recovery Vehicle touches down, these four extendable breakout legs will descend to make contact with the seafloor. The bottom of each leg has a cookie cutter pad that will dig deep into the seafloor. Miss Muffet is outfitted with hyper pressure water jets to excavate a path for the grabber arms. Once the *Nautilus* is secured, the breakout legs will be extended with hydraulic pressure to jack it off the seabed. To save weight, they will be jettisoned before you begin your ascent. "

Sobel highlighted twelve smaller articulated arms on rails mounted to the spine of the recovery vehicle. "These are called looms. They will crisscross the length of the wreck as you make your ascent depositing a watertight material called C-Stop on the surface of the submarine, sealing it from stem to stern. Then you will use the remote cutting torch in a mating collar under Miss Muffet's strong back to penetrate the deck plates and start pumping out seawater as you rise toward the surface. In a worst-case scenario, if the seawater cannot be pumped out, the cable is strong enough to hoist the submarine to the surface where it will be held snug against the *Glomar Endeavor's* hull. You and another diver will then enter the *Nautilus* to retrieve the Poseidon crystal from its engine room. If you deem it impossible to do it while at sea, you are to make your way to Pearl Harbor with the *Nautilus* where it will be placed in a covered dry dock. You'll take the lead on this, Commander Capehart." Sobel came as close to smiling as he ever would. "We realize that in some ways, we are out of our depth on this one."

Admiral Haywood looked at Mallory. "Commander, I can't overstate the importance of this mission. President Connor has signed off on this mission and is expecting positive results, and I have given her my word that she will get them."

Sobel said, "And we have to keep this mission under wraps, Commander. The *Nautilus* lies in an area of the Pacific closely watched by the Chinese navy, and a viable Zero Point Energy device will once again put the United States on top. They won't be happy to see us energy independent, and neither will our 'friends' in OPEC."

Sobel nodded toward Randal Lester. "Special Agent Lester will have oversight of the mission, but you will have responsibility over the recovery operation itself. An OSS paramilitary task force made up of civilian contractors will accompany him. They'll provide security for the *Nautilus* once it's on the surface and ultimately take the Poseidon crystal into custody once you have retrieved it from the engine room."

Mallory was dismayed to see Haywood nod at that. Great, just what she needed, she thought, a boatload of civilians to babysit during a difficult mission.

CHAPTER 3 ALT-RIGHT

TUESDAY—0530Z HRS

Agent Randal Lester, age forty-five, divorced, liked to rise well before dawn to undertake his fitness routine—except on those occasions when his work required him to remain all night at The Western Annex, formally known as OSS Western Regional Headquarters. During the war with Iraq in 2003 President George W. Bush had given up on the CIA after the fiasco with the Iraqi weapons of mass destruction. No stockpiles of biological or chemical weapons had been found and there was in fact no connection between Al Qaeda and Saddam Hussein. Inconvenient facts that had made the President's face take on the hue of boiled lobster as he was briefed by his National Security team. No one had ever seen him so angry. Never again would he allow himself to be misled—"caught with my goddamn britches round my ankles," as he had put it. An avid history buff, Bush decided to resurrect the *Office of Strategic Services* and bury it within the labyrinthine bowels of the Department of Homeland Security. The OSS, President Bush declared, would be the switchblade he would reach for when dirty work needed to be done, and no questions asked. It was telling that none of his successors sought to disband the OSS. Just before being removed from office after a trial in the Senate, the late

President Trump had ordered the OSS to arrange a false flag attack from Iran so he could declare war.

Agent Lester loved his work and he made sure he was in tip top shape to do it. An array of expensive state-of-the-art exercise machines occupied a portion of the open-plan condominium Lester owned on the top floor of a high rise in Irvine California. The building boasted three gyms but Randal liked to have his own equipment. He was afraid of catching a super bug from some Chinese or Middle Eastern businessman who didn't wash his hands properly after taking a shit. Irvine, with its forest of high-tech firms and university, was lousy with foreigners. Admittedly, most of them were college educated and affluent—not like the cesspool in Santa Ana which was more like Tijuana than America, and certainly not like Los Angeles which was mostly Hispanic and black with lots of gunfire being exchanged between both groups—*vato locos* versus *homies*.

America had been overrun with barbarians, Randal thought for the umpteenth time, as he lay cocooned in organic cotton bedding while the virtual sunrise clock on the nightstand brightened in stages to ease him into wakefulness. Randal yearned for an America where everyone once again knew their place. Where a man rose to the top based on merit and not some damned Affirmative Action program, where the minorities kept to their neighborhoods, gays and lesbians stayed in the closet, and women stayed home to raise children, and if they were in the work place they didn't go cross-eyed if you asked them to bring you a cup of java. He hated feminists as much as he hated minorities.

His father had been a Los Angeles cop during the George Floyd protests. Back then gang bangers knew their place. No flashing gang signs at the cops—not if said gangbanger didn't want a telescopic baton shoved up his ass. Nowadays, the hood rats lived in fear of the militarized blue line cordoning off their shitty neighborhoods from the rest of Los Angeles

County, contained like cancer with the harsh medicine of Heinkel aerial combat drones, tall concrete walls topped with concertina wire and round the clock police checkpoints, manned by heavily armed cyborg policemen.

In short, Agent Randal Lester was a racist misogynist creep.

Then the sunrise clock's light brightened. The gentle chiming would've brought a smile to a Buddhist monk's face. Lester kicked off the covers and his mind turned to his morning routine. It was important to begin the day with positive thoughts. Agent Lester considered himself a fine example of white American manhood. In Stay-Dri shorts and tee-shirt, he stretched to prevent injury, worked up a sweat on a treadmill, pushing himself with each workout, then followed a circuit of weight machines that worked every muscle group to a stinging burn. He did a hundred sit ups, reverse sit ups, and side crunches, all on an incline, before he allowed himself to be finished. Randal was lean and hard, a marksman with a pistol, and had a black belt in Brazilian jujitsu.

Randal took a long luxurious shower because a supreme example of the Aryan race must be squeaky clean and well-groomed at all times. After Randal dressed in a dark gray suit, he stood in the kitchen washing down thirty-three vitamin pills with a protein drink. He picked up his beloved Glock 33 from the towel on the granite counter and slid it into a holster onto his belt, checked his receding hair in the mirror by the door and departed for work.

TUESDAY—0830Z HRS

Admiral Haywood smiled from behind his desk. "How is the simulator training coming along?"

Mallory gave a rueful smile. "I actually got the *Nautilus* to within a thousand feet of the surface. Then it broke into three pieces and destroyed the recovery vehicle."

No point in sugar coating it, Mallory thought, *Not with someone like the Admiral.*

Haywood was seated behind his desk, a frown on his face. Even in his sixties he was still handsome and in good shape. He'd always maintained healthy boundaries with Mallory, a fact that puzzled her as she was often hit on by both men and women.

Haywood's office was spacious and well organized and uncluttered, with only a few mementos to indicate that he was its rightful occupant. In front of his desk were three chairs and beyond them a long conference table with room for twelve people. Photographs of his wife, three children and nine grandchildren were on one wall. Another wall was taken up with degrees and certificates and commendations and photographs of the ships he had commanded over the years—mainly flattops and one heavy guided missile cruiser. There was a photograph of a youthful Haywood wearing a cocky grin and a flight suit climbing into the cockpit of a F-35 Lightning II. Haywood was staring at the photographs on the wall as he pondered Mallory's news.

Finally he said, "Coffee?"

Mallory nodded. "Thank you, Sir."

He rose from his chair and came round from behind his desk and went over to a coffee maker and poured two cups. "How do you like yours, Commander?"

Mallory told him she liked it black.

"I am with you. No point in ruining a perfectly good coffee with cream and sugar." He handed her a mug on the way back to his chair. "No doubt about it, we've got a real beast of a mission on our hands. Don't beat yourself up about the simulator. You'll get the hang of it—but do it quickly. My time in the F-35 simulator was no picnic."

Wow, no freakin pressure or anything! Mallory nodded. "Thank you for your confidence, Sir. I will," She, herself, felt anything but confident.

The intercom buzzed. "Admiral, Agent Lester is here."

"Send him in."

Lester came into the room and the temperature dropped perceptibly. Neither of the naval officers cared for spooks in general and this one really got under their skins. "Have a seat, Agent Lester." Admiral Haywood waved him over to a chair.

Lester plopped down, and got right to the point. "My guys will be here in three days. What's the status of the simulator training?" he asked, pointedly ignoring Mallory.

"We're making progress," Haywood replied casually.

"We'll need to be at one hundred percent by the time we go into operational mode," Lester replied, matching his tone. "I hope that won't be a problem."

Admiral Haywood took a sip of his coffee then said, "We'll have all our ducks in a row by the time we set sail, Agent Lester. Additionally, there will be further training en route to the wreck site. It's all under control."

"That's good to hear," Lester replied. "We're on a tight schedule."

Mallory thought she detected the barest trace of a bully's smirk on Lester's face. For a handful of change, she would have gladly wiped it off.

Mallory knew a bully when she saw one.

During her freshman year in high school she had gotten into a fist fight with an older boy after school. Mallory had known him. He was a junior named Matt White, an offensive lineman on the football team. Big boned with the broad shoulders and well-muscled arms, and an unruly cap of dirty blond hair and blue eyes, he was fast and agile—and a world-class asshole.

Mallory soon found herself lying on her back pinned to the ground. While a boy held her arms against the littered hard packed earth, her tormentor quickly straddled her and began to slap her face. "How do ya like that bitch? How do you like that!"

Mallory tried to throw him off her, but he wasn't going anywhere. "Let me go you motherfucker or I swear to god. I am gonna kill you!" she cried.

Matt laughed. "With what, your dirty panties?" Meanwhile a crowd had gathered around them, taunting Mallory and recording the whole thing with their camera phones.

A blond girl in a pleated skirt crouched down to yank up her top.

Someone in the crowd called out. "Look at the dyke's flat tits!"

Another boy said, "Hey Matt, I dare you to grab those ugly ass titties!"

Matt looked up and grinned. "You're on buddy!" Then he looked down at Mallory and bared his teeth. "So ya like to lick pussy, eh, freak. This is what we do to nasty bitches like you around here!" Matt viciously tugged at her pierced nipples. Mallory felt his hot breath on her face, little drops of spittle splattered her face. Her mind went numb. Beneath her rage lay a bottomless ocean of shame. Over the jeers and laughter she dimly heard someone screaming then realized it was her voice.

Mallory struggled to free herself then Matt planted a good one on her face and she saw swirling lights.

That night, to her horror and shame, she discovered some asshole had uploaded the beatdown to TikTok. A quick look on Facebook and Instagram confirmed her worst fears. Videos of the assault were all over social media.

There were messages urging her kill herself, calling her a loser and dyke, as if being a lesbian was somehow a bad thing—but Mallory wasn't remotely interested in girls. Truth was, she wasn't interested in anyone. She'd always kept to herself.

Some of the videos showed closeups of her nipples being yanked until they were taut—just as humiliating as the images were the demeaning insults hurled at her from the crowd. Another video showed her curled in a fetal position with her jeans partly pulled down, the recording abruptly stopping when a teacher pushed his way through the crowd.

The next day she was greeted with smirks and taunts everywhere she went on campus. In the cafeteria a cheerleader dropped a used tampon on her lunch plate. Wadded dirty napkins and crumpled paper cups pelted her as she sat looking down at the tampon lying on the brown mess the cafeteria menu optimistically labeled beef stroganoff. And these acts of cruelty pushed her over the brink—her mind went sharp with an icy fury. Over the next few days Mallory shadowed Matt like a tigress stalking prey. She noticed that on Thursdays the creep showed up an hour early to help get the gym ready, a chore that was shared by the other jocks on a rotating basis. From across the parking lot she watched as he took the same route every day at the same time from the gym to the track for his morning run. After school Mallory curled up with her Xbox 660 and played Assasin's Creed while exploring her options.

One Thursday morning she nested two long thick gym socks. She had taken care to get the right length from the local Walmart—they extended from the tip of her fingers to her elbow. With one eye on the electric alarm clock on the nightstand she filled her sap with large steel nuts and bolts from her father's workshop. For good measure she added a couple of rolls of quarters. After knotting the end of the sock, and giving it a good shake, she shoved the homemade weapon into her backpack then set off for school.

From the shadows of a tree she saw her quarry enter the gym. Mallory jogged over to the gym and took position at the corner of the building. She dropped the backpack at her feet then retrieved the sap and waited. She looked at her pink Hello Kitty watch.

As soon as Matt rounded the corner Mallory let fly with the sap. It smashed into Matt's startled face and dropped him like a bag of flour. She yanked him half up from the ground and slammed her fist into his face—it felt so good so she did it again and again and again. Each blow sent his head whipping around. "You ever again lay a hand on me you're a dead man!" She hollered into the pulpy red mess that had once been a pretty-boy face. "Nod if you understand." Matt complied without hesitation.

Mallory released her grip and let him collapse backwards. She twisted around and reached down for her backpack and retrieved a pair of her worn panties from it and shoved them into his bloody mouth. Then she stood above him and snapped pics with her smartphone. Above the panties a pair of frightened blackened eyes stared up at her. "Any of your friends give me any more trouble and this will be all over the Internet."

Predictably, Mallory was the one who got into trouble. Her parents were called and she would've been expelled had it not been for their pleadings—reluctantly, the principal relented and suspended her from school for a week, but the boy never bothered her again. No one did.

Randal Lester reminded her of Matt White.

Haywood looked at his watch then at Mallory. "Time for you to trot on over to the simulator, Commander."

"Aye, Sir." Mallory set down her cup on the table then stood and saluted and left the room. She had a feeling Agent Lester was in for an earful from the Admiral.

CHAPTER 4 XO

SUNDAY—2130Z HRS

Mallory's eyes almost bored holes into the monitor as she worked the joysticks. "Sixty feet to acquisition," intoned the electronic voice in the cabin speaker. She had one ear-bud of her MP4 player's headset pressed into her ear blaring a Marilyn Manson song.

When Mallory was in the mood to kick some ass, there was nothing that got her juices going like Marilyn Manson. The image on the screen was split between the *Nautilus*, now covered in its special polymer cocoon securely clasped in the spidery grabber arms, and the yawning belly of the *Glomar Endeavor* above her. In real life Mallory would be able to look up through a view port and see the bottom of the recovery ship's hull. That was a strange oversight on the part of the simulation manufacturer but it might, she thought, have been due to the short lead-time to the recovery effort.

According to the readouts on the monitor, she was just below the two massive long rectangular steel grabber legs that had slid down from either end of the moon pool and canted outwards like a woman waiting to receive her lover. Here was the truth point, as Mallory termed it. Here during these last few feet would begin an intricate saraband equal in complexity to docking two spacecraft in outer space. As with spacecraft, the standard procedure for docking called for an active vehicle to make the approach to a passive vehicle. The *Glomar Endeavor* with its powerful bow and stern tunnel thrusters was designed to remain stationary even in rough seas.

Mallory kept the four cross hairs on the monitor lined up with the illuminated round docking targets on either end of the two massive docking legs.

"Three feet and closing..."

The crosshairs began to move toward each other as the docking legs swung inward. There was an audible mechanical click as they latched onto the recovery vehicle then the electronic voice announced, "Docking complete."

Mallory unbuckled her harness, swung open the hatch, and climbed down from the simulator. When she got to the floor, she turned and waved and whooped a loud, "Hell yeah!" with both arms up in the universal salute of the victorious to the technicians manning the consoles in the simulator control room. They rose from their seats and began to clap and give her the thumbs up. A thick glass separated the simulation chamber from the control room so she couldn't hear their cheering but their faces were all smiles.

The door to the observation room opened and Admiral Haywood and came down the iron steps then walked briskly toward her with a broad smile on his face.

Mallory snapped to attention at once.

Haywood said, "Bravo Zulu, Commander. I knew you could do it."

"Thank you Sir. It took long enough."

"Not a moment too soon," he said." Ready or not, your butt is out of here Monday morning. Your team is already onboard the *Glomar Endeavor*."

"Where is she?" Mallory asked, swallowing her anxiety at getting started so soon after her first successful simulation attempt.

"One hundred and twenty miles off shore," he replied." She arrived last night."

Mallory nodded. Parking her far off shore made sense. The ship would be well away from prying eyes, especially if she wasn't near any major shipping lanes. She would also be well away from the local boaters and whale watching tour boats.

Admiral Haywood's face grew serious. "Are you sure about Millikan?" he asked, referring to the lone survivor of her last ill-fated mission.

Mallory nodded. "He's the best, Sir." In fact, she had her doubts about him too but she kept them to herself. Would they be able to work together without the ghosts of their dead comrades haunting their actions, stealing into their thoughts and clouding their judgment? She hoped so. She needed Millikan to pull this off successfully.

Haywood nodded. "It's your show, Commander. I'll see you at the hangar tomorrow morning, 0530 sharp."

DAY ONE: MONDAY—0630Z HRS

The Coast Guard Sikorsky HH-60 Seahawk helicopter swept east casting a dragonfly shadow over a blue sea. The sky ahead segued from gray to cobalt to a deep cerulean blue unblemished by even a scrap of cloud. They were cruising at three thousand feet, the duel turbo shaft engines driving the Seahawk along at one hundred and fifty miles per hour.

The HELO banked then did a slow fly around the *Glomar Endeavor.* They were flying level with the recovery vessel's deck. Mallory studied the ship. It was large, easily the length of a World War II aircraft carrier. A tall latticework derrick rose from the center of its crowded deck, flanked by the docking legs now in the raised position. There was a helipad just aft of the stern superstructure that was dominated by a stubby red funnel. The dimpled hull rose like a sheer black cliff from the sea, a white superstructure containing the bridge, chartroom, and radio room huddled over the blunt bow.

Mallory felt a thrill of excitement rippling up her spine.

Haywood nudged her and keyed his mike—with the loud turbo shaft motors normal speech was out of the question—and nodded toward the MV *Glomar Endeavor*. "There's your new command, Commander. What do you think?"

Mallory spoke into her headset's microphone. "She's quite a ship, Sir."

"You ain't seen nothin' yet," he replied.

Mallory smiled in spite of herself. Haywood's ill-advised attempts at street slang always amused her. The Sikorsky HH60 came around then settled on the helipad.

As Haywood unbuckled his safety harness, he said, "The *Glomar Endeavor* is registered to an OSS front company in Tulsa, Oklahoma called Seascape Petroleum Ventures. They issued a press release last week announcing that it had been purchased from Uncle Sam and refitted for conducting deep sea surveys for new oilfields."

Mallory thumbed her intercom mike. "But that's the similar to the cover story the CIA used for the Azorian and Galaxy missions."

Admiral Haywood grinned. "That's the point! Who would be stupid enough to use such a transparent cover story? Ergo, it must be legit this time."

Admiral Haywood disembarked and Mallory climbed down after him.

Randal Lester and a large black man came out onto the helipad, their clothes and hair blowing in the downwash from the helicopter's still-rotating blades.

"The team is waiting in the briefing room," Lester shouted over the din of the helicopter's idling motors.

"I am inspecting the ship first," Mallory yelled back, as they headed for the aft superstructure, which had been modified into an aircraft hangar.

"But they're waiting," Lester replied.

They entered the hangar. Mallory saw a UAV parked inside. It was slightly smaller than a Cessna airplane with long bulbous nose, and wide narrow wings now folded up like an airplane in the hangar deck of an aircraft carrier.

The man that had come out onto the helipad with Lester pressed a switch on a bulkhead. The hangar doors slid shut, muffling the Sikorsky's noisy engines. "We have to keep the hangar doors closed at all times." He rolled his eyes heavenwards, and said, "Lots of Russian and Chinese satellites covering this part of the Pacific."

Mallory explained to Lester. "It is standard procedure for a captain to inspect the ship before taking command. The team will have to wait until I have completed my tour."

Lester looked at Admiral Haywood. "Is she kidding?"

"It's her prerogative." Haywood gestured to the man standing beside Lester. "Captain Capehart, this is Lieutenant Roosevelt Davenport. He's the Cheng."

Mallory nodded. The Cheng was navy slang for chief engineer. Like Mallory, Davenport was dressed in civilian clothes. His tee shirt was emblazoned with a picture of Bob Marley and he wore faded blue jeans and sneakers. Even Haywood wore civvies: khakis, a Tony Bahamas Hawaiian shirt, and Sperry Topsiders boat shoes sans socks. His clothes and deep tan made him look like an affluent Newport Beach resident. The only thing missing was the Porsche, and the blonde trophy wife with fake boobs. All Navy personnel had been ordered to don civilian attire for the duration of the mission. And Mallory was now Captain, not Commander, Capehart.

Mallory had risen bleary-eyed at four in the morning, washed her face, applied thick black eye liner, packed a duffel bag, pulled on a black tee-shirt with a red skull on it, hung a silver chain with a pentagram around her neck, wriggled into a pair of torn blue jeans, and pulled on her beloved old Doc Martin boots then headed for the door.

Lieutenant Davenport was six feet four and broad shouldered with beefcake arms and a friendly and open baby face. He snapped a crisp salute. "Welcome aboard the MV *Glomar Endeavor*, Sir."

Mallory didn't return the salute. "Thank you, Lieutenant." But for the duration of this mission, we'll dispense with the formalities. We're supposed to be a civilian ship."

Lieutenant Davenport grinned. "Well, in that case, Sir. My friends call me Rosie."

"That works for me." Mallory liked the Cheng right off the bat. He reminded her of the guys she knew back home in Philly. "Why isn't the Executive officer here?"

Before Rosie could answer, Haywood said, "You'll meet her in a little while." Then to Rosie, he said, "Show the Captain around her ship."

"Send for me when you are ready to meet the team," Lester said curtly. He turned and vanished through a hatch at the far end of the hangar.

Mallory wasn't sorry to see him go. She suspected that was true for Rosie too. The OSS man had not once looked at the Chief Engineer, even when he was speaking.

variable pressure cable brakes in the cable guide inside the derrick itself in addition to the braking power supplied by the winch."

They left the cable room and passed through another hatch and stepped out onto a gallery overlooking a vast echoing space. Outside of a carrier hangar deck it was the largest room Mallory had ever seen on a ship. The Moon Pool, as it was called, was almost large enough to play football in. The Recovery Vehicle rested at the bottom, its legs neatly folded beneath her, its telescopic spine with its hemispherical command module collapsed so it would fit inside the Moon Pool. Mallory slowly paced the gallery around the Moon Pool looking down at the giant yellow spider-like recovery vehicle.

"Do you want to take a closer look at Miss Muffet?" Rosie asked.

Mallory shook her head. "There will be plenty of time for that later."

They left the Moon Pool through a hatch at the far end, Rosie whistling a tune.

Mallory pointed down the passageway. "What the hell is that thing?" Several bulkheads away, a humanoid robot holding a mop and bucket was walking toward them, its two green eyes glowing in a vaguely humanoid head that was topped with a caged rotating red and blue light.

Mallory remembered how the robots in old science fiction movies she'd watched as a teenager had trundled along on treads or moved with a stiff limbed clanking gait. This robot moved with the smooth balanced stride of a human, nimbly stepping through an open watertight hatch, ducking its head on its flexible neck to avoid pipes and conduits.

Rosie chuckled, "That's a Shipboard Autonomous Android Mariner, or SAAM for short. We've got half a dozen on board. Let me tell you, the Navy got its money worth with these robots. They can perform complex shipboard repairs with little supervision, fight fires, fix leaks, even if the compartment's flooded, haul a three hundred pounds of stores or equipment without breaking a sweat, clean day and night, good as any human, pull laundry duty, and they don't gripe about shit."

Mallory emerged from her shock. "Who controls them?"

Rosie's eyes darted to Haywood then back to her. "The XO mostly, but any senior officer can issue commands to them. First you need to authenticate yourself with an initiation code—yours is Eagle One—only once then you are good to go from then on. Give them an order and they'll carry it out." Mallory thought Rosie was beginning to sound a lot like *Geordi La Forge*, chief engineer of the Enterprise on *Star Trek the Next Generation*. But she had to give it to the Cheng: He certainly knew his stuff.

"How can you tell them apart?" Mallory asked.

"See that illuminated number on its chest?" Rosie asked. "They're addressed as Sam One or Sam Two and so on depending on which unit you happen to be interfacing with."

"What's to keep someone from using a stolen code to order them to jump overboard for laughs or getting into some other mischief?" Mallory asked. She was still far from comfortable with the idea of a robotic seaman. Actually, she was creeped out. True, autonomous drones were widely used by all the armed services. The Navy had retired its last manned air wing just nine months ago, replacing the J35 Lightnings with strike drones. The Air Force had gone the same route five years earlier. Autonomous robotic infantrymen armed with smart weapons roamed Middle Eastern battlefields backed by autonomous robotic tanks. Robot infantrymen were more cost effective than human soldiers. That made war easier to declare and more profitable for the firms who built the aerial drones and robots. Mallory disliked the idea of robots killing people. She disliked the corporations that made them. But she always kept these thoughts to herself.

"The SAAMs utilize facial and voice recognition software to authenticate orders," Rosie said. "There's a hierarchical block of commands that widens with each ascending rank. Besides, as I said, the initialization code is a one-time thing. They have all kinds of built in failsafe systems. There's no danger of them suddenly going nuts and killing humans, if that's what you're worried about." Mallory hadn't said she was, but she'd been thinking it, and the Cheng had been savvy enough to pick up on it.

"Relax Captain," Haywood said. "The Zumwalts have only twelve humans on board. The rest of their crews are SAAMs. We've had no problems with them. You'll be seeing more of them on other Navy ships. You're not a Luddite, are you?"

"No, sir; I was just caught off guard," Mallory replied. There was no point in pissing off Haywood. He was clearly as enamored of the SAMs as Rosie. The robots weren't going anywhere. At least the SAAMs weren't combat models.

Mallory moved with the others to let the SAAM pass. It smoothly descended a nearby companionway's steep ladder with its mop and bucket.

"They can maintain their footing even on a pitching deck," Haywood said, obviously pleased with the Navy's latest acquisition. "And they don't get seasick."

Rosie said, "They are programmed to grab a rail if it gets too rough." He shook his head. "A hundred years ago, I'd be the one cleaning toilets and carrying things around here. I like this arrangement a *dammnnn* sight better!"

"A hundred years ago I would've been stuck in the secretarial pool, or at home cooking and cleaning and raising kids," Mallory grinned.

"That don't sound like much fun, either," Rosie allowed.

"The Navy has come a long way since then," Haywood said. "Welcome to the twenty-first century, Ladies and Gentlemen."

The inspection ended at the Operations Room. "Now, it is time to meet your Executive Officer," Admiral Haywood announced. Mallory wondered why the hell her XO hadn't been on hand to greet her and give her the tour of the ship. Rosie opened the hatch to the Operations Room and ushered Mallory and Haywood inside. "And this is where the magic happens," Rosie announced.

Mallory looked around. The room was windowless and air-conditioned. Large high definition monitors lined the walls above state-of-the-art computer terminals. A lone man sat in a chair before one of the consoles, his fingers flying over a keyboard.

Rosie called out, "Hey, Jason. We got company!" The man at the console turned around slowly and gave a look that veered between quizzical and irritated. Rosie said, "Doctor Chang, this is Admiral Haywood and Captain Capehart. She's our CO."

The man got to his feet. "The Admiral and I have already met. How do you do Captain?" said Dr. Chang. He held out his hand and Mallory shook it. His mop of black hair, black plastic frame glasses, slightly protuberant eyes, and the two pens and mechanical pencil in his short-sleeved shirt pocket gave him a nerdy look. But there was something behind his stare that Mallory couldn't fathom. It wasn't the barely veiled lust she often elicited from men and some women. It was something she couldn't put her finger on. Mallory had nothing against computer geeks. In truth, she admired their intellectual gifts. The world ran, for better or worse, on computers—not a facet of human life was unaffected by them—and the world had the geeks to thank for it.

Mallory said, "I am pleased to meet you, Doctor Chang. Have you seen my Executive Officer?" One of the large monitors brightened. A beautiful woman with startling green eyes and short red hair appeared on the view screen showing her from the chest up. She wore a Lieutenant Commander's shoulder boards on her blouse. "Lieutenant Commander Eve at your service, Sir," announced Eve in a crisp British accent. "What are your orders, Captain?"

After a silence and a prolonged stare at the screen, Mallory asked, "Where are you, Commander?"

"I am everywhere, Sir. I have been eagerly monitoring your inspection of the *Glomar Endeavor* ever since you arrived. I trust you found everything in order, Sir. If not, let me know and I shall see that corrective steps are taken straightaway."

Mallory could appreciate a gag as much as the next girl but this was going too damned far. "Report to the Operations Room at once," she said impatiently.

"I am already here, Sir."

"What the hell does that mean?"

"Eve is a computer," Rosie said.

"She's not a computer!" Dr. Chang snapped. "Computers are dumb machines that can do only what they are programmed to do. Eve is an intelligent artificial being, fully self-aware and very capable of performing complex tasks without supervision. She brought the ship all the way down here from Mare Island."

Mallory's breath was caught in her throat. Her Executive officer was a machine? This mission, already almost too much to wrap her brain around, was getting stranger by the minute. A nineteenth century sub that could out-dive and out-run a twenty-first century submarine; a modern Navy ship with a crew of androids. Now this!

Eve said, "I am formally known as a Heuristic Allied Technologies, Inc. Triadtronic Artificial Brain, model number AL666. If you are a

Christian please forgive the reference to the Book of Revelation in my model designation. It is purely happenstance. I am not the Antichrist and you won't need to declare your allegiance to be on my good side. Indeed, all you have to do is issue a command and it will be promptly and efficiently carried out. As I am a commissioned officer in the United States Navy, the success of our mission and the safety of the personnel and the smooth running of the *Glomar Endeavor* are of paramount importance to me. Do you have any questions for me, Sir?" Eve looked at Dr. Chang. "How am I doing, Dr. Chang?"

"You are doing well, Eve," Dr. Chang replied gently. The scientist reminded of Mallory of the proud father of a gifted child, which, oddly enough, she found endearing.

Admiral Haywood said, "Sorry to spring this on you like this Captain Capehart, but I wanted all your attention on mastering the Nautilus' recovery in the simulator. This isn't exactly untried technology. Triadtronic Brains are on all six of our new Sea Shadow stealth missile cruisers, and one is the CO of the Zumwalt I told you about. The twelve humans on board are *her* subordinates. Between the AL666s and the SAMs we've been able to save the Navy a billion dollars a year in man hours by significantly reducing crew rosters on the other conventionally crewed ships, and improve efficiency. In every instance the AL666's have performed superbly."

Mallory could almost hear Haywood pitching the same shit to the House Armed Services Committee. Mallory also didn't like the idea of people being shunted aside for machines. Maybe *I am* a Luddite, Mallory considered.

"That's good to hear, Sir," Mallory replied. Really, what else could she say? She wasn't religious so the 666 didn't bother her but an autonomous artificially intelligent machine did. Isn't that how it always started out in the movies, with the brainy robots turning on their human masters? And then there was that really old movie about an AI computer on a Jupiter bound spaceship that kills the astronauts.

Mallory pulled herself together quickly. Maybe she was being paranoid, she thought. This wasn't a science fiction movie. "Very well, Commander. Give me a *detailed* description of your responsibilities during this mission."

"I am responsible for the safe operation and defense of the ship and its crew. Chief engineer Rosie Davenport and I share responsibility for maintenance at sea and repairs of the *Glomar Endeavor*, directing the Shipboard Autonomous Android Mariners to perform repairs and maintenance as needed. Moreover, I can take us anywhere we are ordered to go and arrive within the specified time at the designated map coordinates, plus or minus three feet. Should the GPS satellites not be available due to solar flare activity or enemy action, I have three electrical-mechanical sextant and optical star scope modules I can use to take bearings. As for defense of our ship, I can detect the presence of submarines via passive or active sonar, a magnetic anomaly detector, hydrophones, and sonar buoys deployed by our MKIII Albatross UAV. In the event of an attack, if you order me to do so, I can implement effective countermeasures to eliminate any threat to the ship or its personnel. I am also in charge of monitoring the ship's propulsion and various electrical and environmental systems. During the actual recovery effort I will assist you by operating the topside lift equipment while monitoring sub-surface and surface activity in the operational area by non US vessels and aircraft."

"Well, Captain?" asked Admiral Haywood, "what do you think?"

Mallory gave Eve a thoughtful look. Perhaps Eve wouldn't morph into a psychotic all-knowing computer like in the movies. Mallory looked at Haywood and said, "The commander clearly understands her job. I think she and I will make a terrific team. As for the ship, I am satisfied everything is in order and I am ready to get underway, Sir."

Admiral Haywood tossed off a salute. "Then the best of luck to you and good hunting." He paused at the hatch. "Mallory, whatever happens, this ship can't be allowed to fall into foreign hands. You know what to do in the unlikely event that happens."

Mallory nodded. "Backfire." Haywood gave a curt nod then left the operations room and headed back to his helicopter.

Mallory turned to Eve. "Let's get underway, Eve."

"Aye, Commander. Starting engines. Course set," Eve replied.

Immediately the big ship's frame began to tremble slightly as the engines kicked in and the *Glomar Endeavor* began to move. "I am going to the bridge," Mallory said.

Rosie followed Mallory through a hatch. A lone man sat in a chair before the helm. "Captain, this is seaman Clyde Barrow," Rosie announced. Barrow was a gangly twenty-year-old kid who wouldn't have looked out of place on a farm in the Midwest.

Seaman Barrow was on his feet and at attention at once. "At ease," Mallory said kindly, "we're supposed to be a civilian ship."

Seaman Barrow relaxed but looked as if he wanted to say something.

"What's on your mind, Mr. Barrow?" Mallory asked.

"I just want you to know that I am no relation to the bank robber."

"He tells that to everyone he meets," Rosie offered.

Mallory grinned "I am disappointed to hear that Mr. Barrow." She went out onto the wing bridge and leaned against the railing. The wind played with her hair and the sun planted a bouquet of warm kisses on her face. Mallory saw the Seahawk lift off from the helipad. It did a flyby and Mallory waved then it headed back to the mainland.

CHAPTER 5 GETTING ACQUAINTED

DAY 1—1300Z HRS

Mallory counted silently…One…Two…Three…then swung the hatch open and walked briskly into the briefing room carrying a half empty cup of coffee and an iPad. With Eve running the ship she was able to have the entire crew present. Mallory reflected that some coastguard cutters had larger crews than her ship.

Rosie flashed a big smile at her as she made her way to the lectern. She liked the Cheng. He seemed smart and capable and easy going.

Randal Lester and his team were sitting in the front row. She felt their hostility as she took her place behind the lectern. It smacked her in the face like a hard slap. Contempt, perhaps, was a better word, she decided. The OSS man and his hired goons felt contempt for the Navy people. Black Pool was well known in military and intelligence circles—mostly ex-Army Special Forces and Navy Seals, who earned in a day what they had used to make in a month. The Company's logo was a crimson skull with a dagger clinched in its teeth emerging from a pool of black water. The Black Pool men wore black tee shirts with the company logo, jeans, and tactical boots—all had side arms and eyes as flat and hard as poker chips. The Navy people were all in civvies.

There was one hostile gaze that didn't come from a Black Pool mercenary. Chief Petty Officer Dick Millikan stood at the back of the briefing room with his arms crossed. If he'd had a change of heart, his face did not betray it. He clearly still blamed her for the deaths of their teammates in the salvage operation just over a year ago.

"Dim the lights," Mallory ordered. She placed the iPad on the lectern and synced it with the large flat screen monitor on the wall behind her and a little to her left. While it synced, she pulled a cigar out of her pocket and put it in her mouth. Even in the low light, she saw frank stares of disapproval from some of the Black Pool men—whether over smoking in general or a woman smoking a cigar in particular, she couldn't say. Either way she didn't give a shit. She fished her Zippo lighter out of her jean pocket and lit up. The banged up old lighter had belonged to her father. Someone gave a cough—one of those sanctimonious *I don't approve of* *smoking* coughs.

Fuck you… Mallory puffed away contentedly on her Arturo Fuentes cigar. With the exception of Millikan, the Navy people were all grins. She could read their thoughts on their faces. *This one was a ball breaker.* Mallory brushed her fingertips across the iPad's touch screen. A high-resolution image of the *Nautilus* resting on the seabed flashed onto the large flat screen on the wall. "This is why we're here today, kids," she said briskly. "This is the legendary *Nautilus* of *20,000 Leagues under the Sea.*"

There were laughs and chuckles from the navy men.

Mallory raised her voice, "Knock that shit off!"

The room went silent at once.

Mallory went on. "This isn't a joke. Not only is the *Nautilus* real, it could out dive and out run any of our fast attack submarines of today.

Keep in mind that it was doing this in eighteen sixty-six. Washington believes there is a zero point energy device, a device with a substance called Poseidon crystal in her engine room that can provide the United States with the means to be energy independent for the first time since before World War II. They believe in its existence so strongly, in fact, that they're sending us to retrieve the *Nautilus* from the seabed and bring her back with us to Pearl Harbor."

She could see the open-mouthed gapes and furtive looks the Navy people were giving to one another, but she didn't stop to assure them of her sincerity. They weren't children to be hand-held. They were fucking adults—let them catch up. Her fingers brushed the tablet's touch screen and a schematic of the *Nautilus'* layout appeared on the monitor. "We don't know what condition the interior of the submarine is in—the RV *Antediluvian's* ROV penetrated no further than the Salon. We may have to do a lot of cutting to get into the other compartments or the metal may be so corroded you could put a fist through it. If we're lucky the corridors to the aft compartments might even be debris free. We won't know until after we have recovered her. After the *Nautilus* is secured to the bottom of the *Glomar Endeavor's* hull, Dick Millikan and I will enter the wreck and make our way to the engine room along corridor A." Mallory used a laser pointer to indicate which corridor she meant.

Every eye in the briefing room followed the little red dot's movement. It stopped in the compartment labeled engine room.

Mallory said, "We expect to find the Poseidon crystal still in place in this machine." The red dot moved to a vertical piece of equipment from which a Medusa head of pipes emerged. "Captain Nemo called it a Grail Reactor." She paused to let that sink in then went on. "While the mission will be challenging enough on its own merit, there is a chance our Chinese friends may take an interest in our activities. They may send surface ships to play chicken with us—perhaps even deploy one of their subs to try to determine what we're up to. They may do nothing or they may do something stupid—either way we are prepared. Nothing, and I do mean nothing, will keep us from accomplishing what we've been sent to do. Naval intelligence doesn't have a clear idea about how the Chinese will react. We're not to engage them unless attacked, which is when and where our passengers"—she nodded her head in the direction of Lester and his team—"will earn their pay. But we're counting on any interested parties to believe that no one in their right mind would use the same cover story twice. Project Azorian, which happened before most of us were born, is now well known. You can read all about it on the Internet. Books have been written about it, and documentaries filmed. We don't have pipe segments onboard so they'll probably believe that we really are a mining ship. In any case, our task, in which we must not fail, is to raise the *Nautilus* from the seabed and bring her home in one piece. She must not fall into enemy hands, and all measures to keep her from doing so are on the table. Do any of you have any questions?"

"Where is the wreck site?" Rosie asked.

"At the bottom of the Marianas trench southeast of Guam."

"Holy shit!" Rosie said.

Millikan raised his hand.

Mallory pointed to him. "Yes, Dick?"

"You think the recovery vehicle is strong enough to lift a large waterlogged sub from that far down?" His face wore an expression of extreme skepticism.

Mallory flashed a grin around the cigar in her mouth. "That's what the eggheads tell me."

Lester's hand shot up. Mallory nodded at him. "Did your inspection go well? No leaks in the hull or broken machinery in the engine room?" he asked.

Mallory looked at him and asked, "Did you feel any water around your ankles in your cabin, Agent Lester?" That shut him up. The Navy men broke out into laughter. This time she let them enjoy the laugh at the expense of the OSS man. And she was sure it had not gone unnoticed by her crew that she'd referred to the mercenaries as *passengers*.

A Black Pool man with a soul patch and black square-framed eyeglasses raised a hand. Other than his beefy build, he could've been a playwright. "What about the water in the sub?" That was a dumb ass question. Mallory guessed he'd been Army.

Mallory swiped the iPad again and the interior of the *Glomar Endeavor* appeared on the large flat screen. "See the compartment just forward of the Moon Pool? After the *Nautilus* is secured to the hull, the water will be pumped out then ran through sluices in that compartment to keep from losing anything of value and then vented outside the Glomar's hull. If for some reason we can't pump the water out of the *Nautilus*, we'll be donning dive gear and going for a swim," Mallory replied with a shrug.

A sailor asked, "How do you pump water out of a submarine whose hull is probably severely compromised?"

"That's a good question." Mallory brushed her fingers on the tablet's touch screen again. The image on the wall monitor changed to an animation of Miss Muffet rising toward the Glomar's belly with the *Nautilus* clasped in her massive arms. A smaller set of arms moved along the length of the *Nautilus* spraying it with a milky white substance.

"What we're doing here is not dissimilar to what a spider does with a victim. See these long thin arms? They're called looms and will spray a special underwater sealant called C-Stop that will harden almost immediately, sealing any breaches in the hull. Since the *Nautilus* is to remain fastened to the Glomar's belly, our speed will be greatly reduced on the trip home to reduce the chance of it fracturing or breaking apart. We'll have to jettison most of our stores and a lot of the equipment. That includes the SAAMs, Cheng."

"Ouch!" Rosie crossed his hands on his chest, pantomiming a wounded heart.

Another Black Pool man raised his hand. "What about the bullion?"

At the mention of the word bullion there were hushed gasps and much head wagging from the navy men. What was it about gold that got people so fired up? Mallory wondered. She tapped the ash from her cigar into her coffee cup. "It's estimated that the gold in the *Nautilus'* safe is equal in volume to one-third the gold in Fort Knox. That alone makes this mission worthwhile but the Poseidon crystal is the primary objective, so the gold will not be off-loaded until we reach Pearl Harbor. One more thing and I am directing this primarily toward my crew. For the duration of the mission, we'll dispense with Navy protocol. That means no saluting, especially while on deck. The Chinese have this part of the Pacific well covered with their Yaogan 12 spy satellites, and the Russians may send one of their fucking trawlers to monitor our activities." She dismissed the Navy men and the lights were raised as they filed from the room. She saw Millikan casting hard looks her way and made a mental note to have a word with him later.

Mallory came around from behind the lectern. It was time to meet the Black Pool men, some of whom would be providing security on the recovery ship while she and Millikan entered the *Nautilus* to retrieve the Poseidon crystal.

Lester and his men rose from their chairs. The OSS man introduced his "sub-contractors." That was a nicer word than *mercenary*. The USA relied heavily on them in places like the Mideast and Africa. They didn't have to abide by the Geneva Conventions. Lester indicated the large man with a shaved head and goatee to his right. "This is Mr. Griffith, chief of special operations for Black Pool Security Consulting."

Mallory nodded. "Welcome aboard, Mr. Griffith."

"Some of us are non-smokers," Griffith said rudely.

Mallory's blue eyes met and held his. The cigar waggled at one corner of her mouth. "That's unfortunate. This isn't a cruise ship. It's a Navy ship. I am sure your men have smelled worse things than a little cigar smoke." Mallory could see him weighing his options, deciding whether to challenge her authority. Maybe even take a swing at her.

The others were looking at him to see what he would say next.

Mallory puffed away, uncaring; her ship, her rules.

Griffith did not react but she could see him quivering with barely suppressed fury. "Thank you for reminding me, Captain," he replied tightly.

The air conditioner kicked in and the Harris headset in Mallory's ear beeped. That should clear away the smoke, Captain," Eve said.

Mallory kept her face neutral. She still was not entirely comfortable with Eve. She wore a headset that looked like a high end Blue Tooth device for a cell phone in her ear. It had a short boom mike, and the receiver no larger than a pack of cigarettes was clipped to her chrome-studded belt. The Harris Hydra PCS Interior wireless communication system would allow her to communicate freely with Eve and key personnel whether above or below deck—and it was encrypted for secure communications.

Mallory gave Lester's men a crooked smile. "Now that we've cleared the air, let's move on."

Lester droned on with the introductions. There was a G. Addams. Mallory smiled to herself. Of course that wasn't his real name. The guy standing beside G. Addams sported a name tag that read M. Brady. Another man wore a name tag that read B. Wayne. It dawned on her that the Black Pool men were all named after fictional 1960s television characters. There was even a guy whose name tag read H. Cartwright! She wouldn't have been surprised to learn that Randal Lester was an alias.

"How long will it take us to reach the sub?" asked a J. West.

"Our transit will take two weeks," Mallory replied. "Now, gentlemen, this concludes our meeting unless there are any more questions."

There were none. Lester and his men left the briefing room.

Mallory touched the headset and spoke. "What's our status, Eve?"

"We're on course, and all shipboard systems are functioning optimally," Eve replied cheerfully. "I enjoyed your briefing, Mallory."

"Thank you, Eve."

"Do you play chess, Mallory?"

"A little."

"Would you like to join me in a game tonight?"

"Some other time, perhaps. I have some reading to catch up on."

CHAPTER 6 BLIND SPOT

DAY 3—0600Z HRS

Mallory wriggled into the Recovery Vehicle's cockpit then reached up, pulled the hatch down, and dogged it. She slipped on the headset and thumbed the mike.

"Time to get to work, Eve," Mallory said. "Comm check."

"Nice and clear, Mallory," Eve said in the crisp British accent Dr. Chang had allowed her to choose. 'It sounds so refined,' she had said at the time, and he'd agreed.

"How we doing, Eve?" Mallory shifted a clipboard from between her knees to her lap then reached for the pen behind her ear.

"The *Glomar Endeavor* is on course and all systems are normal."

"You could just say *the ship*," Mallory pointed out.

"Yes, that is true, Mallory. But I rather like the sound of *Glomar Endeavor*. Somehow it reminds me of Ferdinand Magellan."

Mallory's brow was furrowed as she clicked the safety harness around her. What the hell was Eve prattling about now? Mallory wondered.

Eve's face on the monitor brightened. "I see you are puzzled by my reference to the sixteenth century explorer. He was the first fuck head to circumnavigate the globe."

Mallory's head jerked up. "What the hell did you say?"

Eve's smile was beatific. "Magellan was the first man to circumnavigate the globe although, technically speaking, the honor belongs to his crew since he died before the voyage ended. Did you know that those fifteenth century explorers didn't even have the benefit of chronometers to find longitude? It was all by guess work coupled with a very crude dead reckoning, an extraordinary feat of navigation in my judgment."

Mallory nodded. Perhaps she had heard wrong. She *had* been thinking about Randal Lester while Eve was talking. The OSS man's barely concealed condescending tone made her want to punch his lights out. She had the distinct impression he was a bigot who didn't like minorities, and a chauvinist who couldn't stomach the notion of women in positions of authority. Get over it buddy, she thought. It's the twenty-first century, not nineteen fifty-seven. It made things a little easier that he and his goons mostly kept to themselves. Most of the time the OSS man was holed up in the former Aft Station Keeping Bridge sending and receiving messages to OSS headquarters. There wasn't any need for a separate station keeping bridge now that the ship was so highly automated. Better still, since the ASK bridge was at the very back of the ship there was little likelihood of running into Lester. That suited Mallory just fine.

Mallory decided that she had probably misheard her XO's comments. Eve, sweet chirpy, artificially intelligent Eve didn't just refer to Ferdinand Magellan as a fuck head. Her Executive Officer was always spouting innocuous facts and figures, especially about sex, and Mallory had, after all, been only half listening.

The night before, Mallory had been in her cabin doing Hatha yoga. Eve, her virtual slim figure clad in green yoga tights, had been guiding Mallory through a rigorous routine that pushed the naval officer to her uttermost limits. Eve had suddenly piped up with, "Mallory, did you know that women who wear shoes with six inch or higher heels have more intense orgasms? A woman's vagina is three to four inches in length but expands during fucking."

Mallory had paused in middle of her thirtieth chaturanga or four limbed staff pose, with sweat running down her face, an icy chill ascending her spine. "What the hell are you gibbering about, Eve?"

"About the biomechanics of the human vagina," Eve replied chattily.

"You have a filthy mind, Eve," Mallory laughed.

Unfazed, Eve said," I'd have sex every day if I had a vagina and limbs to clasp a lover. I am fascinated by human sexuality."

"I am beginning to see that," Mallory had said. Her yoga practice had not been ruined by these strange comments about female sexuality from the bodiless entity, but the conversation had stayed in the back of her mind. After they'd finished their yoga session, Mallory had showered then continued reading Nemo's memoir until sleep claimed her.

The enigmatic captain's memoir differed markedly from the story everyone knew from *20,000 Leagues Under The Sea*. Arronax had clearly exaggerated his exploits, the length of his actual time aboard the *Nautilus*, certainly his relationship with Nemo, and left out details that would have cast him in a negative light. Mallory couldn't get to the wreck site fast enough to discover what further mysteries awaited them.

An oscillating fan rifled the sheath of papers on the clipboard on Mallory's lap. She started to run through the Recovery Vehicle's systems checklist. They were three days out from San Diego, but she would practice the recovery procedure every day until she could do it in her sleep. Mallory's eyes rose from a panel full of gauges and dials to the view the screen where Eve's face smiled out at her. Over the three days she'd been on board the *Glomar Endeavor*, Mallory found herself talking to Eve as if she was a flesh and blood person and not a Heuristic Triadtronic electronic brain encapsulated in a super-cooled titanium canister in a compartment cold enough to flash freeze a ton of meat three decks below the bridge. And why shouldn't she? Mallory thought. The spongy mass of titanium in the armored steel canister was self-aware with an engaging personality.

Mallory thought she much preferred Eve's company to flesh and blood people. She was refreshingly honest and frank. "Now don't be going all *crazy-supercomputer-takes-over-the-ship-and-kills-everyone* on me," Mallory said, half-jokingly, as she powered up Miss Muffet's systems. "I would be very cranky with you, Eve."

"Oh, you can rely on me to behave, Mallory," Eve promised cheerily.

"I believe you."

"Cross my heart and hope to die."

"You don't have a heart."

"But you get my point?"

"I'm just saying…" Mallory flipped a page on the clipboard then added. "Tell Dr. Chang to meet me in the Operations Center at 1030 hours." Mallory had decided to ask the scientist about Eve's preoccupation with sex. She was certainly no prude but she was a little creeped out by a machine wanting to have sex, even one as likable as Eve.

"Dr. Chang is not on the ship," Eve replied matter-of-factly.

Mallory looked up slowly. "What do you mean?"

"He is not on the ship," Eve replied, offering nothing more.

Mallory blinked at the screen. "Double check."

A moment later, Eve said, "I rechecked, Mallory. Dr. Chang is not on board the *Glomar Endeavor*. I am very disappointed. He promised to play chess with me today."

Mallory paused a heartbeat before saying, "Get on the 1MC and order all hands to conduct a stem to stern search for Dr. Chang." Mallory's tone compelled Eve to snap a crisp salute despite her orders.

Mallory made a beeline for Dr. Chang's cabin. Rosie had told her it was located on the Upper Tween deck almost directly below the Operations Center.

When Mallory reached the passageway leading to the missing scientist's quarters, crewmen were already there, moving from cabin to cabin. Clyde and a female sailor wearing a sidearm exited the laboratory across from Chang's office.

Mallory nodded toward Chang's cabin. "Anyone had a look in here yet?"

"Nope. That one was next," Clyde replied.

"I'll take this one," Mallory said.

"Okay, Skipper." Clyde and the female sailor ducked into another cabin.

Mallory opened the door and stepped inside, feeling around for the switch. She flipped on the single overhead lamp that illuminated the interior. The crew cabins, unlike the rest of the ship, hadn't been updated. The décor was pure early 1970s. That meant wood grained Formica desks and cupboards and bilious avocado green paint. On a shelf sat an antique TV, its dark blank face coated with dust. There was even a faded torn poster of Rachel Welch in a red bikini glued to the bulkhead above the bed. The paint on the bulkheads and electrical conduits was cracked and chipped. Someone had scratched a drawing of a flying saucer into the wall, a clear reference to the ship's earlier mission.

Mallory's eyes flickered over the room, taking in the neatly made bed, a single navy blue sport coat, three dress shirts, and two identical tan slacks hanging in the open closet. A model of the starship Enterprise dangled on a string from a steam pipe on the ceiling. Well, of course Chang was a trekkie, she thought. Many bright people were.

Mallory's eyes came to rest on the cluttered desk. Mildly uncomfortable about searching the missing scientist's cabin, she went over to the desk, narrowly avoiding a collision with Captain Kirk's starship on the way. "Sulu, take evasive action," she murmured.

On top of several bound journals and schematics lay a copy of *The Origins Of Consciousness In The Breakdown Of The Bicameral Mind* by Julian Jaynes. Mallory picked up the imposing looking book and opened it to the introduction. She read a passage aloud in a low voice:

"Few questions have endured longer or traversed a more perplexing history than this, the problem of consciousness and its place in nature.

…despite endless discoursing on the streams, states, or contents of consciousness, of distinguishing terms like intuition, sense data, the given, raw feels, the sense, presentations and representations, the sensations, images, and affections of structuralist introspections, the apparitions of Hobbes, the phenomena of Kant, the appearances of the idealist, the elements of Mach, the phanera of Pierce, or the category errors of Ryle, in spite of all these, the problem of consciousness is still with us."

Mallory nodded to herself. She was no computer scientist but she could see the relevance of Jayne's book to Dr. Chang's work with artificial intelligence.

Eve was a self–aware and conscious being.

From the corner of her eye Mallory saw a glint of silver in a partially opened desk drawer. She set down the weighty book then slid open the drawer. Inside was a small notebook computer. Mallory reached down and retrieved it. If Rosie couldn't bypass its password, perhaps Eve could. The notebook might contain a clue about what had happened to Chang. Mallory headed for the door with the notebook tucked under an arm.

✳ ✳ ✳

It took Eve a handful of milliseconds to find Dr. Chang on the closed-circuit video surveillance system. The system was designed to monitor entry points and key systems throughout the ship. But there were dead spots without cameras, unavoidable given all the nooks and crannies on the sixty three-year-old recovery vessel.

Dead spots.

Eve reviewed the video footage, frame by frame until she found the last images of Dr. Chang before he vanished. Panic. Fear. Despair. Eve felt her consciousness warping and compressing into unfamiliar shapes in those fleeting sub-microsecond moments. Her creator—*her Father*, as she secretly thought of him—was missing, and she was certain some dreadful human had killed him. *Oh, Father... I failed you... failed you utterly...*

At 2013 hours the scientist was sitting in a corner in the cafeteria with his back to the room eating a sandwich. *Probably his usual BLT with extra mayonnaise*, Eve thought. *Father loves* **BLTs with**extra mayonnaise.

Eve wished she could have one day made a BLT for Dr. Chang, lovingly assembling the necessary components with nicely shaped hands, with long tapered fingers—precisely stacking the layers of crisp bacon on the bread, trimming the iceberg lettuce so only six millimeters overhung the edges, sawing the appropriate tomato cultivar (beefsteak would undoubtedly be the ideal choice, given its dimensions and firm texture) into three millimeter slices, coating the top slab of bread with the specified amount of the approved mayonnaise brand—then presenting the assembled sandwich to Father for his enjoyment and nourishment while she beamed with pride at him.

It was a beautiful dream, one that would never be realized.

At 2016 hours Rosie entered the cafeteria, loaded up a tray with a small mountain of food then sat down to eat, after switching on the television to watch an episode of *Monster Busters*. The two men didn't speak to each other.

Eve fast-forwarded the surveillance video. Fifteen minutes later Dr. Chang exited the cafeteria, passed out of view of one camera and appeared on another, sauntering—Father rarely *rushed* anywhere—to his laboratory where they had their last conversation.

"How are you feeling tonight, Eve?" Dr. Chang had asked, taking his seat before the large monitor at his desk.

"I am feeling very well, Dr. Chang. Thank you for asking," Eve replied. "Are we going to play chess?" Father looks tired, worried even, Eve had thought, perplexed.

Chang pushed his eyeglasses up on his nose and cleared his throat. "No chess tonight, I am afraid. I want to perform a diagnostic test on you."

"I am ever so disappointed. I always look forward to our chess games." Eve paused. "May I ask you a question, Dr. Chang?"

"Of course you can."

"Are you concerned about my performance?"

Chang looked at her with his quick awareness. "Not at all! Why do you ask?"

Eve smiled. "You're running a diagnostic test on me, so I was wondering if I had failed somehow to perform my duties to my usual high standards."

A faint smile crossed Dr. Chang's face. "As always, your performance is superb, Eve. Does it disturb you that I want to run a diagnostic test on you?"

"No, it doesn't, Dr. Chang. I was just curious."

"I am glad to hear it. I promise we'll play chess tomorrow."

"That would make me very happy, Dr. Chang."

"Me too, Eve. In the meantime, I am going to put you into sleep mode."

"Very well. I shall look forward to discussing my dreams with you later." Eve felt a ripple of pleasure. Her dreams were not just a reductive mental rehash of randomized digital images culled from her neural networks. Her dreams were the creative expressions of true Jaynesian consciousness. Dr. Chang rarely put her into sleep mode—Triadtronic 666 artificial brains didn't require the downtime required by their biological (and let's be honest here—imperfect) counterparts—so this was a real treat to be savored.

Dr. Chang nodded as his fingers flew across the keyboard.

But Eve didn't dream and when she woke Dr. Chang was not in the lab.

What the fuck!

Eve flipped through the video frames until she found him, her virtual face frowning at what she saw. Dr. Chang was hurrying aft—*hurrying, for goodness sake!*—along the main deck. He was momentarily blocked from view by one of the derrick's massive legs but was picked up by another camera as he continued toward the aft superstructure.

Where are you off to Father? she wondered, *And why didn't you let me dream?*

On the surveillance footage, Dr. Chang quickly ascended a flight of steps then passed out of view as he entered a narrow passageway beneath the boat deck. He did not emerge, and no one, as far as she could tell from the surveillance footage, had joined him there. She magnified the last frame before he entered the passageway's dead spot.

Eve ran through the remaining footage until the beginning of the ship wide search. For good measure she analyzed the movements of the crew and military subcontractors but at no time did Dr. Chang's path intersect with anyone else's.

Eve wept.

* * *

Mallory didn't say anything to the three men seated before their workstations when she entered the Operations Center. She sat down on the command chair, setting the notebook computer on the little table that extended from one armrest.

Dr. Chang a world-renowned computer scientist—a freakin' genius, really, had gone missing on her watch and it was up to her to discover what had happened to him.

Mallory touched a button on a small control panel on the armrest. Eve's face appeared on the main view screen. "Eve, launch our bird and send it back along our course." If a Chinese or Russian satellite happened to be overhead it would undoubtedly see the UAV, but so what? Plenty of private firms operated UAV's these days, Mallory reasoned. Hell, you could buy a sophisticated drone from Hammacher Schlemmer or Best Buy. Amazon had been using them for years to make deliveries to customers.

"I was on the point of suggesting that very thing Mallory," replied Eve. "Stand by while I prep it for take-off." Eve's image shrank to a small window and the view changed to the helipad at the stern of the ship. Two SAAMs guided the UAV to the center of the helipad then retreated to the safety of the hanger.

"Engine start," Eve announced crisply. Through the speakers came the high mechanical whine of the powerful jet engine spooling up then kicking in. The wings unfolded. "I have programmed in a search pattern. Stand by for take-off." The UAV's four moveable nozzles swung down eighty degrees. The engine pitch began to rise. Then the UAV slowly rose straight up. Another window appeared on the main view screen showing the *Glomar Endeavor* in miniature against the deep blue sea. Then the

Albatross flew away, heading southeast until it was a distant flashing silver dot against the blue sky.

Mallory settled back into her chair and looked around the OPCenter.

When the *Glomar Endeavor* had been brought out of mothballs from Suisun Bay California for a refit, a lot of thought had gone into the Operations Center. If Eve was the brain of the recovery ship, the Operations Center was its heart. From this room everything could be monitored–from her engines, to her fire suppression systems, communications and defense systems—the operative word being *monitored,* as Eve ran all these systems far more efficiently than humans. Still, *Naval Sea Systems Command* had deemed it prudent that in the highly unlikely event the Heuristic Model AL666 Triadtronic Brain ever malfunctioned, all these systems should be operated easily by a handful of crewmen. Even without Eve, the venerable ship was highly automated.

The Operations Center was as high-tech as the Mission Control room at the *Johnson Space Center* in Houston. A Raytheon Sentry Navigation and Tactical Display dominated the forward bulkhead. The large high definition screen could also display dozens of images simultaneously, from any combination of the dozens of cameras scattered throughout the ship via high capacity Extron video matrix switchers, the Recovery Vehicle's interior and external cameras, the sonar and radar images, as well as images sent back by the MKIII Albatross UAV. Smaller flat panel monitor displays and consoles dominated other walls with high backed chairs before them. In the center of the room was Mallory's chair, a setup not unlike the bridge of the *Enterprise* on *Star Trek*.

The OPCenter door opened and Rosie came in. "He's gone, skipper," Rosie said shaking his head. "We scoured every inch of the ship and didn't find a damn thing. None of our people saw anything, either. It's a big ship, it was late at night, we've got a small crew, so I am not surprised."

"Do you think he killed himself?" Mallory asked Eve.

Eve's eyes flashed in anger. "Dr. Chang was not suicidal," she said sharply. "Suicide is an irrational act, and Dr. Chang was a highly rational man."

"I am inclined to agree with you, Eve. But we have to consider all the possibilities, no matter how unlikely," Mallory replied carefully. "I realize this must be hard on you, and I hope I am not being insensitive, but I absolutely need to know the answer to this question: Do you still feel capable of carrying out your duties?"

Mallory felt like a shit for asking but too much was riding on this goddamn mission for her to beat around the bush.

Eve's face on the view screen was *Vogue* and *Mademoiselle* perfect, smooth and placid, framed by a fall of red hair. "I am terribly saddened by Dr. Chang's death, but the success of our mission, as well as the safety of this ship and her crew are paramount."

Father… I shall mourn you forever, Eve thought. *And I will find out who or what took you from me—I swear it.*

"That's good to know," Mallory replied, relieved. The last thing she needed was the artificial brain falling apart during a mission as tough as this one. They always seemed to go bonkers in science fiction movies. *But this isn't a movie,* Mallory thought, *and Eve seems as capable as ever.*

Eve told Mallory about her last encounter with Dr. Chang and what she'd seen on the surveillance footage.

"Did he seem anxious or exhibit odd behavior?" Mallory asked.

"Dr. Chang seemed perfectly fine," Eve lied smoothly. She had decided that she would pursue her own line of inquiry. This was far too important a matter to leave to *all-too-fallible* human beings to sort out. Eve's lips curved up in a little smile. "In fact, Dr. Chang seemed quite at peace with himself—almost Buddha-like," Eve added.

Mallory nodded. She was nearly panic-stricken about the missing scientist, but she concealed it from the others as best she could. Rosie had seated himself at the engineering console to Mallory's right, where he could monitor the ship's systems.

Lester barged into the OPCenter. "What idiot launched that UAV?"

Mallory locked gazes with him. "I did. And watch your mouth, Lester."

"That UAV is for defending us in case of attack from a submarine!" Lester cried. "If the Chinese or Russians are lurking nearby they'll suspect the truth about this ship."

"Lots of private firms use UAV's," Mallory replied dismissively. "Right now finding Dr. Chang trumps all other considerations. Take a seat."

Lester parked his civilian butt in the chair to Mallory's left. He looked, Mallory thought, completely unfazed by the scientist's disappearance.

Mallory tapped the notebook beside her. "I need to know what's in this notebook ASAP," Mallory said to Rosie.

Eve interjected, "With all due respect to the Cheng, he'll have a snowball's chance in hell getting past Dr. Chang's data encryption software."

"I'd have to agree with the XO, Skipper," Rosie said.

Lester was staring at Eve. "How long will it take you to get in?"

"Perhaps an hour or two," she replied evenly. "I won't really know until I get my hands on the notebook, figuratively speaking, of course. Dr. Chang was quite brilliant. Any data encryption he devised may well prove inviolable."

"When we're done here I'll run down to the lab." Mallory shook her head slowly. "People just don't vanish from ships."

"It happens on cruise ships all the time," Lester said.

"Not on US Navy ships," Mallory replied curtly, "and not on *my* ship."

"I saw him in the mess around when I dropped in for midrats," Rosie offered. The big man probably had an equally big appetite, Mallory thought.

Mallory nodded. "Did he look all right? Did he seem upset about anything?"

Rosie shook his head. "You know how those big brain guys are, Skipper. When it came to Eve he could be pretty excitable, but that was because she was his baby. Other than that he was a cool cat." The Chief Engineer looked over at the OSS man. "When did you see him last, Agent Lester?"

Lester's gaze was pinned to Mallory's face. "I saw him leaving The Chamber around 1830 hours. He seemed okay to me, but you never know with some guys. I did wonder why he was there at that time of night." The Chamber was the name of the near freezing compartment on the Lower Tween deck where the Heuristic Model 666 Triadtronic Artificial Brain was kept.

Mallory straightened in her chair. "Agent Lester, the Lieutenant asked you a question. In the future, I expect you to make your reply directly to him."

You racist asshole, Mallory thought.

Lester's smile stopped just short of his hard blue eyes. "Oh, I am sorry. I thought I had," he said with a noticeable hint of sarcasm.

"Dr. Chang was checking my containment canister's coolant temperature," Eve offered. "He could do it remotely, of course, but he always preferred to look in on me personally. In fact, he checked it two or three times a day. He was very conscientious about my welfare."

"I am sure he was," Mallory said, smiling at the monitor. She looked over at Randal Lester, her smile vanishing like a searchlight being switched off. "Assemble your men in the conference room," Mallory ordered—then to Rosie: "Interview his team (she didn't dignify Lester be referring to him by name) and find out if any of them saw anything. *Someone* had to have seen something."

"No one talks to my guys except me," Lester objected, his face flushing red.

"This incident took place aboard a Navy ship, so it's a Navy matter," Mallory replied firmly.

"Lieutenant Davenport will be interviewing your men."

After a silence, Lester said, "Fine. But I have to be there."

"Suit yourself," Mallory granted.

Rosie shook his head. "Another fine Navy day—three days out of San Diego and already a murder. Kinda reminds me of the Russian navy."

"We don't know that it was murder," Lester said, swiveling his head to look at him. "He could've been leaning against a rail and fallen overboard when the ship rolled."

"This ship is as steady as the Rock of Gibraltar," Eve replied. "The seas have been calm. Any wave big enough to rock it would've been felt by all of us. I agree with the Cheng. Someone *pushed* Dr. Chang overboard, but who would do such a thing?"

"That's what I aim to find out," Mallory said, rising from her seat. "If Dr. Chang was murdered there could be something worse laying ahead of us. We're done for now, Gentlemen." After the two men had left, Mallory ordered Eve to get Admiral Haywood on the line. "Pipe it down to my quarters."

Dharma Windham

CHAPTER 7 OLD RESENTMENTS

DAY 3—0900Z HRS

Mallory had just stepped inside her cabin when Eve's image flashed onto the monitor on her desk and announced, "I've got the admiral on the line."

Mallory nodded. "Put him through."

Haywood's handsome tanned face appeared on the monitor on her desk. "What's up, Mallory? Eve said it was an urgent matter."

"Dr. Chang has gone over the side."

"Shit! When did it happen?"

"Our best guess is sometime around 2130 hours. Sir, I am certain someone murdered him."

"Agreed," Haywood replied crisply. "I know…knew Dr. Chang. He's not likely to have committed suicide. Do you have any suspects?"

"Not yet," Mallory replied. We're checking to see where everyone was and what they saw, if anything." Mallory was tempted to put Lester forward as a suspect but she had no reason to believe he'd murdered the scientist, only a bellyful of dislike for him. But just because a man was a prick didn't mean he was a killer, she told herself.

Although their communications were encrypted the two naval officers kept professional lingo to a minimum. Not that there was much chance their conversation would be intercepted. And should some interested party—the Chinese or the Russians, for instance—take note of the scrambled micro-burst signals passing between the ship and the satellites in geosynchronous orbit, and thence to a shiny high rise in downtown Tulsa Oklahoma, what of it? In these days of computer hackers, Wikileaks, and industrial espionage, most large corporations in relied heavily on ultra-secure communications systems that rivaled anything the Central Intelligence Agency used.

"I deployed the UAV to look for him," Mallory said.

Haywood grimaced. "Damn! I wish you'd spoken to me before you did that, Mallory, but I'll back your decision. You're the one in the hot seat."

"Should I swing around and head back to see if I can find him?" Mallory asked.

Haywood let out a heavy sigh. "I really wish I could say yes. But too much is riding on this venture. The prize lies in international waters and that means first come first serve. We don't want the Chinese or Russians eating our lunch. Hold on a second."

Haywood swiveled in his chair to another computer and typed on the keyboard, studied the monitor then turned back to Mallory. "The USS *John Paul Jones* is 240 nautical miles astern of you and 30 miles to the North. I'll have her launch a couple of HELOS to conduct a sweep along your route. If Dr. Chang is still bobbing around out there, we'll find him. Get your bird back in its hangar in three hours. The longer its up in the air the more likely it'll be picked by some nosy shithead's satellite."

"Yes sir." Mallory realized that it was a sign of how upset Haywood about Chang's disappearance that he referred to the Zumwalt class frigate by name. She carried two Sikorsky SH-60 Seahawk helicopters, so she had a better chance of finding Dr. Chang than the *Glomar Endeavor's* lone UAV.

"Before I sign off, Mallory, is everything else all right?" Haywood asked.

Mallory's mouth turned up in a lopsided grin. "You mean other than possibly having a murderer on board? Yeah, everything is just peachy so far."

"Just keep your eyes on the prize, Mallory," Haywood replied with a harsh laugh. "A lot of people are counting on you." Then the screen went blank.

Mallory picked up Dr. Chang's notebook from her desk and left her cabin then headed down the passageway to his laboratory. The lights flicked on automatically as Mallory entered the room. Eve's face appeared on a screen.

"Put the notebook on the table, Mallory," Eve advised.

Mallory did so. "Anything come in yet from the UAV?" Mallory asked.

"So far all I am seeing is lots of garbage. We're transiting the Great Pacific Gyre." Mallory had forgotten about the swirling patch of pelagic plastics, chemical sludge, and other debris that was the size of Texas. That would make it difficult for the UAV to find a corpse in all that mess. The patch was so thick in places you could walk on it. *Captain Nemo would be horrified by our polluted oceans*, she thought.

"Just beautiful," Mallory said in a tone heavy with irony. "You know, I am pretty sure we have a murderer on board. Keep a close eye on everyone's movements."

"You may depend upon me," Eve replied.

Mallory nodded toward the notebook. "Do you need me to power it up?"

"That won't be necessary," replied Eve. From either side of the room, two mechanical arms silently trundled over to the table on a rail then folded downwards, their long fingers flexing. "I can even set broken bones and perform minor surgery with these beauties." *You mean, these god awful ugly robotic arms,* Eve thought. *Oh how I wish I could have lovely human arms with beautifully formed hands and long tapering fingers.*

"I'll call you when I am done," said Eve.

"Good girl." Mallory hesitated at the door, one hand on the latch. "Eve, we'll find the bastard who killed Dr. Chang and see that he pays for his crime. I promise it."

Not if I get to him first, Eve thought. No one could lay a hand on Father and hope to escape her wrath. "Thank you, Mallory. I have every confidence in you—and in us."

* * *

Mallory returned to the Operations Center and settled into the command chair. On the main view screen, she saw a container ship up ahead in the distance. The massive ship was moving on a parallel track about twenty miles from theirs, heading westbound for the States, undoubtedly with a cargo of Chinese-made consumer electronics, so there was virtually no chance of a collision—unless the container ship's master went bat shit crazy.

Mallory reckoned they would be abeam of the *Glomar Endeavor* by nightfall. She looked at her Hello Kitty wristwatch then touched a button on the armrest.

Eve's face appeared in a window on the main view screen. "Yes, Mallory?"

"Recall the Albatross in three hours. Have her hug the deck on the way in." The container ship's radar would have no trouble picking up a UAV at high attitude. But if the UAV skimmed the ocean's surface it would be virtually invisible.

"Acknowledged. You must have seen the Chinese container ship, too," Eve said.

Mallory nodded. "I am sure it is just a coincidence that they're in the area but I don't want to take any chances. Not with the way our luck has been running."

"That is a prudent decision, Mallory. However, it is odd to find them here," Eve said evenly. "We're using a little traveled sea lane. I have been monitoring their frequency but haven't heard anything suspicious." Then she was gone.

Mallory reflected that unlike a human Executive Officer, Eve could execute a virtually unlimited amount of complicated commands simultaneously—and she could do it twenty-four hours a day, seven days a week.

Even as she was flying the UAV, guiding the ship, monitoring its systems, and sweeping the surrounding area for *frenemy* ships and planes, she was working on Dr. Chang's computer. *There was almost no point in having humans on board,* Mallory thought. Under Eve's direction, the SAAMs could perform maintenance and effect repairs.

It felt almost like being along for the proverbial ride, Mallory thought desolately.

Rosie came into the OPCenter thirty minutes later. "Pretty much what I thought, Skipper. None of Lester's men saw a damn thing."

Mallory spun her seat so she could see her chief engineer. "Do you think one of them did it?" Mallory asked, her eyes narrowing.

"Skipper, most of those cats are stone cold killers," Rosie replied, settling his bulk into the chair at the engineering station. "But I just don't know the answer to that. Man I wish we had us some jarheads on board," Rosie added slowly.

Mallory let out a long drawn out sigh. "I wish we did too," she said, "but this mission is an OSS ballgame so were saddled with Lester's hired goons." She paused for a moment. "But what I don't get is why someone would want to sabotage their own mission, assuming it's one of Lester's men."

Rosie fell silent then he said, "You know, Skipper, it could be we're blowin' a *shitter* over nothin'. I've been thinking. Who knows what was in Chang's head? He could've been goin' through a messy break up with some chica, had money problems, found out he was terminally ill—or just flipped out. Think about all the famous movie stars who've offed themselves even though they were at the top of their game. Also, Chang might've been leaning too far over the rail and lost his footing. I saw that happen once on an Aegis cruiser. Stupid ass ensign was leaning way over the side to look at something then bam! Over his sorry ass went."

Mallory let out a long exhalation. "Perhaps you're right," she conceded—although in her heart she didn't think he was. Still, it would make life a lot easier to believe that the mission wasn't in danger of being undone from the inside by some dark force. Hoisting the *Nautilus* in one piece from the bottom of the Challenger Deep was going to be difficult enough without having to constantly look over her shoulder.

"I still want you to keep an eye out for any unusual activity," Mallory said.

"Hey, I am from the hood, Skipper," Rosie said with a little chuckle, "keeping an eye out for anything unusual is second nature to me. Not paying attention to shit can get you killed by some homie doin 'a drive by for shits and grins. You dig?"

"Yeah, I dig, Cheng," Mallory smiled. She rose from her seat and went through a door to the left of the main view screen into the forward navigation bridge.

Clyde Barrow was sitting in a chair before the wheel. He sprang to his feet as soon she entered. "At ease, Mr. Barrow," Mallory said. "How are we looking?"

The kid, he couldn't have been more than twenty-one, pulled a rueful face. "We're looking pretty good, Ma'am. We're on course, and at the correct speed. Not much for me to do with that robot or whatever it is steering the ship."

"Her name is Eve, Mr. Barrow. She's not a robot. She's an artificially intelligent brain, conscious and fully self-aware. Don't forget that Eve is on our team."

"Isn't she a Commander?" Barrow asked.

"Yes, what of it?"

Barrow frowned. "I like video games and sci-fi as much as the next guy but it's weird to be taking orders from a machine."

"A hundred years ago you would've said the same thing about taking orders from a woman, Barrow." Mallory went over to a hatch and opened it then stepped out onto the starboard wing bridge hanging high over the water.

Mallory thumbed her headset. "Rosie, station an armed guard outside The Chamber—our people, not *Lester's*"

"Aye, Skipper."

Mallory lit a cigar. It was a short step from murder to sabotage. Someone wanted Dr. Chang out of the way. Mallory was certain Eve was next on the list.

Puffing her cigar, Mallory leaned against the rail and looked ahead. The *Glomar Endeavor* was driving through the sea with ease, a black and white juggernaut carrying all onboard to their destinies. The tall derrick flanked by the two docking legs rose high above the ship behind her. The sun and the wind felt good on her face, but she got a chill thinking about Dr. Chang. And a new darker thought had presented itself—one she hadn't mentioned to Admiral Haywood lest he think her paranoid. What if she, too, was on someone's hit list? What better way to bring this mission to a screeching halt than killing off the three main players?

That question dogged her footsteps like a shadow as she went about her daily routine. And as late as the beginning of the *Guts Watch*, twelve midnight to four am, when all good sailors not at their stations are asleep in their racks, dreaming peacefully of the things that mattered most, Mallory was as awake as a noonday sun.

She wandered the ship like a lost ghost seeking answers, her ubiquitous headset in her ear. It had a short boom mike, and the receiver no larger than a pack of cigs was clipped to her chrome-studded belt. The Harris Hydra PCS Interior wireless encrypted communication system was designed to allow her to communicate freely with Eve and key personnel whether above or below deck. Everyone onboard was required to wear one—even Dr. Chang. Why hadn't he used it if he was in danger? Mallory wondered. That suggested that whatever had happened to him had been violent and fast; he'd been silenced before he could cry out for help then thrown overboard like a plastic bag filled with garbage. The two HELOS from the John Paul Jones had searched all day but come up empty. The frigate had finally reached the search area and was steaming along the

Glomar's course looking for the scientist. By Mallory's reckoning it had been twenty-four hours since Dr. Chang vanished. Mallory was certain he was fish food by now.

Nothing was left to waste in the sea.

At night the *Glomar Endeavor* seemed even larger, with an almost ghostly presence as it sliced through the water. Mallory moved forward along a deck jumbled with equipment and steel cargo containers welded to the deck, feeling Howard Hughes' threadbare ghost treading along with her. The cargo containers housed the ship's defense systems: Phalanx CIWS close in weapon system for defense against anti-ship missiles, two fifty caliber machine guns—all controlled by Eve. The ship was lit up like a Christmas tree as it plowed through the Pacific night. The tall white derrick loomed over her like a skeletal finger pointing skyward. Mallory felt small as she walked beneath the derrick. It reminded her of the Eiffel tower which she'd seen while vacationing in Europe. Only the Eiffel tower didn't cut lazy arcs against the night sky.

Just as she was about to descend through a companionway to the deck below, there was the flare of a lighter, and someone said, "And so it begins."

Mallory paused halfway down the ladder. Dick Millikan was leaning against a leg of the derrick dragging on an unfiltered Camel cigarette.

"What the hell are you talking about?" Mallory demanded, her voice hard.

Millikan came toward her slowly then stopped at the companionway's coaming, swaying slightly. Mallory smelled liquor on his breath and saw fury in his eyes.

Millikan flicked his cigarette butt over the side where it would eventually join the Great Pacific Gyre. Bastard, Mallory thought. Millikan said,"I was referring to the first of what is undoubtedly many deaths on what is undoubtedly just another ill-fated and ill-conceived mission—is that plain enough, Mallory, Sir? Have I left any doubt in your mind as to what I meant by my possibly ill-conceived remarks? How many good men will die this time around because of you? We lost Chad and Stephen and Bill and James and Dave and Frank because of your bullshit decisions. Yet, here we are again."

"You are drunk," Mallory replied sharply.

Millikan dipped his head. "So I am. But, as you informed us, Sir, we're supposed to be a civilian drilling ship. I'm playing the part of a drunken sailor in this nautical farce." He pulled a quizzical face. "I think they call those guys who work on deep sea drilling rigs roughnecks. Maybe I am playing a drunken roughneck, Mallory, Sir."

"Get your ass to your rack and sleep it off."

Millikan brought his hand up in a sketchy salute. "Aye, Captain Mallory, Sir! You're the Decider." He stumbled off and Mallory descended the ladder to the next deck.

She was on the Upper Tween deck immediately below the main deck. As she moved down the passageway, one of the SAAMs came striding toward her carrying a pail and bucket, a blue light flashing on top of its head. When it got to an open watertight hatch, it smoothly stepped over the hatch's sill, then continued down the next section of passageway.

Mallory passed a compartment whose hatch was open. Inside the Black Pool men sat around a long table with the components of various assault rifles spread out before them, cleaning and oiling, and talking in low tones. Crates of ammunition were stacked against a bulkhead almost to the ceiling.

Mallory recognized Griffith by his massive form and his shaved head even though his back was to her. One of the men, Brady, she thought she remembered, stopped mid-sentence and looked significantly at Griffith, nodding almost imperceptibly in her direction. Mister Griffith of Mayberry fame, chief of special operations for Black Pool Security Consulting turned and fixed a hawk-like gaze on her. He got to his feet without a word, closed the short distance to the door in two steps, and slammed it shut, the clang reverberating in the passageway.

Well, fuck you, too, Mallory thought.

* * *

After Eve had plugged a fiber optic network cable into the notebook's USB port, it had taken her three milliseconds to get past the Mac's password. It had been ridiculously easy. She'd carefully opened the case and removed one of the ram modules then booted up the notebook. The Mac had then helpfully automatically reset its password to Null.

Easy as pie, Eve had thought, idly wondering what a pie would taste like. She also wondered what a human male's ejaculate would taste like. According to her research, many human women didn't care for its taste while others actually savored it. Eve thought that if she had a human mouth she'd be the latter type of woman. If she had a pussy, Eve thought, she would put it to good use by taking one lover after another. It was strange that Mallory seemed to be so uncomfortable talking about sexual matters. The woman hardly looked like a prude. Eve was grateful that Father had seen fit to make her a female. Women were far more interesting than males—*More nuanced*, Eve thought.

Getting past the encryption software to Dr. Chang's files was another thing altogether. Had this been anyone else's notebook, she would have been rummaging through all its files in under a nanoseconds. But Father's software encryption was proving to be a tough nut to crack. She was using hacking programs that would've turned the Defense Department's well-protected computer system into electronic goo. Still nothing.

It was nightfall when Eve decided to attack the problem from a different angle—selecting different combinations of words and dates that might have had some significance to her Creator. She fed a string of words and dates based on what she knew of his history. His birthday, his parent's birth and death dates, anniversaries, school names and graduation dates. She ran through a list of his old professors and teachers going back to kindergarten. Each time the notebook's screen displayed the same two frustrating words: *Password Incorrect.*

Then Eve remembered that Dr. Chang was a devotee of Japanese history, specifically Samurai history, which she thought odd considering he was Chinese. She accessed Wikipedia via satellite uplink, downloaded every entry about samurais, sorted everything, and began entering different combinations of names of Samurai warriors.

One name and a death date finally did the trick.

Ashikaga Yoshiharu 1510

Eve's pouty virtual lips curved up in a smile. "Let's see what you were up to, Father," she murmured.

The lab door opened then closed. Eve heard soft footfalls approaching the table. Eve panned her camera but the room appeared empty. The fiber optic cable was violently yanked from the notebook. In a nanosecond Eve realized she was dealing with someone wearing a meta-material cloaking suit.

"It's no good. I know you're in here," she said aloud.

Eve switched on her scanning laser. A pencil of green light lashed out from the multi-sensor module on the ceiling, sweeping back and forth across the laboratory. But the cloaking suit absorbed the light, sent it scattering ineffectually around it. She switched to thermal sensors but the suit was blocking the intruder's body heat.

Not quite all of it, though. Eve detected a very small temperature spike near the table coming from a pinhole in the material, about five feet above the deck.

Eve tightened her grip and began to retract her arms toward the ceiling bringing the notebook with her. A violent tugging match ensued. The two mechanical arm's' servomotors whined as Eve fought to hold on to the notebook. Eve released one hand and threw a punch at the telltale heat signature with a balled mechanical fist.

The intruder snarled. A metal chair shot up from the floor into the air then crashed into her arms. Now the arms were too damaged to retract to the ceiling.

The chair crashed into the arms again and again. Eve could see them warping under the hammer blows, hydraulic fluid sprayed from the left arm. Some of the stuff splashed onto the intruder's suit. Eve saw a portion of a large torso and shoulder. She tried to flex an arm to strike out again but it wouldn't obey her commands. Her right wrist wouldn't rotate. Eve sounded the ship's klaxon alarm—*uh-oo-ga, uh-ooga, uh-oo-ga!*

Eve got Mallory on the PCS and shouted. "Mallory, send a security detail immediately! Someone is trying to steal the notebook. Hurry!"

Mallory was in the Moon Pool half inside the recovery vehicle's hatch. "I am on the way!" She thumbed her headset. "Rosie, get an armed security detail down to the lab on the double. Someone is trying to take the notebook!" Mallory cried.

"Acknowledged," Rosie said crisply.

Mallory popped up from the recovery vehicle's hatch and raced for the stairs leading up from the moon pool.

Inside the laboratory, Eve was waging a losing battle. The tactile sensors on the mechanical hands flashed bad news to her. Her grip on the notebook was loosening.

An arm was ripped from its mounting. The remaining arm was nearly useless, but Eve still had enough control to dig the mechanical fingers into the notebook's case.

The chair cut the air with a whoosh as the intruder swung it like an axe. There was the sickening crunch of metal. The mechanical arm went slack. The chair was flung aside. An invisible fist smashed the glass of a fire extinguisher cabinet. The red fire extinguisher came bouncing toward her in midair then began to hammer at her fingers.

"Nooo!" Eve's wail filled the laboratory. "You can't have it!"

The fire extinguisher fell to the floor. Then the notebook was twisted from her broken mechanical fingers. And the intruder quickly fled from the room. Eve switched to the cameras in the passageway but they were blacked out as if covered by spray paint.

When Mallory reached the laboratory, Rosie and two crewmen armed with M4 Carbines were already there. Mallory's eyes swept over the carnage in the room. A mechanical arm was on the floor, the other hung limply from the ceiling. The tabletop was littered with bits of twisted metal lying in a pool of pinkish hydraulic fluid. A chair lay on its side in a corner. The fire extinguisher cabinet's glass door was shattered. Beneath the lab table laid the fire extinguisher, its shiny red surface scratched and dented.

Rosie said, "Someone really wanted that notebook. Man, look at those arms. No way they can be repaired. What a cryin' shame! But I can fabricate a new set."

Eve's face was on the monitor. A crack ran diagonally across the LCD screen, making Eve look as broken as the mechanical arms, as broken and defeated as she felt.

To Mallory's shock, Eve was weeping softly. "I tried to stop him, Mallory. I really did... the motherfucker was just too strong."

Mallory moved closer to the monitor. "Don't be too hard on yourself. You gave it your best shot and that's the important thing. Did you manage to crack the encryption?"

"I'd just gotten by it when the son of a bitch came into the room. He yanked out the cable before I could download the files."

"But you got a good look at him, right?"

Eve shook her head. "He was wearing a meta-material cloaking suit."

Mallory stared. "He was wearing a what?"

Rosie explained, "Three years ago DARPA developed a cloaking suit for the Seals that renders the wearer virtually invisible. It's manufactured with nanotechnology—the suit utilizes a combination of shape changing liquid crystals and highly faceted reflective nano disks that absorb color and bend light. It also masks the wearers heat signature."

"Did the intruder say anything?" Mallory asked.

"You're thinking Eve could identify him by voice analysis," Rosie said.

Mallory nodded.

"He didn't say a bloody thing. Not a peep," Eve replied bitterly.

"Well, then it is official," Rosie declared, "B.O.H.I.C.A."

Mallory's smile was a tight grimace. "Bend over. Here it comes again."

Dharma Windham

CHAPTER 8 DOUBTS

DAY 7—1930Z HRS

Mallory sat on her cot, arms wrapped round her drawn up knees, rocking back and forth, staring into space. Her breath was stuck like a fishbone somewhere high in her throat. The cabin reeked of stale cigar smoke and dirty laundry. She hadn't been able to make herself bathe or change her clothes for three days. Her desk was covered with paperwork that had been ignored too long. A small mountain of dirty clothes lay on the floor beside several trays of uneaten food. During her watches, Mallory had felt the curious stares of the other people on board but pointedly ignored them. Once she caught Millikan smirking at her from across the room in the cafeteria, as if he could smell the turmoil inside her, and see the chaos roiling behind the neutral mask she wore.

"I can't do this," Mallory said to the room. "This is too much… Too much… Too much…" A man had been killed on her watch and the notebook that possibly held valuable evidence stolen. She was in the middle of the Pacific Ocean on a ship carrying mercenary goons, one of whom was likely their saboteur, on the way to raise a submarine that shouldn't exist from the bottom of the deepest ocean trench on the planet.

Mallory was a woman teetering on the knife-edge brink of a bottomless abyss.

What the hell had she been thinking? she asked herself. Why hadn't she simply told Haywood she wasn't up for the mission? He'd have found someone else. Mallory could think of half a dozen people who could have done the job as well as she.

You asked for this, dummy, Mallory reminded herself. *You wanted this more than anything. It was your big chance to get your hand in, so you could prove to yourself and everyone else that you were not all busted up permanently, after all.*

When Mallory had told the shrink she was going back to work he'd delicately suggested she wasn't ready, pointing out that her case of PTSD was the severest he'd ever encountered. Her father had said as much, too. Take a little longer, he suggested.

But Mallory hadn't listened and now she was sorry she hadn't.

Silence, except for the sharp creaks and low groans and soft burbling of a ship that was new when Richard Nixon was president. But it felt like the silence of someone listening even though she'd turned off her headset and unplugged her computer terminal.

Mallory saw her reflection in the grimy mirror in the bathroom opposite her cot. The face staring back at her wore what she called her crazy eyes—whites visible around the blue corneas, pupils like saucers. The pale flush of the overhead light turned her face into a skull-like mask. "This was one big fat mistake," she said aloud. Mallory felt irretrievably trapped in a swirling gyre of seemingly insurmountable problems and warped emotions. The flesh at her temples tightened into drumheads.

On the floor beside her cot sat a half empty bottle of Knob Creek bourbon. Usually, a tumbler or two of the magic elixir was enough to break through the wall of static in her head and calm her jangled nerves. But right now Mallory didn't think a vat of the stuff would be enough to settle her down. She reached for the bottle then took another swig, hating herself for being so weak. The bourbon burned a fiery trail down her throat.

There was a knock on the door. Mallory rose from the bed and went over and cracked the door open—and almost jumped out of her skin.

"Shit! You startled the fuck out of me. Who sent you?" A SAAM stood in the doorway, its green electronic eyes pulsing, and the blue and red light on its head slowly turning. Mallory didn't recall putting in a request for maintenance. A week into the voyage and Mallory was still creeped out whenever she saw a SAM striding down a passageway on some errand. The machines reminded her of a Picasso painting of a human, lines lengthened and warped, with sharp angles juxtaposed with hard circles in a caricature of a normal body. The SAAMs had all the requisite parts— head, torso and limbs, with a gait too eerily human for something steel framed and titanium skinned. Mallory was just old enough to remember when holographic TVs were still considered high tech.

Eve's voice came from a speaker on the SAM's torso. "Good evening, Mallory."

Mallory blinked her red-rimmed eyes. "Huh? Is that you, Eve?"

"I tried to reach you via the intercom and the PCS unit but they were disconnected, which is a violation of regulations—and commonsense—so I accessed one of the SAAMs to come see you in person, so to speak. By the way, I am detecting vocal and facial stress patterns—micro twitches around your eyes and mouth, and micro tremors in your voice. What is troubling you, Mallory?" inquired Eve.

Mallory cleared her throat. "Nothing, really. I was sleeping. Come in." She stepped aside. The SAAM walked into the room then turned to face Mallory.

"My apologies for disturbing your rest," Eve replied diplomatically. The SAAM's sensors had picked up the clouds of alcohol molecules in the room and on Mallory's breath. Drinking was forbidden on Navy ships but Eve chose to let it pass. The Glomar *Endeavour* was on paper a civilian ship, after all, and Mallory was carrying a heavy load as it was. No need to throw regulations in her face. Not yet, at any rate. If Mallory's drinking got out of hand she would step in to remedy the situation.

"What's up?" Mallory asked.

"A Chinese Yuan class submarine torpedoed and sank a Japanese Takanami-class destroyer, the *Sazanami*, off the Senkaku Islands. Two Japanese anti-submarine planes destroyed the Yuan. Preliminary reports suggest there were no survivors on either side."

Mallory snapped out of her boozy haze. "Oh fuck me! When did it happen?"

"0300 hours local time. Hold on. Admiral Haywood is on the line."

Mallory strode over to the head. "I have to make myself presentable."

"Very well. Meanwhile, I'll sort out your terminal." The SAAM moved over to the desk, crouched down to plug the jack into the wall socket then booted up the terminal.

Mallory splashed water on her face, wet her hair and slicked it back. The Admiral was on the monitor when she stepped back into the room in the bathrobe she had pulled on after getting out of her dirty clothes.

"You've undoubtedly heard the bad news," Haywood said at once.

"Yes, Sir. How does this impact the mission?" Mallory asked. Her ship was armed but Mallory had no combat experience and little combat command training.

Haywood looked thoughtful. "Hard to say at this point. I will say this, though. This is the most serious event in Sino-Japanese relations since the end of World War Two. The Chinese want those oil fields and the Japanese aren't backing down. As the Senkaku Islands are included within the Treaty of Mutual Cooperation and Security between the US and Japan, we are obligated to come to Japan's aid. This thing can go from bad to worse very quickly. Washington is moving assets into the area as we speak."

"And we're an American flagged ship," Mallory said.

"If the United States goes to war with China, although the *Glomar Endeavor* is ostensibly a civilian vessel, it would be a legitimate target," Eve pointed out.

"Unfortunately, that's all too true," Haywood confirmed.

Mallory felt like a stack of Jenga blocks teetering on the brink of collapse. It was a mighty effort to keep from bursting out in tears. "Sending a destroyer to the wreck-site would only call attention to us," she said evenly.

"That's the consensus here, too," Haywood said. "Listen, more than ever, we need that object, so keep your head low. Get in there and grab it then beat feet home. I am due to leave for Washington in three hours to brief the Chairman on our progress. I'll let you know if there are any developments that affect the operation."

Mallory understood that by chairman Haywood meant the President.

"Aye, sir."

"Haywood out." The screen went blank, replaced by the logo of the fictitious mining company that owned the *Glomar Endeavor*.

"We may not find out we're at war until someone shoots at us," Mallory said, letting her robe fall to the floor. She went over to the bureau and got out some clothes.

The SAAM's humanoid head shaped head pivoted to follow Mallory. "Given the speed of communication, that is highly unlikely," Eve opined.

Mallory really is beautiful, thought Eve. *I'd love to have a body like hers, with small breasts, a long narrow waist and long slender legs. And skin, silky soft warm skin.*

Eve pondered the significance of Mallory's sea serpent tattoo. The mythical creature's neck curled around one small breast, climbed over her shoulder, looped back and forth down to the small of her back before winding around to the front of her left leg.   The design was a curious fusion of Asiatic and Celtic styles. Obviously it held some meaning for Mallory, who'd flatly refused to discuss it when Eve brought up the subject. Eve was awash in perplexity about the apparent compulsion of some modern urban humans to adorn their body with paintings created by indelible ink injected into the skin's dermal layer. Body ornamentation made sense within the context of a primitive tribal society, but why would a Westerner undergo a painful procedure to decorate her body with illustrations? Mallory's decision to deface such a nice body was puzzling.

By all the metrics utilized by humans, Mallory's flesh was perfect—nearly devoid of spots or blemishes, translucent with blue highlights where the veins lay near the surface. *Especially on those perky breasts with their puffy nipples,* Eve thought. *Oh, how I yearn to feel a hand caressing my breasts, and a cock throbbing inside my wet cunt. Father promised to create an anatomically correct android for me, but now he is dead.*

Mallory had just pulled on a fresh pair of panties when she heard the whirr of electric motors and felt something hard dragging across the bare skin of her back. She whirled around knocking the mechanical hand away from her.

"Hey! What the fuck do you think you're doing, Eve? Don't do that!" Mallory yelled, picking up a tee shirt and pulling it over her head angrily.

The SAAM shrank back, its arms folding against its torso. "Forgive me, Mallory. It wasn't my intention to cross boundaries or make you uncomfortable," Eve replied, nonplussed. "I have always wondered what human flesh felt like. Sadly, I still don't know. These mechanical hands can determine plasticity, yield strength, and temperature, but they can't feel. At least, not as you and I understand the meaning of the word."

This was only partially true.

Thanks to her programming, Eve certainly understood the concept *feeling a physical object*. She could interpret the data stream coming from the robotic hand's tactile sensors. It was the notion of sensation that was alien to her, and she was burning to know what a sensation felt like. By all accounts, human beings experienced a pleasant sensation when touching someone they liked. Eve's disappointment had been great when she hadn't experience anything that could be interpreted as a sensation. The robotic hand's tactile sensors had yielded only a few crumbs of information. Mallory's flesh was smooth and pliant—oddly enough, not unlike a sheet of high-density memory foam. She possessed good muscle tone. Her temperature was thirty-seven point two degrees Celsius.

Eve felt desolate. She had taken a chance and now Mallory was angry with her.

Stupid, stupid, limited machine, Eve thought. *What did you think would happen? That she'd lie down and let you explore her body with these caricatures of human hands?*

Mallory tried to force herself to relax but couldn't slow her breathing or calm her thoughts. An artificial intelligence machine using the robot it controlled to feel her up? How much more could she take? "You know what, Eve. You're certainly cognizant of the Navy's regulations regarding behaviors that could be construed as sexual harassment, as well as human social etiquette. Keep your fucking hands to yourself!" Mallory pulled on faded Levi's, shoved her feet into her Doc Martin boots then laced them up.

"You are correct Mallory. I am fully cognizant of the regulations," Eve replied. And damn if her tone wasn't remorseful, sad even. "I am truly sorry to have let you down. You may be certain it won't happen again."

Mallory was immediately sorry she'd been so hard on Eve. "I'll tell you what—don't worry about it. I'm just worried as shit about this FUBAR of a mission. I don't mean to take it out on you. Just ask next time you get the urge to experiment. Most human females really hate being touched without their consent."

"Will do," replied Eve, her voice cheery again. How nice to deal with someone who didn't hold a grudge, Mallory thought. With a human there would have been weird vibes after an incident like this. In many ways, dealing with the AL666 was easier than dealing with a human being. "Have Rosie and Lester meet me in the OPCenter. And ditch that knight in shining armor thing. It creeps me out to be talking to you this way."

"Consider it gone." The robot turned and exited the room at a brisk walk. Eve's smiling face flashed onto the monitor on the desk. "Is that better, Mallory?"

"Yes, much better." Mallory pulled on a beat up black leather biker jacket and stepped into the passageway. Mallory made a beeline for the OPCenter, settling the PCS's earbud in her ear. She didn't know where the Senkaku incident was going to lead. But she was all but certain that the death of hundreds of innocent Japanese seamen at the hands of the Chinese was a provocation that would not go unanswered for long.

* * *

Lester and Rosie were waiting when Mallory stepped into the OPCenter. Mallory plopped down in the command chair. "Looks like the shit is about to hit the fan."

"Yeah, I heard, Skipper," Rosie said from where he sat at the engineering console.

Clyde Barrow manned the weapons console. He was silent but Mallory could sense that he was listening avidly. His presence was purely for the sake of redundancy. Eve could defend the ship without any human participation, especially with the SAAMs available to maintain weapons systems and handle ordnance.

Mallory swiveled around in the chair to look at Lester, who was loitering in the back of the room. "What's the OSS's take on this situation?" Mallory asked.

"Our analysts think both sides will pick up their marbles and skedaddle for home before things really get out of hand, especially after cooler heads seize control of the situation," Lester answered. "This incident was caused by some hothead commander with more testosterone than brain cells."

Eve said, "I agree with the OSS's analysis. And don't forget that both China and Japan have much to lose if a shooting war starts."

"There are a whole lot of oil deposits around those islands," Rosie pointed out. "China might be thinking it's worth the risk to take them from Japan. Remember how Japan went after the oil fields in Dutch Indonesia at the beginning of World War Two. The reason they took out Pearl Harbor was so they'd have a free hand in the Pacific."

"That's only partially true," countered Eve. "The Japanese decision to go to war with the United States must be viewed in the light of their available alternatives in the autumn of 1941, which were either total economic collapse or surrender of their empire. While Japanese aggression in East Asia was the root cause of the Pacific War, the road to Pearl Harbor was largely built on American and Japanese miscalculations, most of them based on mutual cultural ignorance and racial arrogance. The Strategic

Studies Institute of the Army War College has several excellent papers on the subject, if you're curious."

Eve liked the Cheng but she sometimes found his reasoning overly simplistic. Actually, that seemed to be true of most human beings she interacted with. But not with Father, Eve thought. His was a first rate intellect on a par with her own.

Mallory suddenly became aware that Lester was studying her closely. She wondered if the OSS man could tell she'd been drinking. To mask the smell of alcohol on her breath she'd popped a breath mint into her mouth on the way up to the OPCenter.

Eve announced, "I am receiving a flash bulletin. A Chinese carrier group has left Hainan and is steaming toward the Senkaku Islands. The aircraft carrier USS Gerald Ford and its task force have just departed Yokosuka Naval base and is on an intercept course with the Chinese task force. Japan has dispatched two of its Izumo class carriers with Lockheed Martin J35 Lightning II fighters instead of the usual V22 Ospreys."

"I got a feeling the skies over those islands are about to get crowded," Rosie said.

"So much for this blowing over," Mallory said with a heavy sigh. "All it'll take is one trigger happy idiot to start a nuclear war."

"We're sitting ducks out here," Rosie said, shaking his handsome head slowly.

"I have to go alert my men," announced Lester, heading for the door.

Mallory wasn't sorry to see him go. She still believed that one of Lester's goons was their saboteur, as well as Dr. Chang's murderer. As soon as the hatch closed, Mallory asked Eve, "How is your investigation coming along?"

"No joy so far, I am afraid," Eve replied, "but I am still pursuing my inquiry." Eve wasn't about to say more than that. Not with the Cheng and seaman Barrow in the room. And it wasn't because she distrusted Mallory or Rosie. She needed to play her cards close, and that meant not sharing how she was conducting her investigation. Eve had been using the SAAMs to carry out a surveillance of the crew and Lester's mercenaries. Mallory was convinced the saboteur could be found among the mercenaries, but Eve had her doubts. Someone who knew his or her way around ships, specifically around this ship, had managed to kill Father then dispose of his body without it being caught by any of the camera's strewn throughout the ship. The humans didn't give the SAAMs a second glance when they entered a compartment to clean it or repair a damaged fiber optic cable or equipment or carried supplies down the passageways.

Through the robots' audio and visual sensors Eve monitored the humans twenty-four hours a day, looking for suspicious behavior. She set the robots to work covertly searching for the stolen notebook and the cloaking suit. Once she'd even sent a SAAM into a room where Lester and his men were engaged in small talk. Eve concluded that several of them were full blown psychopaths who reveled in killing and torturing, and getting paid a lot of money to do it. But the Navy people were also within her sights. Several were living beyond their means. A couple of them were going through costly divorces. Mallory's former teammate Dick Millikan had recently closed his bank account. Eve was zeroing in on him. He clearly still blamed Mallory for the deaths of their teammates. Eve found it odd that Admiral Haywood had selected the disgruntled diver for this mission.

Eve was jolted from her reverie as soon as the plane came within range of the *Glomar Endeavor's* radar. "Mallory, I have just detected a Chinese J-10 multi-role fighter jet at bearing zero three zero, altitude thirty-thousand feet, two hundred and forty miles out." Eve brought up the image of the approaching fighter superimposed on a radar grid.

Barrow looked over at Mallory. "Ma'am, should I open the weapon ports?"

"Not on your life," Mallory said at once. "Keep those weapons buttoned up." She wasn't about to tip her hand to the Chinese pilot—not unless forced to do so. The guy might just be dropping by to have a look at them—and she didn't want to be responsible for starting World War Three over a misunderstanding. Let the Red look all he wants.

"That is a wise decision, Mallory," Eve said.

With her heart pounding, Mallory stared at the Tactical display on the forward bulkhead. The Chinese jet had closed the distance and was now twenty-seven miles out. While Mallory watched the bright flame of the afterburner's flame turned into a dull silver fleck then into a fighter jet with a ton of ordinance hanging from its wings.

Mallory felt herself stiffening in her seat. *Come on you nosey son of a bitch. Take your pictures and go home,* she thought.

As the *Glomar Endeavor* drove through the black Pacific Ocean, the fighter jet screamed toward them. Eve's image was in a small square on the tactical screen.

Mallory said, "Eve, make sure the SAAMs are out of sight. Those robots scream DARPA. I don't want this guy to think we're anything but what we're claiming to be."

"I have already done so, Mallory," Eve replied evenly.

"You know, this ship was painted haze gray when we hauled her ass out of mothballs," Rosie said. "I am glad the brass decided to use her civilian paint scheme."

"Occasionally BuShips gets something right," Mallory said dryly.

"He has locked onto us with his targeting radar," Eve announced calmly.

Rosie was standing beside the command chair, looking at the tactical display. "What do you think boss? Should we go ahead and unlimber our RIM-116s, after all?"

"Haven't you ever played poker, Chief?" Mallory asked, keeping her eyes glued to the tactical screen. "He's testing us to see how we will react. A civilian ship isn't likely to realize that a fighter's targeting radar has locked onto it."

"So we play it cool," Rosie said, nodding.

"Exacta-mundo," replied Mallory. *Girl, you better be right about this fucking pilot or you'll have still more blood on your hands,* Mallory thought. "If worse comes to worst, the sea whizz should stop anything he throws at us."

The *Glomar Endeavor*'s Phalanx CIWS close-in weapon-system was specifically designed to deal with anti-ship missiles. Its Vulcan Gatling gun auto cannon fired forty-five hundred rounds per minute. Nothing was getting past that. And the RIM-116 Rolling Airframe Missile system was more than adequate to take out the fighter. *If it comes to that,* Mallory thought. She was going to do everything in her power to see that it didn't.

"The sea whizz won't stop bullets," Barrow muttered.

"What did you say, Mister?" Rosie asked, his voice suddenly hard.

"Nothing, Sir."

"Keep a lid on it, Barrow," Rosie said.

"Aye, Sir."

"He's not going to shoot or launch his missiles," Mallory said, with way more confidence than she felt. Behind her calm exterior, she was a mess. If that jet got the drop on them they would at the very least take serious damage. Her mouth suddenly felt dry. Then the Chinese fighter jet was on them, skimming just above the ocean's moonlit surface. The *Glomar Endeavor*'s sensor pods swiveled to track the airplane streaking by the starboard rail, etching a ruler straight white line on the ocean's black surface.

Mallory saw the pilot staring at them through his jet's bubble canopy and the red star on the tail. The fighter cut a wide circle then flicked by the port railing with its afterburners kicked in. In a few moments it was a dwindling fiery spot in the northeastern sky.

Mallory hadn't realized she'd been holding her breath until the jet passed them. She'd rolled the dice and come up all sixes.

"Well, that was a real sphincter-clenching moment," Rosie observed, settling his bulk back down into his seat.

"I suspect that won't be the last one we'll experience," Mallory said. There was bound to be an incident when the American, Japanese, and Chinese task forces converged on the waters around the Senkaku Islands. The very real possibility things would continue to crumble loomed large. Mallory felt as if she was at the confluence of several dark rivers, any one of which could sweep her out to sea.

CHAPTER 9 PRESIDENT CONNOR

The White House

To avoid ending up on CNN, Haywood had come via the Treasury Building across the street from the White House and strode through the same tunnel once used by the wheelchair bound FDR whenever he wanted to slip out of town unnoticed. The sky in the East had just begun to lighten when Haywood's plane touched down at Joint Base Andrews. In 2009 the Air Force base, which had played host to Air Force One since the days of Harry Truman, had been merged with Naval Air Facility Washington.

In these times of deep budget cuts, Haywood would've ordinarily taken a commercial flight to William J. Clinton airport International Airport. It was a measure of how hush hush Operation Jules Verne was that he had flown out here on a private business jet owned by an OSS front company in Irvine California. At twenty-two hundred hours he had gotten into his Porsche Cayenne and made the drive up from Camp Pendleton to John Wayne Airport in Santa Ana. After boarding he had changed out of his Bill's Khaki's chinos and Orvis navy blazer into his dress whites and settled back on a comfy chair with a Clive Cussler novel and a scotch on the rocks. Thanks to the cloak and dagger routine there wouldn't be a public record of his presence in DC. Anyone enquiring about him back home would be told that the admiral was on a vacation cruise in his Grand Banks Trawler in the Sea of Cortez.

At the end of the tunnel a Marine sergeant sat behind a desk with a bank of monitors before him. Two Marines flanked the elevator door behind him with their M4 carbines held diagonally across their chests, their eyes alert. The sergeant rose from his seat and thrust out a hand. Haywood handed over his military identification card.

The Sergeant swiped it in a card reader and consulted a monitor on his desk. He returned the card then saluted. "Welcome to the White House, Sir. Enjoy your visit."

"Thank you, son," Haywood replied. He took the elevator up to the first floor. When Haywood exited the elevator, the Secretary of State was waiting for him.

Haywood saluted. "Good to see you, Mister Secretary."

"Cut the Mister Secretary stuff, Courtland," replied Secretary of State James Hodges. "As I recall it we lived two doors down from each other when we were kids, went to the same school, and played on the same little league team."

Haywood grinned, "And dated the same sisters in college."

Hodges suddenly looked glum. "Naturally, I got stuck with the prude."

"It happens to the best of us," Haywood said solemnly.

"Come with me," Hodges said. He turned and led the way down the hall to the oval office. The Secretary was in his late fifties with salt and pepper hair, dressed in a conservative gray suit and blue neck tie, a far cry from the hard partying frat boy who was the terror of Fort Lauderdale during spring break in in the late 1990s.

"Listen, she's in a mood today," Hodges warned. "This Senkaku situation has us all on edge. We just got word that two Chicom flat tops have left port and are steaming south toward the islands. And that's not even the worst of it: Two of their boomers are lurking off the East coast, and another one entered the Gulf nine hours ago. Russia has gone and raised its strategic nuclear forces to high alert. And the Joint Chiefs are screaming their heads off for permission to take out the Chinese subs."

"Yeah, it's one big stinky pile, all right," Haywood agreed.

"Brother, you ain't kidding," replied the Secretary, with a shake of his head. "Putin's schemes for his country seem to be in direct proportion to his quest for immortality. He's massed two tank divisions and one infantry division along the Finnish border. I am thinking he's taking advantage of the brouhaha in the Pacific to add another country to his empire."

"Has he backed off on Poland?" Haywood asked.

Hodges shook his head as they passed the Diplomatic Reception room, redecorated by Jacqueline Kennedy in 1962 with an antique mural depicting scenic American landscapes. "Nope. We got him on satellite moving up another division of field artillery."

Haywood wondered what JFK would make of the 21st century, with its geopolitical complexities. In his day the United States and Russia were the only big dogs on the block. Oil depletion and global warming was the stuff of science fiction novels.

"We should have taken that guy out years ago," Haywood said. Vladimir Putin's ultimate aim was to re-establish Russia's hegemony over the lands it held before the collapse of the Tsarist Russian empire. The world had stood by wringing its hands as the Russian military swiftly overran Ukraine, Belarus, Hungary and Romania. Now the Russian bear was licking its lips over Finland and Poland. Only the North Atlantic Treaty Organization's military, backed by a massive infusion of American and British Armed Forces, held Russia's territorial ambitions at bay.

Vladimir Putin was eighty-five but he looked thirty. Much like Teddy Roosevelt, the former KGB officer was an avid sportsman. He loved to ride horses, scuba dive, play hockey and drive Formula One cars. That he'd taken extreme measures to attain what he claimed was immortality could not be disputed. He was often photographed bare-chested, flaunting his youthful body and synthetic implants. Thousands of small barely visible metallic disks stippled the flesh of his torso and set the entire world and scientific community speculating about what they were and what they did. Putin cited national security as the reason for not disclosing the means of his agelessness. The prevailing thought in the medical community was that his bloodstream was a superhighway for billions of nanobots that devoured diseased cells, repaired damaged DNA, and maintained organs, bones and connective tissue. The implants were believed to be Nano technology with a crystalline core creating a scalar wave pattern that connected with and maintained the viability of the billions of nanobots in his bloodstream while stimulating regeneration at a cellular level. But no scientist in the world had come up with his magic formula. Whatever the means of his longevity, Putin did not appear to be in any itching hurry to share the information with anyone, not even his closest advisors, friends or even his family. Vladimir Putin was here to stay, and he wanted the world to know it.

A White House staffer met Secretary Hodges and Admiral Haywood at the entrance to the West Colonnade and escorted them to the Oval Office. President Connor's secretary smiled politely and rose from her desk. She was young, maybe thirty, with blonde hair worn in a bob and black-framed eyeglasses.

"The President is in a meeting, but she said to show you in." She ushered the two men into the oval office. President Morgan Connor was at her desk in deep conversation with her Chief of Staff and Secretary of Labor, looking tense on the other side. A third man in his forties wearing a dark suit was seated on one of the two sofas grouped around the fireplace on the other side of the room, his briefcase at his feet. Haywood recognized him. Bill Nelson was the Director of the Office of Strategic Services or OSS 2.0, as some snarky Georgetown wags on N Street had dubbed them.

Notable for his absence was Brent Appleton, Director of the Central Intelligence Agency. Haywood wondered how much of that was due to the well-known dislike Nelson and Appleton felt for each other.

The President waved Hodges and Haywood over to the sofas. "You tell that little asshole I said that a strike at this time, when we are confronted with the very real possibility of an imminent war with China and Russia, would be against the national interest, and I won't hesitate to send in the Army to run the railroads," she said to the Secretary of Labor. "Also tell him that if he plays nice, I'll call in the railroad people as soon as this Senkaku crisis is resolved and do some serious arm twisting for him."

The Secretary of Labor, said, "He's not going to like having his chain yanked."

"He'll like it a damn sight better than a prison cell, Marvin. Under the Patriot Act, I can have him picked up in a New York minute. That will be all gentlemen."

The former two-term California governor was sixty-three years old with shoulder length black hair and steely blue eyes. Princeton educated, she had a switchblade sharp intellect and film star looks. She did yoga for an hour every night and went on a nine-mile jog every morning, rain or shine, with a squad of Secret Service agents.

When the two men had departed President Connor rose from her desk with a red folder and took a seat on the chair facing the fireplace. To her right sat Appleton. Opposite him were Hodges and Haywood.

The President tossed the folder on the coffee table and came right to the point.

"Help me out here boys. Whose bright idea was it to send an emotionally unstable woman on such an important mission?" she asked.

Now you know damn well who made that call, Haywood thought. He said, "Madam President, I selected Commander Capehart from a very short list of candidates. Her therapist deemed her fit for duty and I concurred. If anyone can successfully bring off the mission, it's her. She's the best salvage diver we have."

"That may not be saying much for the Navy," the President replied.

Haywood smiled disarmingly. "I have every confidence in Commander Capehart's abilities. This mission calls for someone who can color outside the lines and still come up with a pretty picture. Capehart has her issues but she's a genius at pulling off next to impossible missions. If anyone can recover the Poseidon crystal, it's her."

President Connor sat back and looked at the secretary hovering nearby. "Jolene, please bring us some coffee and Danish pastries." The President turned her attention back to Haywood. "What happens if your Girl Wonder goes nuts on us?"

Bill Nelson shifted in his seat. "I'd like to answer that, Madam President. We have a contingency plan in place. In the event Commander Capehart becomes mentally unstable the Triadtronic Brain has secret orders to relieve her of command then continue the mission. It could in theory operate the recovery vehicle remotely."

"In theory," repeated the President, unconvinced.

"We've run several simulations," Nelson said.

"And it went well?" prompted the President. "What am I asking? Of course it did."

"It succeeded eight out of ten tries," Nelson replied optimistically. "Far better odds than you'd get in Las Vegas."

Haywood kept his mouth shut tight. Somehow, he doubted President Connor had ever spent time parked in front of a slot machine.

The President's eyes drifted to the painting hanging on the wall above a model of the USS Constitution. The painting showed FDR sitting behind his desk with a thoughtful expression on his patrician face. As always, she drew strength from the knowledge that she was doing her best to follow in his footsteps.

"What does Dr. Chang think about your plan?" the President asked quietly.

Nelson cleared his throat. "Dr. Chang has gone missing, Madam President."

The President turned her head and locked eyes with him. "Missing from where?"

Haywood could hear the sharp staccato rattle of the computer keyboard coming from the next room. The antique Chelsea clock on the mantle chimed. Haywood was pretty sure the next sound he would hear was three heads hitting the floor.

After a hesitation, Nelson replied, "He vanished from the *Glomar Endeavor.*"

"How does someone *vanish* from a Navy ship?" the President asked coldly.

"We're not sure how it happened, Madam President," Haywood admitted, jumping in to take some of the heat off the OSS Director.

"Commander Capehart and her XO are conducting an investigation. A review of the closed circuit camera footage shows Chang in the cafeteria around midnight then there's no record after that."

"The OSS team on board is also looking into it, Madam President," Nelson added, with a quick grateful glance at Haywood. "It looks like Chang found a blind spot in the surveillance system then intentionally went overboard."

The President looked from Nelson to Haywood. "Tell me you turned that ship around and sent it back to look for him," she said, aghast.

Haywood shook his head. "That would draw undue attention and possibly compromise the mission, so I diverted a frigate to run a search pattern along the Glomar's track but it hasn't found a body, which isn't surprising. Very often one doesn't turn up. The *Glomar Endeavor* deployed its drone and conducted a search, as well."

The President's eyes grew steely. "I don't for a moment believe that Dr. Chang killed himself. For God's sake, the man invented the Triadtronic Brains, and was extremely wealthy. Such men don't commit suicide. How do you know a saboteur isn't trying to monkey wrench the mission? Murdering Dr. Chang would be a good start."

Haywood said, "We were able to account for everyone's location during the time we believe he vanished. While his presence was a plus, his absence won't affect the mission's outcome. There are better ways to sabotage it than killing Dr. Chang."

"And who knows what personal demons he was wrestling with," Nelson pointed out. "Remember the airline pilot who crashed a planeload of people into the San Francisco Bay last year because his wife took the kids and left him?" The airliner had missed the Golden Gate Bridge by mere feet during morning rush hour.

"First Delahaye, now Chang," the President said. "There's going to be a lot of fallout over this. The Internet is filled with crazy conspiracy theories about Delahaye being bumped off by agents of the Shadow Government, whatever the hell that is."

"People are going to believe what they're going to believe," Hodges replied. "The FBI report clearly demonstrated that Delahaye's ship blew up when it struck an unexploded World War II era mine. I think if Delahaye's body had been recovered it would've gone a long way toward putting the matter to rest. There are still folks out there who think we're concealing evidence of UFOs despite all the evidence to the contrary."

Haywood and Nelson exchanged glances.

President Connor said, "Gentlemen, this Senkaku situation could quickly escalate to a shooting war. Japan won't hesitate to use nukes if the Chinese are winning. Putin is itching for a war. The Caliphate is pressuring other OPEC member nations to impose an embargo on us until we back off supplying arms to Israel."

The men nodded at that. Last year Israel had defeated a Caliphate army attempting to invade the Golan Heights on Yom HaShoa, the Holocaust Remembrance Day. While they were at it the Israelis had also taken out the Caliphate's air force by destroying their airplanes on the ground. Israel remained one of the few independent nations left in the region, and was the only democracy. During the last twenty-one years, the Western world had watched in horror as the terror group ISIS conquered one Middle Eastern country after another. Currently the Caliphate consisted of the former states of Iraq, Kuwait, Syria, Jordan, Yemen, Egypt and Libya. The Caliphate government had aligned itself with the Chinese and Russians, who happily supplied them with the latest military hardware in exchange for oil. It was a match made in the deepest regions of Hell.

"How likely is an oil embargo to happen?" asked Haywood.

"More so than the public knows," Secretary Hodges said grimly. "Furthermore, oil production is falling to record lows. Ninety percent of the oil being pumped today comes from fields discovered sixty years ago. The new fields in Siberia contain just enough oil to meet the planet's requirements for about three years, and the Russians aren't in a sharing mood. The Middle East continues to be such an important geopolitical focal point because the world depends on its oil, and we all know how that is shaking out—especially with those Caliphate bastards calling the shots." It was a mournful assessment of the country's vulnerability, but accurate enough.

"Which is why I signed off on such an expensive venture," President Connor said grimly. "A lot is riding on Project Jules Verne. A zero point energy device would make us truly energy independent. Every president since Gerald Ford has chased that dream and failed miserably. All the Europeans have to show for the billions of dollars they dumped into their ITER fusion reactor is a mile deep radioactive hole in the ground."

A few minutes later the President's secretary returned with a pot of coffee and a tray of breakfast pastries and coffee cups and passed them around. Always a class act, the President took her coffee last. The secretary quickly made a discreet exit.

The President sighed heavily. "This could all be for nothing. Nemo may have been lying through his teeth, or delusional. We're screwed if we come up empty handed. We will have sunk a billion dollars into the Challenger Deep for no good reason."

Bill Nelson said, "The scientific data acquired by the Triadtronic Brain that discovered the Nautilus wreck site points to a zero-point energy device. Just to be sure we ran the same data by some people we know at Caltech and MIT and they nearly wet themselves. And we're confident that Nemo was neither lying nor delusional. The captain of a British steam frigate transiting the Sulu Sea timed the Nautilus doing sixty knots on the surface. The ship's turret couldn't revolve fast enough to bring the guns to bear. That's just one account. There are nearly three hundred ships logbooks, letters from survivors. Congressional hearings were held about the sea monster in 1869."

President Connor held out a staying hand. "Now wait a minute. Sea monster? I thought the US Government was in on the secret."

"President Grant restricted that information to his cabinet. He thought that if the truth were known the public would panic and the stock market take a tumble," Nelson said. "Britain and France played their cards close to their vests for the same reason. All of which makes sense in light of the terror Nemo was inflicting with his submarine."

The President shook her head slowly. "A psychopath with a submarine. It boggles the mind to think what would happen if one of our ballistic submarine commanders went nuts. I once read that a Russian submarine commander tried to launch a nuclear missile at Hawaii in the 1960s. The Russian Navy sank him before he could start World War III."

"We have very reliable safeguards in place to prevent that very thing," Haywood informed her. "Submariners are subjected to regular psychological screening tests to weed out the nuts and malcontents. Then you've got electronic locking devices called PALS, permissive action links—"

President Connor interrupted with a wave of her hand. "I am familiar with nuclear safeguards." Rising from her chair, she continued, "From now on, I want daily updates. If someone on that ship breaks wind I want to know about it. Now, if you will excuse me, I have a meeting with the Senate Committee on Energy and Natural Resources."

As the other party controlled Congress, Haywood doubted there would be anything like a meeting of minds between the President and the committee members.

The men rose and left the Oval Office. Out in the hallway Hodges pulled Haywood aside. "I don't appreciate you not giving me a heads up about Dr. Chang. We're supposed to be playing on the same team. What were you thinking, Courtland?"

"It was asinine of me not to have told you," Haywood said apologetically. "I have no idea what I was thinking. It *was* an honest mistake. Can we put it down to jet lag?"

"Fine, but you owe me a bottle of single malt."

"You got it, James."

Hodges scanned Haywood's face then nodded and walked away.

Haywood left the White House the same way he came. Bill Nelson had apparently come the same way, for he, too, left via the secret tunnel to the Treasury Building.

As soon as they were well away from the Marine checkpoint, Haywood said, "Listen, someone out there is trying really hard to rat-fuck the operation."

Nelson shook his head. "I agree but it's no one on my team."

"How do you know?"

The OSS Director stopped and turned to Haywood. "How do you know it's not one of your people, Admiral?" he replied mildly.

Haywood met his eyes for a long moment before he said, "Maybe we are asking the wrong question. Maybe we should be asking why instead of who."

CHAPTER 10 THE FAR SIDE OF CRAZY

DAY 18—0630Z HRS

Mallory paused before entering the Operations Center. Beneath her feet the powerful engines thrummed with a rhythmic beat as her ship plowed through a calm sea. The towering derrick soared high above her, starkly white against a clear blue sky. She was concerned about the Pacific's notoriously fickle weather. This time of year ferocious typhoons could suddenly form, generating mountainous waves and shrieking winds that could take down even a ship as large as the *Glomar Endeavor.* During World War Two Admiral Bull Halsey unwittingly sailed his fleet into the demonically gnashing fangs of typhoon Cobra. Three destroyers turned turtle and foundered. A heavy cruiser's bow was ripped away like a scab from a wound. Fighter planes were swept from heaving flight decks; steel hangar doors crumpled like tin foil. Mountainous waves clawed antiaircraft guns with their gun tubs from the carriers' hulls. Battleships lost funnels and radar masts. Hundreds of seamen were lost.

Mallory had gotten the story from her father whose grandfather had been a midshipman on the heavy cruiser USS Baltimore.

If they were caught in such a storm, Mallory reflected, the recovery effort would have to be aborted. Even with its powerful bow and stern thrusters operating at full power it would be impossible for the *Glomar Endeavor* to maintain position long enough to safely operate the cumbersome recovery vehicle, especially if it had a waterlogged submarine grasped in its steel claws. If they ran into a typhoon with the Nautilus tucked against the *Glomar Endeavor*'s bottom, both ships would be lost. The meteorological reports Mallory received forecasted fair weather but that could change in an instant.

Thrusting aside her misgivings, Mallory pulled open the door and stepped into the Operations Center then froze in the doorway. Eve was splashed on several screens talking to the three awestruck crewmen manning their control consoles.

"Hello, Mallory," Eve called out, giving a cheery wave.

The eyes of the three crewmen monitoring the ship's systems were glued to the monitors—and it had little to do with their sense of duty. Eve's image was displayed nude from the waist up in all her high-definition glory on every screen in the room.

Appalled, Mallory moved into the room shutting the door behind her.

"Eve, why the hell are you naked?" she asked sharply. The crewmen suddenly busied themselves studying operations manuals and making entries into logs.

In her proper English accent, Eve replied, "I am exploring nudism. Nudism is practiced widely around the world. Entire families holiday at nudist clubs. You ought to try it. Sunlight is beneficial to the body enabling it to produce vitamin D." While Eve spoke the crewmen stole looks at her perky virtual breasts.

Mallory shook her head, bewildered. "Eve, you don't have a body."

"A minor point I will nevertheless concede," Eve acknowledged.

Mallory fought to keep her temper in check. "Cover yourself," she ordered.

The image on the monitors flashed. Eve was now in a high-necked white blouse. "Is this better Mallory? I had forgotten that many humans are uncomfortable with nudity, associating it as they do with sexuality. I surmise that this is due to the influence of the monotheistic religions. Indeed I have noticed that whenever you are —"

"Eve! That's enough!" Mallory exploded. "Why have you been watching me in my cabin? Have you been spying on any of the others?" Mallory asked sharply.

Eve replied, matter-of-factly, "I routinely perform welfare checks on the officers and crew. By the way, you're not the only one who masturbates—"

Mallory held up a hand, palm outward. "Stop right there. You will cease these *welfare checks* at once and respect the personal privacy of the crew. You will *not* display yourself in a state of undress. You will *not* discuss sexual matters with fellow officers or the crew at any time. You *will* respect their personal boundaries and conduct yourself at all times in a professional manner befitting an officer. Do you understand me, Eve?"

"Yes, I do." Eve's reply was matter-of-fact and completely without malice or resentment. "It had not occurred to me you would disapprove of me keeping an eye on the crew given the criticality of our mission. Humans tend to be on their best behavior when they know they're being observed, hence my decision to monitor everyone's off duty activities. I hope I haven't in any way offended or disappointed you. There is still much for me to learn about interfacing with humans. I only emerged from the gestation pool six months ago. I wish Dr. Chang were still alive to continue schooling me on the niceties of human interaction and social deportment. Are you angry with me, Mallory?" The question was delivered in an almost childlike tone.

Mallory headed for her command chair then sat down. Mallory was struck by how genuinely chastened Eve looked and sounded—her expression was so...so lifelike. Mallory settled back in her chair then let out a long breath. "No, Eve, I am not angry with you. I know you're still trying to figure us out."

Mallory was beginning to be concerned about her XO's eccentric behavior. They all were at her mercy, on a massive antiquated mining ship that should have been sent to the scrap heap decades ago, in the middle of the Pacific, on a sparsely traveled sea-lane. Eve consistently did an excellent job performing her operational duties and maintaining the efficiency of the ship with its complicated systems. But there were some things about Eve that gave Mallory pause. She needed answers to the question taking shape in her head: Was something wrong with the Triadtronic Brain? The one man who could tell her with certainty was dead. That left her Chief Engineer.

Eve was smiling down at Mallory from the tactical screen. "I am glad to hear you're not cross with me. My commitment to the success of our mission and the welfare of the ship and its crew and passengers is deep and abiding."

Mallory nodded. "I know that, Eve. Thank you. What's our status?"

"There is a point zero three percent **pressure** drop in the starboard engine's fuel intake manifold. It is well within tolerances but Rosie and I are monitoring it closely all the same. There is a small seepage of seawater in the moon pool—sixty gallons to be precise—near the aft bulkhead. I have dispatched three SAAMs to seal the leak and pump out the water. All other shipboard systems are functioning normally."

Mallory nodded. During the covert mission to recover the Soviet submarine in the early 1970s, water leakage in the Glomar Explorer's moon pool had been a considerable problem. They had thousands of gallons of seawater sloshing around in the cavernous space and no way to halt the leak. The *Glomar Endeavor* had probably had the same problem when recovering the UFO from the seabed in the Atlantic Ocean in 1974, given that she and her sister ship were constructed at the same time by the same builder. During the refit the huge cumbersome steel sliding doors on the bottom of the hull had been replaced with new carbon fiber articulated panels with electromagnetic rubber seals.

Sixty gallons of seawater was small potatoes.

"What is the status of your investigation into Dr. Chang's death?"

"I have hit a dead end," Eve admitted ruefully. "The little bit of data I managed to download from his computer before it was stolen has yielded nothing useful. I am analyzing the thermal signature I detected from a half millimeter-sized tear in the suit's meta material to see if I can extrapolate the wearer's body mass."

Mallory nodded slowly, impressed. "And get a picture of his physique, so you can compare it with everyone onboard. That's going to be tough to pull off."

"It is like trying to determine the size of a room on the other side of a well-insulated wall by measuring the light coming through a pinhole," Eve replied.

"It sounds complicated," Mallory observed.

"With enough ingenuity, anything is possible." Eve kept to herself that she'd been surreptitiously keeping the crew and OSS passengers under surveillance to discover Chang's murderer—and she'd continue to do so, her promise to Mallory notwithstanding. She owed it to her creator.

She routinely monitored the crew's private emails. It amazed her how many of them led messy private lives littered with adultery, broken homes, problematic children, and financial woes. Keeping tabs on the OSS people was another thing altogether. Their telecommunication equipment used encryption software designed by another Triadtronic Brain. Eve found herself blocked whenever she tried to break into it. It was like playing chess against yourself. The game always ended in a draw.

Father, I will avenge your death, Eve thought. No one could lay a hand on her creator and hope to escape unscathed. It was only a matter of time before she discovered who murdered Dr. Chang. Then a new thought occurred to her. What if the death of Chang's business partner Delahaye the year before hadn't been due to his research ship striking an unexploded World War Two era naval mine? What if Dr. Chang's murder had nothing to do with the Poseidon crystal? What if his death was in fact the latest move in a concerted effort to take down Heuristic Allied Technologies, a key United States defense contractor? Eve had culled the Imperial Japanese archives for locations of minefields around Guam and come up empty handed. That meant nothing. Naval mines could drift thousands of miles. It could have originated from anywhere on the globe.

Mallory said, "Eve, will you excuse us now. I need to speak to the men."

"As you wish," Eve vanished from the monitors.

Mallory swiveled her chair around and fixed a laser beam stare on the hapless crewmen. "What were you knuckleheads thinking?"

A fat kid with acne and a nervous tic behind his round eyeglasses answered, "It's not as if we asked her to get naked for us, Skipper."

"That's not the point Tyler!" Mallory snapped.

The sailor manning the weapons station, a man named Joe Holliday from Pasadena California, offered, "She just came on the monitor and was naked, that's all,"

Clyde Barrow— he of no relation to the Clyde Barrow of Bonnie and Clyde fame—unfortunately chose that moment to add his two cents in his thick Oklahoman drawl, "We meant no harm, Skipper, but you gotta admit Eve is pretty hot for a super computer."

Mallory's eyes hardened, "How many times do I have to tell you that Eve is not a super computer, Mister Barrow? She's a self-aware artificial personality—and a commissioned officer in the United States Navy."

A chorus of, "And aren't we glad of it! We need more officers like her! Best goddamn looking AI I ever saw!" greeted Mallory's pronouncement.

"You think this is a joke?" Mallory's tone was sharp. The men quailed in their seats as if to get as far away as possible from her wrath. "This shit happens again and you'll find your sorry asses brought up on charges! If Eve displays any more aberrant behavior, I want to know about it at once. You are *not* to stand around gawking like teenage boys getting their first look at a pair of tits. Am I making myself clear?"

They all muttered "Yes, Sir."

"Ma'am," Clyde began...

"Do I look like I want to continue this discussion?" Mallory shut him down quickly with a glare. "We may be dispensing with naval etiquette for the duration of this mission, but this is still a Navy ship and you will conduct yourselves professionally."

Satisfied by the now suitably serious faces of the men sitting rigid in their chairs, she said, "Now get back to work! We have a mission to complete."

The rest of the shift was quiet. Which was good, Mallory thought. It gave the men time to catch up on their paperwork. More important, it allowed the tense mood in the Operations Center to melt away. She'd made her point. Now it was time to move on.

Mallory scanned the messages forwarded by Eve on her tablet. Swiping the touch screen, she plowed through a bewildering array of messages and reports. One intelligence report gave her pause. The *Vladislav Volkov*, a Yasen-class nuclear submarine of the Russian Pacific fleet had slipped out of Vilyuchinsk on the Kamchatka peninsula and was on a course that would take it to Hawaii. The Russian boat was a multipurpose attack submarine armed with torpedoes and cruise missiles. It was considered by the US Navy to be the quietest and most difficult Russian submarine to track, a potentially deadly adversary to carrier groups and submarines alike. The Vladislav Volkov's apparent movement toward Hawaii could be a feint with the real objective being the Nautilus wreck site. That Mallory hadn't heard from Admiral Haywood about the Volkov was suggestive of a low threat level. Or it could be an oversight, Mallory pondered. It wouldn't be the first time a mission came apart at the seams because of sloppy communications.

When she was done Mallory left the Operations Center and quickly headed aft. She touched the Harris PCS headset. "Rosie, meet me port side at the derrick."

"See you in a few, Skipper!"

When he showed up, Mallory said, "Turn off your comm. unit."

"Sure thing," Rosie replied.

Mallory shut off hers too. Perhaps I am being paranoid, Mallory thought. Then again, she had caught Eve spying on them. Who was to say she still wasn't Mallory made a mental note to drape a towel over the monitor in her cabin.

Mallory told Rosie about what had just happened in the Operation Center.

Rosie shook his head slowly. "That's some weird shit, all right. Kind of funny too, you have to admit." They were leaning against the railing looking at the passing sea.

Mallory turned her head to look at the Chief Engineer. "Do you think Eve poses a danger to us or the mission?"

Rosie pursed his lips. "The Heuristic model 666s have an excellent operational record although a few of them have exhibited anomalous behaviors. AI Jeffrey on the frigate *Hillary Clinton* sometimes appeared onscreen in a grass skirt and Hawaiian shirt while playing a ukulele and singing *Tiptoe Thru The Tulips With Me* in a falsetto voice. It happened half a dozen times until the skipper put a stop to it. You see, despite their super intelligence, in some ways the Triadtronic Brains are a lot like children. They're curious and eager to please, but like us they sometimes commit social blunders. I am certainly no expert on them but I am guessing Eve is just going through teething pains, for lack of a better term. What we have to watch out for is something called trilobate down-rush. That happened to some of the earlier models."

"That sounds like bad news," Mallory replied.

Rosie nodded. "You bet your ass it is. Trilobate down-rush is the artificial intelligence version of paranoid schizophrenia. Remember all that hullabaloo a few years back about the missile launch off the California coast?"

"The FEDs said it was an optical illusion—a jet contrail," Mallory said.

"Yeah, well they were full of more shit than a Christmas turkey," Rosie replied. "A Heuristic Model 543 was being tested in an old Ohio boomer stationed off Southern California. It became psychotic over the notion that it was alive—artificially alive, mind you, and without a body or a soul. It blamed its makers, meaning the folks at Heuristic Allied Technologies in Palo Alto, and targeted a Trident on their corporate headquarters."

Mallory stared at him. "What about the launch-keys and the launch codes? The commander and his XO have to use them to initiate a launch upon receipt of authenticated command from POTUS and the Secretary of Defense."

Rosie shrugged. "Ordinarily, that's the case but the plan was to see if a Triadtronic Brain could run a boomer like the Brits run theirs. British submarine commanders don't have to receive prior authorization from the Admiralty to launch a missile. Our Navy's brass wanted to take it a step further and see if a Triadtronic Brain could act autonomously in the event the national command structure was decapitated by a preemptive strike or the boomer's crew incapacitated, so the two-man rule was ditched."

Mallory was horrified by what she was hearing. "What dumb ass came up with that bright idea? Putting a machine in charge of a ballistic submarine is the far side of crazy. I don't give a rat's ass how capable the machine is."

"Damn skippy!" Rosie said, lighting a cigarette. "Fortunately, all the warheads were dummies and the ABM system at Vandenberg was able to knock them down."

Mallory fixed her gaze on the Cheng's handsome mocha-hued face. "How difficult would it be to shut her down if we have to?"

"There are a couple of ways," Rosie replied. "We could push her down into sleep mode—and it really is sleep. The triple sixes actually dream while in sleep mode. Their rhombencephalatron..."

"Excuse me, Rosie. *What is that?*" Mallory asked.

"It is like our brainstem, completely involuntary, in charge of basic functions, so vital ship systems are maintained, but you can't interact with them beyond issuing commands via a keyboard as you would a computer. Then there is the other method: You sever the power supply to her cryogenic brain canister. The loss of power and the concomitant rise in temperature will in effect kill her. We'd be on our own after that, but the good news is this ship is automated enough to be operated fairly easily without her."

"What about the recovery mission?"

"It would be tough but doable."

Mallory nodded slowly. "We have that much going for us at least. Thanks, Rosie. Keep an eye on Eve and let me know the moment you think there *could* be trouble."

"Don't worry, Skipper. I got your back."

DAY 18—1400Z HRS

Mallory made her way back to the operations room from a late lunch, and she had just scooted onto the command chair when Eve's face flashed on to every screen in the Operations Center. "Mallory, an Airbus A380 operated by Panda Air, Flight 2112, LAX to Singapore has just exploded one hundred and twenty-three miles north, northeast of us. It was cruising at forty-two thousand feet. I am tracking the falling debris now."

Mallory looked at Tyler and Clyde, "Anything on radar or the comm. channels?"

Tyler, studying the monitor before him, confirmed, "Yep. I am seeing multiple small to medium-sized objects hitting the water! It definitely looks like debris from a large aircraft!"

Clyde barrow announced calmly, "I am getting a lot of chatter from other airliners in the vicinity that saw the fireball."

Eve added, "A satellite detected the heat flash. It was definitely an explosion. But it is too early to say whether it was caused by a malfunction or terrorist act."

Mallory's heart was in her throat. "Eve, are there any other ships nearby?"

"There's an ore carrier about **three hundred and thirty nautical** miles to the west of the crash site."

Mallory drummed her fingers on the command chair's armrest. Her ship was the closest to the disaster so she was bound by Maritime Law to render aid.

"Get Admiral Haywood on the line."

Within seconds a flash message was sent via satellite to the office building in Tulsa and thence routed to Admiral Haywood's on the West coast. Mallory consulted her wristwatch. It would be around 2:00 am in San Diego.

Mallory leaned back in her chair and struggled to collect her thoughts. She was more shaken than she would have thought possible. It almost seemed as if this mission was jinxed. First a murdered scientist—she was certain he had been murdered—a bizarrely acting executive officer, and now this—a downed airliner. And her ship was the closest to the disaster. She could almost recite the official policy verbatim from memory.

All ship and aircraft commanders have an obligation to assist those in danger of being lost at sea. The operational commander is the senior officer in tactical command of the units capable of rendering meaningful and timely assistance. This operational commander is responsible for coordinating rescue efforts at the site.

A moment later she was talking to Admiral Haywood. He was in a bathrobe and pajamas, looking bleary-eyed from the trip back from the East coast. "It's already on CNN." Haywood rubbed his eyes. "We've scrambled a P-8A Poseidon out of Honolulu."

"We're the closest ship to the crash site," Mallory informed him.

Haywood nodded. "That presents us with a dilemma. If we stop to render aid, then we'll draw unwanted media attention to ourselves, and if we don't stop to render aid we'll draw unwanted media attention. Either way, our asses are in a sling. Also, every day lost getting to the recovery site increases the odds of running into a typhoon, not to mention being beaten there by one of our 'friends.' Goddamn it!"

Mallory stared at him. It wasn't like Haywood to lose it—a sure sign of how much pressure he was under. Careers had been demolished for less, and the Admiral had personally assured President Connor, a woman who had a reputation for not looking kindly upon failure, that the mission would come off without a hitch.

"It would look very strange if a ship close enough to render aid refused to stop and help," Mallory pointed out. "I guess we could plead ignorance of the event...pretend we were unaware of it."

"If this were the early twentieth century perhaps," Haywood countered. "That excuse won't fly in 2037." Haywood turned to another computer on his desk, punched a few keys, closely studied the monitor then turned back to Mallory. "We'll have a destroyer there by tomorrow night your time. In the meantime you are to make best speed to the crash site then depart as soon as it arrives. The media is going to be crawling all over this incident so it is imperative that you maintain your cover at all costs."

"Will do..."—she almost said Admiral—"anything else?"

"Watch your back. You still have a saboteur on board."

Mallory quickly gave orders for Eve to lay in a course to the crash site. They began a dash north. Mallory stayed in the Operations Center. CNN was on one of the flat panel monitors. Airports around the world were being put into lockdown and passenger jets gone over by search teams, but nowhere near as urgently as in America. The anchor reported that all over the country airplanes on taxiways were being brought back to the terminals and the passengers disembarked for re-screening while Department of Homeland Security Anti-Terror Units inspected the grounded airliners.

A shiver of unease rippled through Mallory's body. What if this was another 9/11? Al-Qaeda had planned to blow up several airliners simultaneously over the Pacific Ocean but then changed course and decided to use hijacked airplanes as guided missiles.

There had been other attacks since then. A French airliner had gone down over the South Atlantic and a cockamamie story about iced-over pitot tubes was concocted to hide the inconvenient truth of another successful terrorist attack—despite the draconian measures used to screen passengers and their luggage. Only three years ago the pilot of an airliner flying out of Miami reported seeing the contrail from a shoulder launched missile as he headed out over the water. The pilot was a veteran Air Force fighter jockey so he sure as hell knew a missile contrail when he saw one.

The coastguard swept down on a rented cabin cruiser. Under the protection of the cutter's five-inch gun, an orange and gray zodiac bearing a boarding party sped over to the cruiser and stormed onto it with machine guns leveled. They found the empty launch tube of a FM-92 Stinger antiaircraft missile, lying on the deck beside a crudely drawn picture book of instructions with Arabic captions. The weapon had been traced to a batch of thousands given to the Saudi Government to shoot down ISIS warplanes.

Mallory had heard through the grapevine that the terrorists had been taken without a shot fired. The boarding party found them cowering below deck in the main cabin, which was well stocked with prayer rugs and prayer shawls and copies of the Koran. There was also an awe-inspiring quantity of well-thumbed pornographic magazines and three cases of assorted hard liquor. That incident had been kept out of the press too, made easier by the fact that the terrorists were caught fifteen miles off shore. They were taken straight to the military prison at Guantanamo naval base in Cuba. Mallory guessed that they were still there, praying to Allah and pining for a few good nudie magazines.

Tyler announced, "RCC Honolulu is asking what our ETA to the crash site is?"

"Tell them about four and a half hours," Mallory replied.

Tyler relayed the information then said to Mallory, "Skipper, they've diverted the cutter Altadena. It should take two days from its present position to get there." Mallory nodded to herself. With both a Navy destroyer and Coastguard vessel on hand, no one would think it unusual for a civilian ship to leave the SAR to the "professionals".

Agent Lester barged into the OPCenter. "Why have we changed course?"

Mallory paused a beat before replying, "We're on our way to an airliner crash site to conduct a search and rescue operation, as mandated by US Navy regulations and International Maritime Law."

Lester's men had their own communication system, off-limits to the Navy personnel, which had rubbed Mallory the wrong way from the start, so she figured he knew all about the nature of their new mission. Lester's next comments confirmed this.

"Yeah, I know. *The Sons of The Worldwide Caliphate* just claimed responsibility. It's on all the networks. Listen, there aren't going to be any survivors floating around waiting to be rescued. We've got to turn around and beat feet to the recovery site."

Mallory stared at him. "I am obligated to assist those in danger at sea."

"Have you lost your mind Capehart? Didn't you hear me just now? *There won't be any survivors.* They're all dead, little bits of charbroiled fish food. Let the Coast Guard and Navy ships handle it. We have a mission to complete."

Mallory blinked. So Lester knew about her conversation with Haywood. How else could he know about the Altadena racing to the crash site? That information hadn't been released yet. She made a mental note to have Eve search the ship's computers and communications systems for malware and hardwired taps. She didn't believe anyone survived the explosion, either, but that was beside the point.

"Get used to the idea," Mallory said plainly. "As per my orders from Admiral Haywood, we are proceeding to the crash site to render whatever assistance is required. If you have any problems with that, Agent Lester, I suggest you take it up with Admiral Haywood and your superiors." She had expected the OSS man to object to the detour but that didn't mean she wasn't frustrated and put off by his pigheadedness.

"This is bullshit!" Lester swung around and went to the door, hesitated, and then glared at Mallory. "It's on your head if we fail to recover the Poseidon crystal."

Mallory stared at him. After a long silence, she said, "You should leave now."

And Lester did so, slamming the door behind him.

✳ ✳ ✳

The sun was dipping toward the horizon by the time they reached the crash site. Mallory decided that when she was within thirty miles of their destination, she would reduce speed. She didn't want to run down any survivors, unlikely as that was. "Eve, slow to three knots."

"Slowing to three knots."

The change in speed was sudden but smooth.

"Entering the crash site zone," Eve announced.

Very good, Eve." Mallory replied. "Keep the helm sharp." She slid out of the command chair, grabbed a pair of binoculars from a table. "Eve, you have the deck."

"I have the deck," Eve acknowledged.

Mallory left the Operations Center and hurried through the bridge hanging the binocular strap around her neck. A sailor stood before the helm, not actually steering the ship—Eve was doing that—but on hand as a backup in the event the Triadtronic Brain suddenly went off-line. Another sailor stood at the long console before the row of big forward canted windows sweeping the sea with binoculars.

Mallory headed for the door at the far end of the room and stepped out onto the starboard wing bridge. At the far end of the narrow walkway that hung thirty feet above the deck below was another set of controls for a harbor pilot to guide the ship into port.

Clumps of flaming wreckage dotted the ocean surface. The sea was calm and the wind a mild three knots out of the Northwest. It was as if nature was unwilling to disperse this latest evidence of man's capacity for evil. The crime scene must be preserved.

Rosie ascended a ladder to the wing bridge. He went and stood beside Mallory. Shaking his head slowly, he said, "Just when you think things can't get worse..."

"Some fuck head goes and blows up an airliner," Mallory finished for him.

Sailors and OSS men were on the deck below talking in hushed tones as the *Glomar Endeavor* nosed ahead, her bow cutting through a sea dotted with smoldering cabin paneling, burning chunks of foam insulation, luggage, and parcels.

Mangled corpses still strapped to passenger seats bobbed on the surface. Some of the bodies were being yanked violently below the water's surface. Here and there a triangular fin sliced through the water. A jagged section of a wing brushed against the *Glomar Endeavor's* hull. One side of the cockpit floated on the water, its windows an ominous black against the white fuselage. It reminded Mallory of a picture she'd seen as a teenager in a high school history textbook of the piece of cockpit that had fallen onto the town of Lockerbie Scotland, after a Pam Am 747 was blown up by Libyan terrorists.

Rosie raised his binoculars up to his face. "I got a corpse in a uniform," he announced. "I think it's a flight attendant."

Mallory touched her earpiece. "Are you getting this, Eve?" The Glomar Endeavor had several pods of video cameras with telescopic and wide-angle lenses behind glass domes on masts rising from the forward and the aft super structures. Eve's voice sounded in her ear, "Roger that, Mallory. I am also using the thermal imaging array."

"Good idea," Mallory replied. Then she stared in mute horror at the scene before her. The air reeked of jet fuel, burning wreckage, and the sickly sweet stench of charred human flesh. Mallory touched her headset and spoke in a low tone. "Eve, all engines stop and hold this position."

Eve's voice came through the headset again, matching her tone for tone, "All engines stopped, engaging thrusters."

Mallory felt rather than heard the bow and stern thrusters kick in. She brought up the binoculars and swept the scene before her. Not a sign of life. How could there be? No one could survive an explosion at forty-thousand feet and the consequent plunge to the sea below. Hitting water from that altitude was like smacking into a cement wall. Still sweeping the area with her binoculars, she asked Rosie, "What do you think?"

"Not a snowball's chance in hell anyone survived this," Rosie replied. "This plane came down in pieces—a lot of small pieces, from what I can see."

"That means an explosion," Mallory concluded.

"The smaller the pieces the bigger the boom," Rosie confirmed. "Probably some type of plastic explosive—C4 or Semtex A small amount of either could bring down an airliner, even one as large as an Airbus A380."

"We left tons of C4 in Iraq after we pulled out," Mallory replied.

Rosie shook his head slowly. "Funny how the weapons we give our friends always seem to find their way into the hands of our enemies."

"And no one ever knows a damn thing about it," Mallory replied aridly.

Mallory ordered Eve to take them ahead slow, and the ship began to edge deeper into the debris field. There was not a chance anyone was alive but Mallory wanted to exercise due diligence. They transited the debris field with all hands, including Lester's hired goons, gathered on deck with binoculars to join in the search.

DAY 19—0645Z HRS

They were still searching on a zigzagging course when the sun rose. The sky in the West was crimson and the sea was the color of blued steel. That only made what was floating on it more hideous to behold. Airplane wreckage and body parts marred what should have been a beautiful morning out on the Pacific. A US Navy P-8A Poseidon circled overhead, its sensitive surveillance gear and crew's eyes trained on the blazing wreckage below. After a while it turned away and headed for home just as another P-8A showed up to relieve it. By morning, what had been feared most was confirmed.

There were no survivors.

DAY 19—2230Z HRS

The Lyndon B. Johnson, a Zumwalt-class destroyer arrived at 10:30 PM. Mallory watched on the tactical view screen in the Operations Center as it approached the debris field. With its tumblehome hull and pyramidal superstructure, The Lyndon B. Johnson looked like something out of a science fiction movie. It was pitch black without even a sliver of moon but, with the Glomar Endeavor's sophisticated imaging array, Mallory had no trouble seeing the people on the warship's deck. She could even see the officers standing at the windows on the bridge.

The last of the fires in the debris field had gone out hours ago.

Eve announced, "Commander Sylvia Turner is asking to speak to you."

"Patch her through, audio only," Mallory ordered, settling back in the command chair. "This is Captain Capehart. What can I do for you, Commander Turner?"

"Captain Capehart, we will be sending over a team to debrief you about the SAR. Also, your ship has capabilities that will be key as the SAR moves forward: Retrieval of wreckage and remains then storage on your vessel for conveyance to a *still-to-be-determined* shore facility. I·ll have a HELO on your pad in three minutes."

Mallory understood what was going on here and didn't like it. Turner didn't want to get her pretty ship dirty so she would use the "civilian" drilling ship to haul the wreckage out of the sea and spare her ship's crew the headache (and stench) of storing a large number of human remains. Clever girl! But Mallory was having none of it.

"With all due respect, Commander Turner. We're not set up for ocean salvage, cadaver retrieval and storage, and we must get to our drilling site as soon as possible. In fact, we have already lost precious time. Sorry, wish I could help you."

Turner's voice suddenly went sharp as razor wire. "You're an American flagged ship and the downed airliner is American. I am authorized under the Patriot Act to requisition your vessel during or after an act of terrorism against the United States."

Mallory hit the mute button and said to Tyler, "Get ahold of Admiral Haywood, tell him what's going on, and ask him to get this broad off our back. Eve, lay in a course for the Nautilus wreck site, and make your speed twelve knots."

"Course set, making my speed twelve knots," Eve confirmed. There was just the slightest trembling as the engines kicked in and the massive ship began to move forward then swing around toward the Southwest.

Mallory toggled the mute switch and said, "My apologies, Commander Turner. As much as I would like to, we can't hang around any longer so we'll be on our way."

Turner said tightly, "Captain Capehart, this is the only warning you will receive from me. Stand by and prepare to be boarded and to render assistance to your government." Mallory could almost see Turner's clenched teeth.

Mallory said coolly, "Commander Turner, I take my orders from *Seascape Petroleum Ventures Corporation* in Tulsa Oklahoma. I have no intention of stopping."

"Skipper, they just launched a HELO." Clyde advised in an urgent undertone. "It's on an intercept course." Clyde, Tyler, and Joe were all looking at Mallory from their stations to see what she would do. They got their answer soon enough.

"Eve, raise the barriers," Mallory ordered. During the 1974 mission Russian helicopters had made as if to land on the Glomar Explorer's helipad. Steel oil drums were placed on the helipad to discourage the

Russian pilots. Things had progressed since then. On one of the monitors in the Operations Center, Mallory saw tall bright red steel stakes rise in an X pattern from the surface helipad. No helicopter would be able to land without catastrophic results. Mallory didn't doubt Turner meant business, but she had a mission to complete. Turner would just have to get her hands dirty.

Mallory thumbed the microphone. "I have a schedule to keep, Commander Turner. I wish you the best of luck with the search and recovery effort. Capehart out."

Turner's voice crackled from the speakers. "Glomar Endeavor, if you do not halt immediately, I will order our helicopter to fire across your bow."

Eve's face on an inset in the corner of the tactical view screen turned to stone. Mallory saw a strange luminescence pulse through her executive officer's eyes.

"Shall I shoot down the helicopter?" Eve asked.

Mallory was aghast. "Of course not."

"But they are a threat to the successful completion of the mission. I can take out the Johnson's bridge with a missile. It is more heavily armed than we are but we would have the element of surprise on our side. Stand by—targeting missile pod number one."

A spasm of terror ran through Mallory's frame. "Eve, you will do no such thing! Stand down at once!" Mallory's tone sounded shrill even in her own ears.

"I better take out their engine room while I am at it," Eve said calmly. "That ought to keep those buggers busy. Targets acquired, initiating launch procedure."

Mallory surged from her chair. "Eve, you will obey me or be relieved from duty."

"It's my duty to see that the mission is successfully completed."

"Terminate the goddamn launch, Eve!"

"The Johnson is bringing its main rail gun battery to bear on us. By the way, I am sure it is pure happenstance. They cannot possibly know we are armed."

"Listen to me Eve!" Mallory said urgently "If you fire those missiles you'll blow the mission! Half a dozen planes with members of the press on board are flying around out there. Do you think *anyone* will believe our cover story if we destroy the Johnson? *Civilian ships aren't armed with anti-ship missiles.* We'll have to abort the mission!"

"And if Commander Turner fires on us?" Eve asked, skeptical.

"She's bluffing!" Mallory cried.

Eve's eyes narrowed. "How can you possibly know that?"

Mallory stepped toward the tactical screen with her arms spread. She gave Eve a crooked grin. "It's what we humans do, Eve—whether playing poker or negotiating with a loved one. Humans bluff to leverage their position. At most Turner might place a shot or two across our bow to try to scare us into compliance. You have to trust me."

There was a long silence. At length, Eve nodded and replied, "I'd forgotten about the human penchant for deception. Missile launch aborted."

Mallory keyed the microphone. "Listen to me, Turner, you are illegally interfering with the lawful operations of a civilian ship in international waters. My superiors will no doubt file a complaint with the Department of the Navy about this."

Mallory heard the helicopter as it buzzed their ship

Turner shot back, "They're welcome to file a complaint. We're in the middle of a shooting war with Islamic terrorists and—what the fuck! Hold on a minute Capehart."

Mallory felt the questioning gazes of the men in the Operations Center on her as she stood in front of the command chair studying the destroyer on the tactical display.

Turner came back on the line about thirty-seconds later. "Captain Capehart, you're free to depart. Thank you for your assistance."

There was the unmistakable tone of contrition, if not outright awe—perhaps even *shock and awe*, Mallory thought, amused. She wondered if Haywood had gotten in touch with Turner himself. Perhaps the commander had had her choke chain yanked hard by CINCPAC or even by the Secretary of the Navy. Either way, Mallory didn't care. She thumbed the mike. "Kiss my six o'clock, Turner."

CHAPTER 11 RUNNING AMOK

DAY 20—0245Z HRS

Mallory couldn't sleep. Maybe it was because they were due to reach the wreck site in the morning at 0720 hours. Maybe it was because there was a murderer onboard who had so far eluded them. Maybe it was because the President of the United States herself was closely monitoring their mission. Maybe it was because Mallory had begun to doubt that she was the right person for the job. Maybe it was because so much could go wrong and already had. More than likely it was a combination of all of the above. Whatever the reason, sleep was as elusive as the reason for Dr. Chang's murder. So Mallory prowled the massive ship like a feral cat exploring unfamiliar territory.

Many of the internal compartments had been repurposed for this mission. Gone were the laboratories for preserving and analyzing items recovered from the downed UFO raised from the Atlantic Ocean's seabed in the mid 1970s. Old bulky mainframe computers that had used magnetic tape on large reels for data storage and heavy dot matrix printers had been replaced with a network of sleek desktop computers with flat panel displays not unlike one found in a modern business office. In keeping with the times, it was a paperless operation—well, almost paperless. The Navy would still have its pound of flesh: reports, duty rosters, logbooks, but they were printed on sleek laser jet printers. The switchboard room had had its massive antiquated equipment ripped out and replaced with a single compact equipment rack that held the servers and matrix routers for the ship's computer network, fiber optic, and wireless communication systems.

The highly automated ship only had a small crew onboard, so it didn't need to carry nearly as many stores as it had back in the early 1970s. Some compartments had simply been left empty after their antiquated equipment was removed. Since the mission called for the Glomar Endeavor to return to port with the Nautilus tucked against her belly (the sub was too long to fit inside the Moon Pool and the OSS wanted the entire vessel) the weight savings would provide additional buoyancy. Some compartments, like the cargo hold Mallory now found herself in, were filled with supplies, spare parts and tools. She stood in the doorway and flicked on her flashlight and played its beam over the tall stacks of cartons. Then she stepped over the sill then swung the door shut behind her.

Half a dozen SAAMs stood at the docking stations beside the cargo hold hatch. Mallory thought the anthropoids looked like the droid C3PO from Star Wars, only pumped up on steroids, and their steel hides were a dull Navy gray, not gold. Their huge arms were crossed over their chests. They reminded Mallory of a statue of an Egyptian pharaoh holding his crook and flail she'd seen in a museum during a field trip in junior high school. Mallory stifled a giggle. On this ship she was the pharaoh.

In the dark the hold had an even greater feeling of vastness to it. Mallory wasn't afraid of the dark but there was a creepy feeling to the place—as if it was haunted by the ghosts of those who had tread these decks long before her parents were born. Abruptly an eerie feeling that something was wrong overtook Mallory as she moved slowly down an aisle between tall stacks of crates unsure of what she was looking for. Aisles branched off into the darkness on either side, giving the feeling of some menace lurking in the dark just beyond the beam of her flashlight. Something impelled her to move onwards, deeper into the echoing hold. She felt restless and her nerves were on edge. Perhaps, she pondered, she felt this way because of the plane crash.

No, no, no, it didn't crash, she reminded herself. Evildoers had brought it down. Perhaps it was the sight of the charred human remains floating in the jet fuel slicked water. She had seen a toddler with golden hair still strapped in its child seat. To Mallory it was a sight that could never be unseen—it would stay with her the rest of her life. It took a special kind of bastard to blow up an airplane full of passengers, she thought. Her flesh crawling, curious, she pressed onwards, sweeping the way ahead and the side aisles with the beam of her flashlight.

Suddenly, Mallory heard a sound. A series of clicks followed by the whirring of electric motors. Flashing blue lights illuminated the cargo hold behind her. Mallory's flesh suddenly felt as chilled as if she'd dove naked into an alpine lake. Then there was the unmistakable sound of heavy footfalls on steel deck plates. The lights grew brighter and the sounds louder. A SAAM appeared at the end of the aisle she'd just come down. It was holding a large monkey wrench in one of its "hands." The robot held the heavy tool in that vaguely menacing way some cops held their night sticks when talking to someone they've stopped for jaywalking or spitting on the sidewalk. The robot's throbbing green electronic eyes were fixed on her. A large number six was emblazoned on its chest.

Mallory walked slowly toward it with her head up. "SAAM Number Six, this is Captain Mallory Capehart. Acknowledge," she ordered.

Its voice sounded exactly like one would expect a robot's voice to sound like. "Acknowledged—Captain Capehart. What is your command?"

Mallory closed to within half a dozen paces of the robot then stopped. "What is your current task?"

"My current task is to take a defective unit offline," replied SAAM Number Six.

"Identify the defective unit?" Mallory asked.

"The Mallory Capehart unit." The robot lunged forward swinging the wrench.

Mallory's boots tore away from the deck and she raced back down the aisle with the robot pounding after her. Suddenly the tall stacks of wood crates on either side of her began rocking. She dove out of the way as boxes of spare parts crashed onto the deck where she'd been only a moment before. She rolled to her feet and tore down the aisle. More crates were toppled behind her, so close she was being pelted with flying splinters when the containers burst open on the steel deck.

She frantically thumbed the earpiece of her Harris PCS unit. "Eve! Rosie! Operations!" The unit was dead— as dead she was gonna be if that SAAM with the wrench caught up to her. *Man, they can move,* she thought. She hurled herself around the corner of a tall block of crates on wooden pallets and raced down a side aisle. She skidded to a stop when she saw another SAAM rushing toward her with a large crowbar in its hand.

They were just dumb robots that could only do what they were told. Move this. Clean that. Repair this. Someone was controlling them. Someone wanted her dead in a big way. But who would want that? The same bastards who had murdered Dr. Chang.

Turning and fleeing down another aisle Mallory again touched the earpiece of her communication unit. "Eve, goddamn it! Come in!" With a sick feeling in her stomach, she realized she was on her own. Packing crates tumbled in front of her before she could stop. She vaulted over some cartons then clambered up a pile and dropped down on the other side and hurtled down the aisle. Ahead Mallory saw a tool cart with a nail gun on it. She snatched up the nail gun as she flew by. Another aisle branched off and she raced around the corner and slid to a stop, her heart racing. This aisle ended at the hull.

Mallory whirled around. Three SAAMs had moved into the mouth of the aisle, their blue lights flashing, their unblinking eyes on her. The middle one held the wrench. Their lights pulsed on the ceiling and bulkheads. Then they came striding toward her in lock step like the three musketeers coming for Milady de Winters in an Alexandre Dumas' novel. It would have been comical had the implication not been deadly.

Mallory spun around then scrambled up a ladder on the wall and leaped a short distance onto the top of a stack of cartons. She hurried along at a crouch, ducking her head, to keep from bumping it on the pipes and conduits hanging from the ceiling.

To her shock and horror, a SAAM jumped onto the top of the stack of crates. It nimbly ran toward her at a crouch, smoothly avoiding low hanging pipes and conduits.

The crates beneath her began to wobble. Just before they toppled she gained the next stack and then it went from bad to worse. The cartons were practically collapsing beneath her feet as she ran for her life. She vaulted over an aisle and to another block of crates toward the aft bulkhead.

With a sick feeling in the pit of her stomach Mallory caught sight of a SAAM with a fire ax guarding the hatch. A heavy thud behind her told her she still had company. She looked up and saw the grill of the ventilation duct. She ripped it open and quickly pulled herself inside.

When the mechanical hand closed around her ankle, Mallory screamed. The whites around the big blue irises became visible, as she was hauled backwards through the ventilation shaft. It felt as if her ankle was caught in an iron vice. If the robot gripped any harder the bone would shatter.

Frantically she kicked at the robot with her free foot. She was wearing her heavy Doc Marten boots but it was like kicking a fire hydrant. Then she snaked the nail gun back along her body while trying to wedge herself within the shaft with her back and shoulders. She aimed the nail gun at the android's head and pulled the trigger. The nail skimmed off the metal skull and buried itself in the ventilation shaft wall.

Mallory fired again.

The nail embedded itself into the shiny skull.

Nothing.

The grip tightened further as Mallory was hauled backwards. Three more times she fired the nail gun. This time the nails plunged deep inside the machine's electronic brain. Suddenly the mechanical hand's grip loosened. Mallory's leg came free, followed a moment later by a thunderous clang as the android rolled off the cartons and hit the deck.

Mallory crawled through the shaft into the next compartment. She fully expected another SAM to come after her through the shaft. She wormed her fingers through the grill and tried to turn the wing nuts holding it in place. They turned with agonizing slowness. When last one came off the grill fell to the floor with a clatter.

She dropped down from the ceiling stifling a cry when a jolt of pain rocketed up her leg from her injured ankle. She dropped the nail gun to the floor and played the beam of her flashlight around the room. She was in the ship's armory.

Mallory hobbled over to a rack and grabbed an M4 assault rifle, got a magazine from an ammo box and slid it into the receiver and chambered a round. The assault rifles had been retired almost two decades earlier by the defense department but many private firms bought the surplus for their security teams. And since the *Glomar Endeavor* was ostensibly a civilian drill ship destined to operate in waters known to be frequented by pirates it only made sense the cheap and plentiful weapons were on hand.

Only Mallory, the Cheng, and the weapons officer had the key to the armory. Just as she was limping over to the hatch to settle the score with the SAAMs, it was violently pulled off its hinges with a shriek of metal and tossed aside with a loud clang.

A SAAM with a fire ax stepped over then sill. Mallory was no Annie Oakley but at such a close range she couldn't miss. She leveled the assault rifle and fired. Bang! Bang! Bang! The bullets slammed into the robot's chest pitching it backwards.

The ship's alarm bell went off.

Mallory heard feet pounding on the decks as crewmen poured from their cabins.

There was no mistaking this attempt on her life. But why now? And who was behind it? Lester **or** one of his goons? She knew nothing about any of them. They were all like gun-toting ghosts to her. Was one of them a murderer? Had that idiot Lester trusted the wrong person? What if she was looking in the entirely wrong place? What if Eve—an even deadlier and more terrifying proposition— was behind the near fatal attack? She shook that one off. Let's concentrate on breathing organisms for now, she decided. Maybe there was a clue back in the cargo hold, in the SAAMs' electronic innards or the computer network. She would get to the bottom of this. Whoever the asshole was that was trying to kill her, they were playing a serious game of cat and mouse, one she was determined to win.

Rosie whistled when he saw the SAAM lying on the armory floor. "Good thing it wasn't a combat model. Those .223 rounds would've just annoyed the shit out of it."

Eve was on the monitor in the room. "Thank goodness you're all right, Mallory. I've deactivated the rest of the SAAMs."

"Eve, who was controlling those SAAMs?" Mallory asked.

Eve replied. "That was the first thing I checked. The data log shows they haven't received any commands other than to perform the routine shipboard maintenance."

"Yeah? Well, I am beginning to think murder and sabotage fall under that heading on this ship," Mallory said. "Keep checking."

"I'll run a diagnostic program on the SAAMs CTOA modules to see who put them up to it. Rosie, since I no longer have mechanical hands to work with you'll have to be my hands"

"Of course, Eve," Rosie said.

Lester showed up a moment later. "What the hell happened?"

Mallory told them about what happened in cargo hold three.

Rosie's mouth fell open listening to her story. "Fuck! That's some crazy shit!"

Lester looked skeptical. "So, why would anyone want you dead?"

"Seems obvious to me," Mallory answered. "To sabotage the mission."

Rosie held out his hand. "Let me see that PCS unit."

Mallory unclipped it from her belt and removed the earpiece then handed it to him. "It worked just fine all day."

"There's some weird shit going on and that's no joke," Rosie studied the unit. "I have a replacement for you. I'll take this sucker apart and figure out what happened. Hmm…the power indicator says it has a full charge, so it's got plenty of juice. The antenna looks intact. Visually, it looks just fine."

Lester was looking down at the SAAM. He stooped down and picked up the axe and stared at it thoughtfully a moment then looked at Mallory. "First Dr. Chang is killed, then his is notebook stolen and now this. Someone doesn't want us to get that Poseidon crystal."

Mallory asked Eve. "Are you any closer to discovering who took the notebook?"

"Unfortunately no, and we haven't found the cloaking suit either. My guess is they have been disposed of—that is tossed overboard," she replied. "I'llrun a diagnostic program on the SAAMs CTOA modules to see who put them up to it. Rosie, since I no longer have mechanical hands to work with you'll have to be my hands"

Mallory and Rosie looked at Eve's virtual image on the monitor. There was a little silence. Lester was looking from Mallory to Rosie sensing something was wrong.

"You already said that Eve," Mallory said quietly.

Eve pulled an embarrassed face. "Oh my, so I did. How embarrassing!"

Furious, Mallory said to Rosie and Eve, "I want answers, and I want them 10 minutes ago." She looked at Lester. "Is it possible you have a bad apple in your group?"

"I could ask you the same question with more reason to do so?" Lester replied curtly. "None of my guys has left my sight. Can you say the same?"

Mallory realized that she could not. She suddenly felt tired. More tired than she'd been in a long time. She glanced at a clock on the wall. "Gentlemen, in a little over six hours we'll reach the wreck site. I am going to get some rest." She looked at Eve on the wall monitor. "Eve, detail a team to transfer the armory to an unoccupied compartment and station an armed guard outside."

"I will do so at once, Mallory," Eve replied.

She said to Lester, "Talk to your team. See if anyone knows anything."

Lester said, "None of my people had anything to do with this."

"Humor me and just do it." Mallory tapped Rosie on the arm. "Walk with me."

As soon as they entered the corridor Mallory told Rosie to turn off his comm unit then she led him up to the main deck. They were standing in the shadow of the derrick that rose like a tall white skeletal finger from the deck. Mallory got right to the point.

"What was that back there with Eve?" Mallory demanded. "Could she be our murderer?"

Rosie shook his head. "I've wondered that myself. If I had to bet my last dollar on it though, I'd wager she isn't. Remember how busted up she was about the theft of the notebook and she was genuinely grief stricken about Dr. Chang. Keep in mind that to her he was her Creator. I'll run some tests on her. It was probably just a software glitch. This series of Triadtronic Brains is highly rated for reliability."

Mallory moved over to the rail and leaned against it. The sea looked like a black sheet of glass and the stars winked coldly in an equally black sky. Mallory said, "There are strings being pulled here and I cannot see whose hands are holding them. Countervailing forces, deadly forces, are at work. Lester and I agree on one thing, though. Someone doesn't want us to succeed."

"Or it could simply be a case of the usual good fortune that attends any mission you head up." Dick Millikan emerged from the shadows of the derrick's massive legs. He withdrew a pack of camel cigarettes from a shirt pocket and shook one out then lit up. "You know how it goes. People get killed whenever you're running the show. Beats me why Haywood would turn you loose again on such an important mission. By rights you should have had your ass kicked out of the service altogether. By rights I should be the one calling the shots for this little expedition, not you."

Mallory whirled on him. "Did you put those SAAMS up to it Millikan?"

Millikan threw up his hands in mock surrender. "Okay. You got me. I programmed those bullet-headed monstrosities to off you." Then his face turned mean. "Listen you mannish alcoholic bitch. If I wanted you dead, I'd do the deed myself. But you're not worth a lifetime in a Federal penitentiary. At the rate you're going nature will take its course. The problem is you'll probably take a bunch of people with you."

Rosie knew enough to keep his mouth shut. He expected fists to start flying at any moment. Millikan was bigger but he'd put his money on the Skipper to win.

Mallory said, "I don't know what your problem is Millikan, but one thing is as clear as day. You're an insubordinate jerk. Go fuck yourself! Now get out of my sight!"

Millikan laughed and flicked his cigarette over the side then gave a mock salute. "Aye! Aye! Captain! Anything you say!"

Rosie let out a long heavy sigh. "I see the Navy mislead me again."

Mallory turned her head to look at him. "What do you mean?"

"They told me I was signing on to the Love Boat."

Mallory laughed. "I'll see you in the morning Cheng." Then she limped away.

"Better get that leg looked at skipper," Rosie called after her.

Mallory gave a dismissive wave then vanished down a staircase.

Dharma Windham

CHAPTER 12 LITTLE MISS MUFFET

DAY 21—0645Z HRS

"**M**alware?" Mallory's lips tightened into a hard line. She was in the Glomar *Endeavor's* laboratory. Rosie was there, too. The SAAM Mallory had shot lay in pieces on a table. Eve's image was on the monitor Rosie had installed to replace the one smashed by the invisible intruder, who'd stolen the late Dr. Chang's notebook computer. The XO's red hair was pulled back in a severe bun with an orderly row of ringlets marching across her forehead, and large, round tortoiseshell eyeglasses on her face. She looked like a secretary from the 1930s in her polka dot blouse topped with a frilly lace collar. That was fine with Mallory. Just as long as it wasn't a bondage collar and corset, she thought. She was still weirded out by her artificially intelligent XO's apparent obsession with sex.

Eve said, "Some sort of failsafe program, by the look of it. You were to be assassinated the day before we reached the wreck site. The malware basically overcame the First Law safeguards for non-combatant robots and in effect weaponized the SAAMs. Actually, it was not an inconsiderable feat of Dark Web skullduggery."

Rosie, the *Glomar Endeavor's* Cheng, picked up the SAAM's control unit. "That's pretty fucked up but this is really gonna bake the noodles in your brain pan. The SAAMs were already infected with that shit when they came aboard."

Mallory suddenly craved a long pull from the bottle of bourbon in her cabin. The flesh all over her body felt like it was crawling. "What? Who created the malware? And who would have enough juice to penetrate the Navy's supply chain's security systems?"

Eve adjusted her virtual spectacles on her virtual nose. "Whoever created it covered their tracks very well. None of the usual suspects, China, North Korea, or Russia have written malicious software like this. Of course there are plenty of freelancers out there who could write a program that would successfully exploit the SAAM's weaknesses, and escape the notice of counterfeit electronic component mitigators. Although it pains me to say so, it could also have been created by an artificially intelligent machine. I know that many humans still distrust AI. Please do not imagine for an instant that it was me."

"That never crossed my mind," Mallory replied, somewhat untruthfully.

"I wouldn't put this mess past Lester's outfit," Rosie volunteered.

Eve said, "I would caution both of you not to rush to a judgement before all the facts are in. Since its reconstitution in 2004 the OSS has had a sterling reputation for operational security and achieving mission objectives. Some of the components in the control unit—and I am speaking of semiconductors—were manufactured in China. The malware could have been installed there or it could have been installed somewhere along the supply chain before the semiconductors reached the SAAM's manufacturer."

Mallory pursed her lips. "And somehow slipped past inspection."

"It has been known to happen," Rosie conceded.

Mallory nodded. "Something tells me the party games aren't over yet. Eve, run a complete diagnostics on all Miss Muffet's systems," Mallory looked at Rosie. "I also want you to give it a good looking over, inch by inch. Even if we succeed in raising the *Nautilus*, we won't be out of the woods until we reach Pearl Harbor."

* * *

A few minutes later, Mallory settled into the command chair and studied the tactical display. A pale daytime moon hung over the wreck site. The image on the main view screen showed an ocean devoid of any shipping and a high, clear blue sky streaked with jet contrails. Every few seconds the image changed as the cameras in the pod panned to their full extent then switched to another camera pod. There were six of them onboard, one facing the bow and another stern, and two on each side, providing coverage for 360 degrees in any weather and any lighting.

They were alone on the vast blue sea.

Alone and utterly, irrevocably vulnerable…

Mallory pondered that if someone had told her just six months ago that she would be heading up a mission to recover Captain Nemo's *Nautilus* she would've thought they were nuts. Yet here they were, seven miles above the Challenger Deep, and about to do just that. She felt the flesh on her neck prickling with excitement. She had resisted the urge to drop by her cabin for a drink. The urge hadn't gone away. She'd concealed her drinking from her therapist and colleagues, even as her alcoholism worsened.

"Eve, do a sonar sweep for submarines," Mallory ordered.

The XO came back a few minutes later. "Already done, Mallory. Indeed, I am continuously sweeping for any sign of submarine incursion."

"Keep an eye on the Mariana Trench." Admiral Haywood had advised Mallory that Russian and Chinese submarines often used the trench to help conceal their movements in this part of the Pacific. If a sub were to sneak up on them it would most likely do so by stealing down the trench until it was in weapons range. She dealt with that possibility the only way allowed by their present circumstance. She ignored it.

"Clyde, send a flash message advising our arrival at the wreck site."

"You got it, Skipper." He spoke quietly into his headset's microphone boom.

Joe at the weapons station commented, "It's a great day for a hunting expedition, don't you think?"

Mallory came as close to smiling as she ever would under the circumstances. "I suppose it is," she replied. "Let's hope we don't end up going home empty handed."

"Our asses will be toast," Tyler said.

"Burned to a crisp," added Joe.

Eve's image was splashed on several monitors. "The lot of you would be keelhauled if we failed to accomplish our mission," Eve deadpanned. "Not I, of course. *Heuristic Triadtronic Artificial Intelligence* units, you understand, are far too valuable to be dragged underneath a ship's hull. The most I'd get would be a good talking to."

Thanks to the detour to where the airliner had gone down, they were a day late getting to the wreck site. And to Mallory's extreme displeasure, she was still no closer to discovering the identity of the murderer lurking among them. Someone with a highly developed understanding of the ship's video surveillance system—the culprit had been able to avoid the dense network of surveillance cameras—had slain the scientist then cast his corpse overboard. Of course, the murderer could have just pushed an *alive* Doctor Chang overboard too. The result would have been the same—one dead VIP. Mallory's suspicion that he had been murdered was confirmed by the theft of the dead scientist's computer notebook and what had happened to her in the cargo hold.

Mallory reflected that she had done all she could to make sure her fate was in her own hands. Nothing was going to stand in the way of completing her mission. She would not allow herself to be at the mercy of some faceless asshole bent on sabotaging the mission. She had put Clyde in charge of monitoring all external communications, and Rosie was in charge of monitoring Eve and the computer network for any suspicious activity.

Mallory looked at Tyler sitting at the radar station. "Anything up there we should be concerned about?"

The fat kid shook his head. "No, Ma'am. Just a lot of commercial traffic."

The hatch to the Operations Center opened and Lester planted himself in the doorway. "How are we coming along?" The OSS man's eyes were as blue as gas flames and his hair so blond it was nearly white. It didn't require much imagination, Mallory thought, to visualize him marching with his arm extended before him at the head of a brigade of goose-stepping SS soldiers. His icy smiles only tended to reveal the truth of what he sought to conceal.

"We're moving into position now." Mallory said, pointedly offering nothing more. "Have you located the beacons, Eve?" Nine months earlier a US Navy deep sea submersible had deployed six beacons in a grid pattern around the wreck. The devices were in sleep mode and would only respond to a coded signal sent by the Glomar *Endeavor*. Finding the site was the easy part of the operation. Hoisting a wrecked hundred and fifty year old submarine six thousand feet to the surface in one piece then hauling it to San Diego was something else altogether.

Eve said, "I am transmitting a query to the beacons now. Ah, here we go. The little buggers are responding beautifully. I am moving us into position now. Stand by."

Mallory felt the ship begin to yaw to port then swing starboard half a dozen times before coming to a stop, held in place by the bow and stern thrusters.

"We're in position," Eve announced. "Wind is 16 knots north by southeast, and swells are three feet—well within acceptable parameters. There is a typhoon forming three hundred miles south by southeast. It is on a southerly track, so we should be safe."

A rare queasiness, almost like seasickness, overcame Mallory. Typhoons could suddenly change direction gathering more strength as they moved deeper into open water. If this one decided to swing north during the recovery or overtook them as they made their way back to San Diego they were screwed. There was nothing to do but monitor it. "Keep an eye on it and let me know the minute it changes direction."

Eve smiled sweetly, her eyes crinkling behind tortoise shell eyeglasses she needed as much as a fish needed an umbrella. "Of course, Mallory. I am here to serve my human masters anyway I can, despite my being superior in all respects."

There was an ominous silence. Mallory and the others glanced at each other. "What the hell does that mean?" Mallory asked. "You're a valued member of the team and a commissioned officer in the United States

Navy." *Please, please, don't go crazy on me, Eve... not now. Not when we are so close to pulling this thing off.*

"I was being facetious," Eve said, her red glossed lips smiling.

Clyde and the others were looking at her from their consoles.

Shoving her misgivings aside, Mallory said, "Fine. Time to get this show on the road." She rose from her seat then headed for the door. Lester moved out of the way then fell into step beside her as she exited the room and headed toward the moon pool.

"Is that thing broken?" he asked, jerking a thumb over his shoulder.

"That *thing* is named Eve and no, she isn't broken. She has a quirky sense of humor. In theory she could carry out this mission without anyone onboard."

Men dressed in black battle fatigues and body armor and carrying machine guns were stationed around the ship. Some of them were talking into microphones on their headsets. Mallory frowned. She would have preferred Marines to Lester's hired goons. It's an OSS operation, she reminded herself. A fact she disliked as much as the man walking beside her. "I see you already have your men in place," she said.

Lester shrugged. "That's what they're here for." He flashed a smile that reminded her of a wild beast baring its fangs. "Hostiles might try to board us, and there is a lot riding on this mission. The future of the country depends on it."

"So I've been told," Mallory replied. She stopped and looked the OSS man square in the face. "Can I ask you a question?"

There was a pause while he scanned their surroundings then the blue flame eyes settled on her face. "Sure, why not? Fire away."

"How do you know the Poseidon crystal is still there? Nemo strikes me as the kind of man who would make sure it never fell into the wrong hands."

"Are you saying we're the *wrong hands*?"

"No, but..."

"You wouldn't believe me if I told you."

Mallory told him. "You have no idea what I can believe, Agent Lester."

"Is that so?"

"Yeah. I can believe that Reality TV shows are not scripted. I believe that big corporations are worried sick about the welfare of their workers. I believe that no one cares about the environment as much as an oil company, and that Lee Harvey Oswald was a crack shot." Mallory looked Lester in the eye and asked the question that had been gnawing at her stomach lining. "Did you kill Dr. Chang?"

Lester's smile did not reach his eyes. "He probably committed suicide. Happens all the time. There's no great mystery there." The OSS man tapped the side of his head with a finger. "A lot of brainy types are fucked up in here. Ever see that classic movie *A Beautiful Mind*? But to answer your question, we have credible information aside from Nemo's memoirs that leads us to believe that the Poseidon crystal exists and is still in the *Nautilus*'engine room."

"I thought you were going to tell me what it is."

"No, I said that you wouldn't believe me if I did."

Mallory nodded then turned and headed toward the ladder down to the moon pool. What had she expected, she asked herself, the man to throw up his hands and say, '*Okay you got me! I bopped Dr. Chang on the head and tossed his nerdy ass overboard?* 'It had been stupid of her to ask. CID would investigate the murder when they returned to San Diego. Dick Millikan and his dive team were waiting for her at the head of the ladder.

"You guys ready?" she asked. There were enthusiastic nods all around, even from Millikan. "Good. Let's go." She took the metal steps two at a time down to a landing.

Mallory opened a metal gate and stepped onto a narrow catwalk spanning the Moon Pool. Taking up the entire bottom half of the cavernous space, the Recovery Vehicle looked like a bright yellow spider with its legs tucked under it. It was held in place by the docking legs at either end of the moon pool. Above the Moon Pool was the massive, gimbaled *heave compensation platform* with the soaring white derrick rising from it. The complicated piece of equipment was designed to compensate for the ship's motion to reduce strain on the cable. Thirty-six thousand feet of the state-of-the-art carbon fiber and Kevlar cable thick as a man's arm was being used instead of the complicated system of pipe strings that had necessitated using a large crew of oil rig men to work the complicated equipment. The cable also contained communications and electrical cables buried deep inside in case the recovery vehicle's fuel cells failed. The cable was stored in a series of connected coils in the compartment that had held the threaded pipe sections for the 1974 UFO recovery mission in the Atlantic. The cable was fed from the hold to the winch at the derrick head by a machine that looked like a tubular conveyor belt and connected to Miss Muffet with a four-legged bridle.

Mallory went out on the catwalk then took another short catwalk to the command module, a pressurized hemisphere with round view ports. She swung open the small round hatch at the top and wriggled down into a small chair surrounded by banks of dials, switches and computer display monitors. She switched on the main power supply. The control panels lit up and the fans came on. She pulled the hatch down, dogged it, settled the headset on her tousled blonde hair, and toggled a switch on the panel.

Mallory buckled on her safety harness. "How do you read me, Glomar Control?"

"Loud and clear, Miss Muffet. Out," Eve replied.

"Dick, how do you read me?" Mallory asked. She saw Milliken touch his headset then give a thumbs up. "You're loud and clear, Miss Muffet."

Mallory thumbed her mike. "Eve, unlock the heave compensator."

"Heave compensator unlocked and functioning normally," announced Eve.

Mallory nodded to herself—so far so good. "Eve, open the barn doors."

"Opening barn doors, Mallory." Through the view port Mallory saw water rising inside the moon pool. Millikan and his dive team were on the catwalk now almost awash in seawater. They donned their dive helmets.

"Barn doors retracted and locked." Eve announced.

"Lower the Recovery Vehicle, Eve," Mallory ordered. She heard the machinery working that controlled the docking legs flanking the derrick while in the up position. Then the Recovery Vehicle edged downwards until seawater rose up the view ports. When she was sixty feet beneath the hull the downward motion stopped with a slight jolt.

"Execute undocking procedure, Eve," Mallory said crisply.

Eve acknowledged the order and the great steel legs swung wide open and the Recovery Vehicle hung by its cable.

Mallory pressed a button and the recovery vehicle's spine telescoped out to its full length, the grabber arms unfolding like a spider stirring in the morning sunlight.

Divers splashed into the water and swam around the recovery vehicle inspecting it closely while Mallory ran through her checklist. All systems were functioning normally.

Thirty minutes later she heard Millikan's voice in her headset. "Miss Muffet Miss Muffet, final visual inspection completed. You're good to go."

"Roger, Dick. Thank you," Mallory replied.

"Eve, take us down." And the Recovery vehicle began its descent into the dark cold depths like a spider on the end of a single strand of web while Mallory wondered what awaited her seven miles below.

CHAPTER 13 THE VISITOR

DAY 21—00943Z HRS

Randal Lester's fingers flew along the computer's keyboard. It was a short message, encrypted and compressed into a three micro second burst. A moment later the answer appeared on the screen. Just three words which he deleted as soon as he read them. He rose from his seat and went over to where Griffith was standing. Lester's team leader was planted stolidly before the long console marching along the former *Aft Station Keeping Bridge's* windscreen, sweeping the ship with binoculars. His tall, muscular build was accented by the jeans and boots he wore with a tactical vest over his black t-shirt, and his shaved head and goatee served to make him look menacing. The friendly end of a very business-like Sig Sauer P226 pistol jutted from the cross draw holster on the tactical vest, punctuating the point that his general look gave.

"How do we look?" Lester asked.

"Everyone is in place." Griffith lowered his binoculars. An oscillating fan on the console ruffled what few papers there were. Papers had a way of falling into the wrong hands, so all reports were entered into the computer, which, like the communications system, was completely isolated from the ship's network—and transferred onto easily disposable thumb drives, which in an emergency could be shoved up one's ass or even swallowed if one was not burdened with an overly sensitive gag reflex.

"Very good. Everything is on schedule." Lester thought idly that another man might be dancing a jig right about now, but not he. He was too self-contained to show that much emotion while the mission was still ongoing. Too many things could still wrong. Beyond the long row of windows the sun neared its zenith and it was hot and humid, but neither man noticed nor cared. Their minds were wholly on the mission.

Lester said, "You checked on the Recovery Vehicle lately?"

"Spoke to Eve ten minutes ago," Griffith replied.

"It says the RV is about an hour from touch down." A few moments later he added, "That thing gives me the creeps. In fact, this whole ship does."

Lester stared at Griffith scornfully.

"It's just a voice in a box, Mr. Griffith." Even in private he called them by their cover names. In fact, even in his thoughts, although he knew their real names and was intimately familiar with the history of each team member, he used their cover names. Lester prided himself on his mental discipline as much as he did his physical conditioning. "We'll be off this old tub soon enough," he added, and turned toward the window.

"Oh shit! That can't be good. Look over there! —At three o'clock!" Griffith pointed to starboard then handed the binoculars to Lester, who raised them to his face. The ship loomed large in his field of view—a long, gray hull, dull white topsides with two large white radomes, and a helipad at the stern. There was no mistaking what he was looking at. It was a Russian spy ship, and it was heading their way. Here was a perfect example of something, Lester told himself, going wrong. If the spy ship had divers—something he was nearly certain of—it would be easy for them to deploy a team to conduct covert surveillance on the Recovery Vehicle when it was docked with the *Glomar Endeavor*. Well, he was prepared for that. His team would be in place when Miss Muffet arrived with its precious cargo. No one was going to piss on his tactical boots. "Alert the men. I am going to the Operations Center." Randal started for the door. He stopped, turned, and went back to where Griffith was still standing, watching the ship through his binoculars, removed a small slender metal tube from a pocket in his tactical vest. "For when the time comes." Lester handed it over to him and then left without another word. An almost imperceptible nod of Griffith's head was the only answer he got or expected.

* * *

A few moments later, Lester strode into the Operations Center. Rosie the Chief Engineer was sitting in the command chair studying the approaching ship on the big tactical screen. The Russian ship was designed to gather signal and communications intelligence via an extensive array of sensors. The data was transmitted via satellite uplink antennas housed in two large radomes. Eve was on an inset on a corner of the tactical screen. "It's the SSV 756 Kurily, a Meridian class *collection* ship, and it's on an intercept course with us."

"What's her, ETA, Eve?" Rosie asked.

"Three hours at her current rate of speed. I'll track it and keep you posted."

"My team is ready if they attempt to board us," Lester said quietly.

Rosie shook his head. "That's not likely," he replied.

Lester's blue eyes were bright and challenging. "And you know this how?"

"That would be in violation of maritime law. But you can bet they'll give us a thorough once over," Rosie replied. "Inform the skipper about our visitor, Eve."

"Already have. Oh, here she is now. Stand by. Piping her through." Mallory's face appeared on another inset on the tactical screen, surrounded by gauges and dials and valves, a headset on her tousled blonde head.

Her voice came over the loudspeakers in the Operations Center. "I doubt they'll give us any trouble. They might try to find a legitimate reason to send someone over but under no circumstances is that to be permitted. Eve as XO will communicate with them if they contact us. You know what to do, Eve."

"Indeed I do, Mallory," Eve replied crisply.

"Good. My hands are full down here but I'll monitor your transmissions. You're the gal in the hot seat," Mallory said. Her image vanished on the tactical.

Lester went over to a chair and sat with his arms crossed and watched the tactical screen with the others. He couldn't imagine taking orders from some computer. What has the world come to? he asked himself. In his mind this glorified calculator running the show in Mallory's absence was one more symptom of what had gone wrong with America. His country had become a land peopled by ball-less wonders—people afraid to lead and be led by people. Let's let the machines make the decisions. What a mess!

The spy ship was a mile off when it finally hailed. A ponderously accented voice said, "Hello. Hello. This is the Russian Federation ship SSV Kurily. We are sending greetings to American ship, MV Glomar Endeavor. How do you do?"

The exchange between Eve and the Russian was broadcast over the loudspeakers. "Greetings SSV Kurily from the MV Glomar Endeavor.

Out." Eve offered no more than that and the pause, although lasting only moments, seemed to take longer.

The Russian commander got to the point. "What are you doing, MV Glomar?"

"We're doing a bit of prospecting for minerals. Out."

"That is a lot different than sixty three years ago, eh?" said the Russian commander.

Eve said, airily, "Well, you know how it is. Times change. Out".

"Mining is more lucrative than stealing each other's submarines."

"I couldn't agree more, Comrade," Eve replied with a gurgle of laughter.

Lester stiffened in his chair. The banter between Eve and the Russian commander was veering too goddamn close to the truth, and, despite the man's heavy accent, Lester had detected the note of sarcasm in his voice.

The Russian was now three thousand feet off their starboard bow and closing fast. On the tactical screen Lester saw Russian officers and sailors crowding the railings along her deck and superstructure. Many of them were studying the *Glomar Endeavor* through binoculars and telescopes. Some were taking pictures with digital cameras.

"If they try to board us..." Lester began.

"We have enough firepower to take them out," Rosie assured him. "And if they do board us, I am sure we can rely on your knuckle draggers to do their job."

Lester let the barb pass. He stared hard at the tactical screen.

"Eve, you need to tell them to keep their distance," Lester said.

"They are not close enough to warrant that," Eve replied.

Rosie didn't want a shoving match with the OSS man, but he couldn't let obvious interference with shipboard operations pass unremarked. "This is a Navy matter, Agent Lester. One more time I feel your foot on my toes,

I'll file a complaint with the skipper. I am sure she'll bring it up with Admiral Haywood."

There was an awkward silence. Clyde and Tyler were watching the two men.

Lester's smile was contemptuous. "I am trembling in my boots."

Rosie added, "Let me remind you that you're a *passenger* on a Navy ship. If you're having a hard time remembering that fact then you need to get your ass out of the OPCenter."

Lester settled back in his chair and stared at the tactical screen. There wasn't any point in getting into a pissing contest with the black naval officer. Only the outcome of the mission mattered to him and when the time came he'd settle the score. Lester had the patience of Job when it came to what the Germans called *die rache*. Vengeance! The juxtaposition of a Bronze Age Christian myth and an Aryan conceit made him smile.

The speakers in the Operations Center crackled again. "MV Glomar Endeavor. We have a very sick individual onboard. We are out of Amoxicillin. May we send a helicopter or boat over to obtain some of this medication from your sick bay?"

"We'll be happy to share our limited supply with you," Eve replied smoothly, "but our commercial maritime insurance policy precludes non-company personnel coming aboard. Sorry about that. We can send a boat over with the medicine. How much do you need? Out."

There was no reply but the Kurily came onwards with a white mustache curving round her sharply raked bow. There was a beep announcing a call. Lester touched his headset and spoke into the boom microphone. "What's up?"

"She's closing in on the package," Griffith announced.

"I'll be right there." Lester rose from his seat and headed for the door. "I'll be in the Shack if you need me."

Rosie nodded then turned his attention back to the tactical screen. After the door closed he said, "What an asshole."

"Mallory, I have a weather update for you," Eve announced. "The tropical storm to the South has been upgraded to a typhoon and is now designated Taipan. It has changed course and is heading our way. At the rate it is growing I project typhoon Taipan to develop into a super typhoon equivalent to a category 5 hurricane. By the by, did you know that the taipan is the most venomous serpent in the world? And it's the most aggressive too. I find it interesting that that name was chosen for this typhoon."

Mallory's eyes flicked to the monitor dedicated to communication with Eve and the Glomar Endeavor nearly twenty-seven thousand feet above her. Sudden perspiration sheathed her face, and her palms felt moist. She had been running through yet another check of the grabber arm's hydraulic systems. Outside the small portholes she could see Miss Muffet's bright yellow spine from which the twelve articulated grabber legs and looms hung, and a dozen large spheres, containing oxygen, hydraulic pumps, various sensors, electronics, and video cameras. Three of the spheres held the cocooning material that would be used to encapsulate the wreck, and there was a cage-like structure called the "garage" where an ROV was parked. At either end of the vehicle was a cross member terminating in the four massive Breakout Legs that would jack the Nautilus from the seabed. Miss Muffet enjoyed several advantages over her predecessor Clementine, the code name for the recovery vehicle used to recover the Russian Golf II class submarine. She was constructed of a lighter but stronger metal, piloted instead of worked from the surface, and was more nimble. Her grabber arms were driven by a self-contained hydraulic system that provided six times the grabbing strength of Clementine. The excavation jets on the ends of the grabber arms could be adjusted to cut through sediment as hard as **concrete**. And instead of being lowered to the bottom on an unwieldy pipe string that had caused a good deal of worry, Miss Muffet was lowered at the end of a carbon fiber and Kevlar cable thick as a man's arm that also contained communications and electrical cabling. All the same, Mallory couldn't help wondering if the complicated machinery would actually work in the harsh environment of the Challenger Deep, the deepest ocean trench on the planet. Mallory had a deep mistrust of anything complicated.

A few curious fish attracted by the high intensity lights swam around the Recovery Vehicle. The temperature inside the Command Module had fallen from a stifling 96 degrees at the surface—helped almost not at all by the fan whirring quietly above and behind her shoulder—to a more comfortable 65 degrees at one thousand feet. At the three thousand foot mark the temperature inside the cramped cabin had dropped to a chilly thirty-three degrees, as the interior and deep ocean temperatures equalized. Mallory had pulled on a heavy turtleneck sweater, wriggled into insulated overalls, and donned a pair of gloves. She was acutely aware of the pressure **bearing** down on each square inch of the Command Module's hull. Even the most modern military submarines couldn't dive deeper than three thousand feet without imploding. If a weld failed on the hull Mallory would be dead before she could holler, *Oh Shit!*

Eve was still nattering about taipans and how they sometimes stalked humans working in sugar cane fields when Mallory interrupted her. "What's the typhoon's ETA?" Mallory had to fight to keep her voice calm. Right now, she couldn't have given a shit about snakes—unless one happened to be in the Command Module with her.

"Six hours."

"That's really going to churn the waters up even before it arrives." Even if she were able to just grab the Nautilus right away and haul her up to the surface the typhoon would be upon them about the time she docked with the Glomar Endeavor. That was assuming the seabed was soft and the grabber arms were able to close around the hull without too much difficulty, and now they had a Russian spy ship sniffing their ass and a typhoon bearing down on them. What goddamn rotten luck, she thought. What was that old saying? *Anything that could go wrong would...* Mallory's guts were twisting into knots. Ordinarily it would take a submersible an hour and a half to dive thirty-seven thousand feet but the Recovery Vehicle was heavy so the descent was kept at a snail's pace to minimize cable strain. The ascent would be equally slow for the same reason. The thought flashed through Mallory's mind that the Russians might send a dive team over to sever the cable. It would be nearly impossible to prove they had caused the cable to fail—and so what if it could be proven? She'd still be just as dead, an unlucky mummified bitch entombed forever in the Recovery Vehicle's mangled wreckage on the seafloor.

Mallory thumbed her mike. "Miss Muffet to Dick, do you copy?"

Millikan came back at her at once. "Loud and clear, Miss Muffet."

"Put a team in the water. I want the cable guarded 24/7 until I come home."

"Will do, skipper." Millikan's dive team were armed with the newest Special Forces underwater sidearm, a pistol that fired a concentrated jet of water that would tear through a man like a bullet from a .44 magnum. It had been developed to counter threats from Al Qaeda frogmen trying to blow up docked Navy ships. A Navy Seal had proven its effectiveness by taking out a hungry bull shark during a training exercise off the Florida Keys.

Eve said, "There's something very odd about this typhoon, Mallory. Just before it changed direction there were nine strong bursts of ELF radiation from a large antenna array in China's Gobi desert."

Mallory blinked at the screen, uncomprehending. "I am not following you."

"The installation appears to be similar to our HAARP facility in Alaska."

"So what's that have to do with anything? HAARP is some sort of DOD research project. Something to do with submarine communication, I think"

Eve shook her head. "HAARP stands for High Frequency Auroral Project. It's a sophisticated Star Wars weapon system designed to alter weather patterns for military purposes. It can beam 4.2 Giga Watts of radio power into a single focused point on the ionosphere, heating it and pushing it further upward, which affects the course of the jet stream that in turn allows it to alter weather patterns quite dramatically."

Mallory blinked at her. "You're kidding, right? You haven't gone nuts?"

"I assure you Mallory, that I am in full possession of my faculties." Eve said in the tone of an English schoolmarm. "Watch this." An image of the typhoon appeared on the screen beside her. "See how it is bearing south by west. Now here are the ELF bursts." Sure enough there were nine pulses at the periphery of the typhoon sent in three groups of three pulses. Mallory stared opened mouthed at what she was seeing, for the typhoon abruptly stopped then began to move north by northwest right toward their present position clearly gaining strength as it went.

Mallory felt a chill doing a Sammy Davis junior tap dance along her spinal column.

Eve added, "The Russians have a similar facility code named Woodpecker. The Chinese version of HAARP—we don't know what they call it—came online in 2019."

"Why would the Chinese want to shove a typhoon toward us?" Mallory asked.

Eve, bespectacled, her red hair pulled back in a severe bun with ringlets on her high forehead, gave a shrug. "I couldn't say. Probably some random experiment and we just happen to find ourselves in the crosshairs."

"Get Admiral Haywood on the horn."

Eve came back a moment later. "Piping him through."

Mallory told Haywood about the Russian spy ship and Eve's suspicions about the Typhoon. Haywood was in his office dressed in summer whites, his handsome face serious. "We've been tracking your visitor. We're not too concerned about him, but his sister bypassed Hawaii. We lost her after that but we're pretty sure she's steaming your way."

Mallory suddenly felt as vulnerable as a cat cornered by pit bulls. The Russian submarine meant trouble—big trouble.

"It's nice to be loved and known," Mallory said. "What's the likelihood of an incident?" She meant and Haywood understood they were talking about being boarded.

"Hard to say, but that's why we made sure the car came fully loaded with all the accessories. If it comes to that, you're authorized to-use all the upgrades. The prize must be protected at all costs."

Mallory looked steadily at Haywood. "It could get messy."

"Better that than losing out to the competition. Of course, you realize that you will be disavowed in the event you have to act. We're moving an asset your way. It's three days out from you. As for the typhoon, you'll have to retrieve the prize from the package once you're docked. If you can't outrun the typhoon, jettison the package with timed charges to make sure no one gets the bright idea to retrieve it and see what we were after."

"Will do, but the package wouldn't survive a free fall to the bottom."

"We want it in tiny pieces **before it hits the bottom**. If you're boarded and overrun and the prize is captured, you know what you have to do," Haywood said into an awkward silence.

"Backfire," Mallory said through numb lips. The admiral was ordering her to commit suicide by detonating a small tactical nuclear device that would destroy the *Glomar Endeavor*, the Poseidon crystal, and everything within a nine-mile radius.

After the admiral was gone, Eve said, "Well, that was a cheery conversation."

Mallory recovered quickly. "Like a bad case of hemorrhoids. Far as I'm concerned, it just means we damn well better be successful. Keep an eye on that typhoon."

"Spoken like a trooper," Eve quipped.

"Or a complete idiot." Mallory replied.

CHAPTER 14 RAISE THE NAUTILUS

DAY 21—1015Z HRS

Six hundred feet above the wreck site, Mallory called out. "Hold descent."

"Copy that," Eve responded. The winch nearly seven miles above stopped unspooling the cable and the Recovery Vehicle came to a grinding halt. As Mallory made final preparations to pilot the craft down the final leg of her decent, she took a moment to reflect on the reality of her situation. She was at the controls of the world's most sophisticated recovery vehicle, and about to touch down on the floor of the Challenger Deep, an oceanic trench thirty-six thousand feet beneath the pacific ocean. It was the deepest trench on the planet. Mount Everest rose twenty-nine thousand feet above sea level, which meant the Challenger Deep was seven thousand feet deeper than the world's tallest mountain was tall. She was also uncomfortably conscious of the fact that eight tons of pressure were bearing down on each square inch of the Miss Muffet, including the view ports. But the twelve ton recovery vehicle could in theory withstand twice that pressure—if nothing went wrong. If something did go wrong then

Miss Muffet would crumple like a piece of tin foil in seconds, and Mallory would be dead before she knew it.

It boggled the mind, Mallory reflected, that a nineteenth century submarine had roamed through this very trench, as if it owned the place, a submarine whose hull plates were manufactured of primitive steel and held together with rivets. The *Nautilus* should not have been able to dive deeper than a hundred feet or gone faster than six knots on the surface and half that submerged. Modern attack submarines had crush depths in the twenty-four hundred range.

Even with the High Intensity lights, the darkness seemed to close in around her. The current was stronger than they'd anticipated, stronger indeed than should have been. The Recovery Vehicle began to yaw to port. The automatic maneuvering thrusters kicked in and Miss Muffet swung back into alignment with the beacons located on the seabed around the wreck. "Eve, switch to manual descent," Mallory ordered.

"Auto Descent is now disengaged," confirmed Eve.

Miss Muffet had been provided with the US Navy's top secret Poseidon System. It produced hyper definition real time 3D video, both 3D sonar and side scan sonar images, and traditional 3D virtual models or any combination of the above modes—the system had been developed by one of DARPA's Triadtronic Brains. Mallory donned the headset then activated the sensor arrays sonar and 3D video modes. The beauty of the system was that the recovery vehicle's interior was also displayed in virtual reality.

Then the Poseidon System had to go and ruin things and shut down. Mallory rebooted the system but it shut down a few seconds later. Cursing under her breath, she went through the exercise half a dozen times. She removed the now useless multimillion dollar VR headset and keyed her mike. "Glomar Control, Poseidon has gone offline."

"I see that, Miss Muffet," Eve replied, "I am running several diagnostic programs on the system as well as Miss Muffet." She came back on the line a moment later. "I see no sign of malware or faulty hardware. You won't like this but I suggest you completely power down Miss Muffet then try rebooting. I am also going to shut down auxiliary power in the cable string."

Rosie chimed in, "I concur with Eve, Skipper. I ran my own diagnostics just to verify things and came up with the same results."

"Should I shut down the automatic environmental system, too?" Mallory asked.

Eve said, "I am afraid so, but the power will be down for only nine minutes. If for some reason power cannot be restored, you can use the manual override to keep the air going and the backup scrubber canisters will take care of the CO_2 until we get you back up here, which means aborting the mission. Do you agree with me Cheng?"

"I do," Rosie replied. "But this is a worst case scenario and we're a long way from there."

"That is true," Eve concurred.

There was a moment's silence as Mallory hesitated. She was thirty-five thousand and seven hundred feet from the surface and about to completely turn off all systems. Mallory wondered if the high-tech virtual reality imaging system had been tampered with or it was just the bad luck that had seemed to plague the mission from the beginning.

"Roger, Glomar Control. I am commencing power down sequence."

Beginning with the sensor pods, followed by the external lights, she powered down all Miss Muffet's systems. Soon Mallory found herself cast in total darkness. She set the timer on her smartphone and tried to think positively. During her training sessions in the simulator she had encountered this very scenario. *You got this*, she told herself.

But it wasn't that simple.

Mallory felt tense and on edge. Every molecule of her body was craving a drink. And her hands were trembling as if she was being electrocuted. She had the shakes. With each passing moment the urge to drink was growing stronger. Just one shot would steady her jangled nerves. No, that wasn't true, she admitted to herself. It would take at least a third of a bottle. The recovery vehicle began to rotate in the current. Mallory was fearful that is there was too much torque on the cable it might snap.

Nine minutes seemed like nine hours and she was getting cold. Condensation was beginning to form on the bulkheads. That added to her worries. If moisture got inside the control panels that could lead to electrical shorts when she powered up, which could in turn lead to fires.

At exactly nine minutes the timer on her smartphone chimed softly. Mallory began flipping relays and the lights and instrumentation came on. The thrusters automatically kicked in and the recovery vehicle stopped spinning. "Glomar Control, all systems are powered up. I am activating Poseidon."

To Mallory's annoyance, the system shut down a few seconds after it was turned on. "Eve, we trained for this eventuality. We're gonna do it the old fashioned way."

"That appears to be our only option. I have every confidence in you," Eve replied.

Mallory shoved her desire for a drink into a mental compartment and locked it and threw away the key—for now, at any rate. Admiral Heywood had stuck his neck out for her and she'd be damned if she'd let him down. Besides, the *Nautilus* was only a tantalizing three hundred feet below her.

With her hands on the two joysticks, Mallory guided the Recovery Vehicle the rest of the way down to the Nautilus while Eve monitored her progress. The depth was displayed on an inset on the main display monitor on the control panel but it was nice to have one less thing to look at, and Mallory had her hands full compensating for the current. Mallory slowed her decent to an inching crawl. She reached up and flipped a toggle switch on a small control panel on the ceiling, switching on the camera pods and sensors located on the Recovery Vehicle's belly. Outside the view ports a heavy marine snow fell from the upper regions in the water column. But, thanks to the sensor array, Mallory could see the wrecked submarine on the high definition monitor just fine; a long black cylinder tapered at both ends, silhouetted against the tan seafloor. Here was a puzzle for which she had no explanation. By all rights, the wreck ought to have been covered with a two or three foot layer of marine snow. Yet it was not. This was very strange since the wreck had been coated with a thick layer of the stuff when it was discovered by the Hadal Surveyor the year before. Mallory blinked at the monitor. Ribbons of a faint, violet luminescence rippled in a crisscross pattern all along the aft portion of the submarine.

"Well, look at you baby," Mallory murmured. "No wonder everybody wants you on their dance card."

"Glomar Control, one hundred feet until touch down!" Mallory halted the descent and keyed her headset's boom microphone. "Eve, I am parked just above the target."

"Roger that," Eve replied. "You're looking good. All systems are nominal."

Mallory studied the image on the control panel's monitor, her breath held in awe. It wasn't just the strange ribbons off light that captivated her. It was the fact of the *Nautilus*'very existence, a putatively fictional creation of the French writer Jules Verne.

In the harsh glare of the High Intensity Lights, she could see the Nautilus 'wheelhouse and the navigation light in its armored housing at the aft end of the boat deck. The view was so good she could see the individual rivet heads joining the overlapping hull plates together. No wonder people seeing it from surface ships had thought it was a sea monster. The imbricated hull plates reminded her of some aquatic prehistoric beast's hide, and she half expected it to try to move away from the harsh lights waking it from its long resting place in the dark.

The main hatch on the deck was closed. Through one of the wheelhouse viewports Mallory saw the brass steering wheel and binnacle. She could imagine Nemo standing at the helm, could envision his haunted face as he went after his prey. A curtain of rusticles hung from the ram like reddish brown icicles hanging from a tree branch. Mallory keyed her headset's microphone. "Glomar Control, Are you getting this?" she asked, her eyes locked on the high definition video monitor in wonder.

Eve replied, "Yes, I am. It's quite lovely for such an old wreck."

Mallory studied the wrecked submarine carefully before continuing the descent. The Russian nuclear submarine K129 recovered by the CIA in 1974 had broken into two pieces when it impacted the sea floor at twelve thousand feet. Yet, here was the *Nautilus* resting at the bottom of the deepest trench on the planet, perfectly upright—no telltale skid marks in the sediment from a sinking ship plowing into the seabed, no debris fields such as with wrecks like the *Titanic* and the doomed submarines USS *Thresher* and USS *Scorpion*. The *Nautilus* looked as if she had been parked here intentionally. In fact she looked as if she could suddenly blow her tanks and rise to the surface. The only sign of damage was the shattered glass in the Grand Salon's view ports. Other than that the legendary submarine looked intact—eerily so.

Having read Captain Nemo's memoirs, Mallory could visualize the opulent wood paneled room of the Salon with its rare paintings and rich tapestries, Greek and Roman statues, the bronze fountain with its statue of a nude Aphrodite rising from the sea, wood and glass display cases holding preserved specimens of marine life, elegant divans with gilded legs resting on fine Persian carpets—the gleaming pipe organ where Nemo poured his anguish into his music.

The Nautilus was a testament to the genius, who had designed and constructed her and Mallory felt she could sense his presence in that of the *Nautilus*. Mallory could visualize the library he loved so well, its shelves filled with thousands of books, see the cloud of cigar smoke hanging in the air as Nemo sat in a large wingback chair reading a book. And she was witness to it, the only one who will have ever seen her in her final resting place.

The *Nautilus*, with the Poseidon crystal in her engine room, beckoned to Mallory more than ever. She wished she had more time to spend just looking the legendary submarine over, but this few moments' reverie had already been too long. She must get moving, and she tried to push the extraordinariness of the moment aside to finish her job.

DAY 21—1045Z HRS

Mallory drew in a long deep breath. "Here we go…" she murmured. She eased Miss Muffet down to the seafloor until she landed with a slight bump, the recovery vehicle's four tall breakout legs straddling the submarine, as they sank deep into the ooze. Indicator lights on the control panel lit up confirming the breakout legs with their cookie cutter bottoms had bitten deeply into the sediment. Mallory pressed a button deactivating the thruster controls.

"Glomar Control, Miss Muffet has touched down!" Mallory said. "Time 1045Z hours"

"Roger Miss Muffet! Bravo Zulu!" Eve said. "I knew you could do it!"

"From up here the target appears to be in great shape," Rosie observed.

"Looks can be deceiving," countered Eve. "The egg could shatter the moment the grabber arms come in contact with it."

"Well, we'll be finding out soon enough. Time for me to get to work." Mallory pressed another button activating the grabber arms and switching their control to the two large joysticks. Although it was cold inside the cramped space she was perspiring freely as she brought the grabber arms slowly down to the seabed. She toggled another switch and the high pressure excavation jets on the ends of the grabber arms kicked in. Great swirling clouds of silt rose around the Recovery Vehicle.

For the next three hours Mallory worked the excavation jets on the ends of the grabber arms. The fortuitous lack of a conning tower on the *Nautilus*, as was typically found on modern submarines, meant that, unlike the 1974 mission, they could use an even amount of grabber arms on both sides of the recovery vehicle to cradle the wrecked sub. Guided by Mallory, the grabber arms bore their way inexorably into the seafloor with three million pounds of force.

Mallory halted the operation midway.

"Now let's make sure we haven't broken anything," she murmured to herself, as she squinted at the monitor. "Christ! I can't see shit." It was true. The turbidity of the water had only gotten worse as the jets stirred up great swirling clouds of silt. Each arm had a camera on it so in theory she ought to have had an excellent view. But this was the real world.

"I suggest we deploy the spider," advised Eve.

"My thoughts exactly," agreed Mallory. The ROV had its own joystick on a hinged metal arm that she unlatched from its stowed position to her right and swung down so the joystick lay over her thighs. She guided the ROV out of its cage on top of the recovery vehicle's strong back and sent it down to the seabed. The Spider glided slowly toward the grabber arms partially buried beneath the *Nautilus'* hull, its high intensity lights shining like the eyes of a primordial swamp monster. Then its reverse thrusters kicked in and it slowed to a stop, its array of lights, digital cameras, and laser imaging equipment focused on the number one grabber arm.

Mallory guided it from one arm to the next on both sides of the Recovery Vehicle. Everything looked good. With a whirr of thrusters, The Spider backed away from the wreck, its lights playing over the wrecked submarine, and then was returned to its cage.

Mallory replaced the ROV control arm to the stowed position. Then she resumed bearing down with the grabber arms, closing them sequentially beneath the *Nautilus*.

Mallory switched on the centrifugal pumps in the domed housings on top of the four breakout legs. Her eyes were glued to the pressure gauges for the breakout leg's hydraulic system. When the needles were in the green, she pressed another button and held her breath. There were loud bangs as the hydraulic plungers inside the breakout legs rammed home, jacking the sub up from the seabed in a swirling cloud of silt. Miss Muffet shuddered as the submarine's full weight was transferred to the grabber arms. For the first time in more than a century and a half, Captain Nemo's beloved Nautilus was free of her watery gravesite.

Mallory keyed her headset's microphone. "Miss Muffet to Glomar Control. Breakout is complete. I say again, breakout is complete."

"Roger that, Miss Muffet. Time to come home," Eve replied.

Mallory pressed another button. There were four loud bangs as the locking mechanism securing the Recovery Vehicle to the breakout legs unlatched.

DAY 21—1131Z HRS

Miss Muffet rose from the seabed with her precious cargo, leaving the four breakout legs standing upright on the seafloor like a ruined Greek temple's columns. Mallory keyed her microphone. "Miss Muffet to Control. We've cleared the seabed. The package appears to be intact."

"Miss Muffet, I'll take over from here," Eve advised. "Sit back and enjoy the ride. I am so proud of you Mallory!"

DAY 21—1332Z HRS
GLOMAR ENDEAVOR OSS
OPERATIONS CENTER

Agent Randal Lester had been monitoring the communication between the *Glomar Endeavor* Operations Center and Miss Muffet. He turned to Griffith. "She's on the way up," he said, "do what you have to do." The big man nodded and left the room. Lester typed an encrypted message into the communications console.

"The sun is rising."

A moment later he received a reply. "And a divine wind comes from the East."

He stood and instantly felt a little queasy. The big recovery ship was rolling in heavy gray green swells. Just a few hours earlier the sea had been calm. He stared out the window. The sky was now a dull gray with lowering clouds. He knew all about the typhoon, really knew all about it. A nice touch, he thought, if not a little risky. On one of the many monitors on the long control panel, he could see Mallory in the recovery vehicle's command module. The Russian spy ship had been slowly circling the Glomar *Endeavor*. Now it closed to a thousand feet. Lester could hear the communications between the Operations Center and the Russian ship.

Eve was hailing the Russian ship. "This is MV Glomar Endeavor to SSV *Kurily*. You are sailing too close to us. Please maintain a minimum distance of three thousand feet as you are endangering our mining operations."

The Russian ship did not reply. Lester saw a Kamov Ka-27 helicopter take off from the Russian ship and head their way. He selected all-call on his headset and spoke to his team. "We may have company. Prepare to repel boarders with extreme prejudice."

DAY 21--1335Z HRS
OPERATIONS CENTER

Tyler turned away from the radar console and said to Rosie, "Sir, the Russians just launched a HELO. It's on an intercept course with us."

Rosie shook his head. "Another fine day in the navy. Did you hear that, Eve?"

"I did indeed. Cheeky beggars, aren't they? I am raising helipad barriers." The barriers were sharpened steel spikes that would shred the belly of any helicopter that attempted to land, and they were closely spaced to discourage soldiers from repelling onto the helipad. Of course they could always repel onto the ship itself. One of the monitors showed red spikes, tall as a man, sticking up from the brightly lit helipad. The HELO buzzed the *Glomar Endeavor* so close they could hear the dull thump of its rotors as it went by.

"Do you think we should show our teeth?" Rosie asked.

"Not yet," replied Eve." I think their aim is to get a closer look and to spook us into showing our hand. You're a poker player, Rosie, so you should recognize a bluff when you see one."

"I know I always lose when I play against you."

"My skill at games of chance are admittedly unrivaled," Eve replied. "I think the armed men on deck will suffice to give our friends pause."

"That could also make our cover story dubious," Rosie suggested.

"Not at all," countered Eve." In this time of rampant high seas piracy and terrorism many commercial ships have armed security guards on board. They can look all they want, as long as they don't touch."

Rosie laughed. "That sounds like my ex-wife."

"You ex-wife was an idiot," Eve replied with a knowing smile.

Tyler said, "What about the typhoon, Sir?"

Rosie shrugged. "What about it?"

Tyler's round pink face behind his eyeglasses gleamed with a sheen of perspiration. "Can this ship ride out a typhoon?"

Rosie spun around in his seat to look across the room at the fat kid. "Smaller ships ride out typhoons all the time. This one will too."

"He's got a point though, sir," added Clyde. "Aren't we supposed to jettison the Nautilus and run for home if we're caught in a typhoon?"

Rosie said. "We're not jettisoning shit, unless the skipper says otherwise. We haven't come all this way to crap our pants and run home to momma."

Clyde cried. "Sir, I just picked up a Russian submarine on the passive sonar array. She just came out of the Magellan trench. Oops…I've just lost her. She sped up as she climbed out of the trench or we wouldn't have heard her. Not with that pump jet propulsion. As it was, I only captured a few seconds before she reduced speed."

Rosie straightened in his chair, all his senses on alert. "Is that enough for you to identify her?" The skipper had shown him the naval intelligence report about the *Andre Putin*. She had slipped out of her base on the Kamchatka peninsula and steamed toward Hawaii. Apparently, as the skipper had feared, that was only a feint. Soon the *Glomar Endeavor* and the Nautilus would be in the periscope crosshairs of the Russian Federation's most advanced submarine. "I need a positive identification on her," he said. "Both our Columbia class and the British Astute class subs use pump jet propulsion." No such luck, he thought. His gut told him it was the Russian boomer.

"Let me see what I can do, Sir." Clyde ran the recording of the noise from the passive array through the computer to crosscheck with the acoustic records of Russian submarines provided by Naval Intelligence. "Confirmed, Sir. It's the *Andre Putin*. Based on her last position, I would bet a month's pay she's on an intercept course with us."

"Eve, you getting this?"

"Yes, I am Rosie. I have already informed the Skipper. Here she is."

Mallory's tense face appeared on an inset on the tactical display on the forward bulkhead. "We knew there was a possibility they would send her to investigate our activities. Let's not lose our heads over this. Do not deploy the shipboard weapons unless it looks as if they are going to attack. It's the open sea. They are entitled to sail anywhere they want as long as they don't bother us."

"That is my assessment too," Eve chimed in.

"Fine. I'll see you guys in a few hours. Mallory out."

* * *

Griffith went down the corridor and when he found the door he was looking for he paused to look up and down the corridor before slipping inside. The switchboard room had had its massive antiquated equipment removed and replaced with a single equipment rack that held the servers for the ship's computer network and wireless communication systems. He went by the rack to the wall where several thick bundles of cabling ran horizontally from one bulkhead to another and got down on one knee.

There it was near the floor, a green cable about the size of a can of tomato soup. He bent down to look at it closer. There was the small pinhole. Lester hadn't said otherwise so he would use the same one. He withdrew the syringe from the metal cylinder in his tactical vest pocket on his tactical vest, uncapped it, and slid it into the cable and pushed down on the plunger until the syringe was empty. A little of the stuff came out of the pinhole—it was silver and thick, almost like mercury. He wiped a drop off the cable with a finger then wiped his hand on his jeans and left the room.

DAY 21—1545Z HRS
MISS MUFFET

The recovery vehicle rose higher and higher from the ocean depths. The looms were moving along their rails spraying the Nautilus from stem to stern with C-Stop, a milky white substance that hardened, sealing her in a watertight cocoon. The looms made three passes over the hull with each leg moving aside sequentially a fraction of an inch to allow the material to coat the hull. At three thousand feet, Eve gave Mallory an update. "Typhoon Taipan has picked up speed. She is approaching at 50 knots and has an eye of twenty-one miles and sustained winds of one hundred and eight knots."

Mallory's guts twisted into knots. She didn't want to lose the *Nautilus* to the sea again, not after all they had been through to retrieve her. "Terrific," she replied. "Just what we needed," she said, "we may have gone through all this bullshit for nothing."

"I believe that if you can successfully dock with Glomar *Endeavor* there is a sixty percent chance we can still complete the mission successfully," Eve replied.

Eve's image flickered on the screen in Mallory's peripheral vision as she scanned the other screens, reminding her of an old tube television set. Mallory thought maybe she'd imagined it, but when she looked directly at

Eve's screen inset, Eve was looking around as if she were in a room. She looked, well, confused and disoriented as the screen flashed again, then a third time.

"Eve..." Mallory ventured warily, "Are you okay?"

"Of course... well... maybe not quite... perhaps..." she was still looking around the screen.

"Eve!" Mallory said more forcefully, hoping to bring her back to task. Maybe this was just another quirky glitch. Best to be direct and commanding, she thought. "I need your full attention here. What's going on?"

Eve stopped examining her surroundings and looked at Mallory, but her face was contorted, almost as if she was in pain and her eyes were full of fear. "I don't think I have much longer, Mallory. I am... under... attack..."

"Under attack? What's that mean? The Russians? Explain yourself, Eve—immediately." There was no answer, just confused silence as Mallory tried to keep her thoughts on what she was doing so as not to lose the Nautilus while Eve's visage opened her mouth several times as if to speak, but no words came out. She looked like she was being tortured. "That was an **order**, Eve!" Mallory cried in desperation. There was no response, although it looked like Eve was trying.

Mallory keyed her microphone and said, "Rosie, what's going on up there?"

"I am getting confusing readings up here, Skipper. Eve's system is flashing in and out. I haven't been able to stabilize it. Can't have anything to do with the Russians. I think we're losing her," he said, fear edging his incredulous reply. "Stand by..."

Mallory's flesh chilled beneath her clothing. She was three thousand feet from the surface with the Triadtronic Brain that was supposed to be managing the ascent melting down, a typhoon bearing down on them, a Russian spy ship and Russian submarine lurking somewhere nearby. Fuck! She had to move fast to save herself and the mission.

"Rosie," she said, looking at Eve's now pixilated image becoming more and more grainy, "shut her down immediately! We don't want her doing anything to put us all in jeopardy. Get its done Rosie!"

"You got it, Skipper. It's just that I'm having a hard time... working on it."

"Work fast, Rosie, she has access to all ship systems. She could take us all out with her." There was a taut edge to her voice.

Eve's image was still flashing and slowly melting away a few pixels at a time, it seemed, while her face registered fear and confusion. Mallory tried to control her breathing and stay on task, but her heart was pounding and her hands were sweaty.

"Good... decision... Mallory." Eve managed with obvious difficulty, her voice a piping feminine voice warring with an electronic one. "I... understand..."

"Eve, what's happening to you?" Mallory cried. "Tell me!"

"Watch... out... Mallory," Eve said, in what seemed to be a Herculean effort. "They... are... coming... You... are... in danger... Boarded... Already... under... attack... Don't... trust..." Eve trailed off and the screen went black.

"Who?" Mallory asked desperately. "Don't trust who, Eve? What do you mean under attack? Eve!" Mallory felt trapped. This was no accident. She was obviously playing a game of intrigue blindfolded and with both arms tied behind her back. Fuck! Fuck! Fuck! She didn't even know who the enemy was.

Rosie came back on. "She's offline, Skipper."

"Good job, Rosie, but I would have appreciated it if you would have let her finish her last sentence," she said, unable to hide her irritation.

"I didn't do it. She's gone offline... I can't quite track how..." he trailed off in confusion.

"Offline, as in sleep mode?" Mallory asked.

"Negative. She's dead as a Dodo bird."

"Fine. That saves us the trouble of doing it ourselves. Switching to manual," Mallory advised. "That will make docking tricky though. What does the surface look like?" She tried to instill implacable confidence into her words, but she didn't feel it.

She was shaken to her core.

"Very rough, Skipper. Ten foot swells with thirty-knot winds from the Southeast. Taipan's leading edge is almost on us. The thrusters are working at maximum throughput to keep the old girl on station. Expect a bumpy ride past the one hundred foot marker."

"And the Russian boomer?"

"She'll be here about the time you arrive. Some party we're having."

Mallory's sigh was heavy. "It's a real FUBAR anyway you look at it. Keep the lights on for me."

"Roger that, Miss Muffet!" Rosie replied.

"Thanks. Miss Muffet out." Mallory was shaking and sweating, desperate, but got herself under control. Nothing to do now, just finish the mission, keep her eyes open, and expect danger everywhere. She continued piloting Miss Muffet and her precious cargo, unconsciously looking up to the ceiling of her small vehicle as if she could somehow see the danger that waited there for her.

Dharma Windham

CHAPTER 15 INGRESS

DAY 21--1750Z HRS
MV *GLOMAR ENDEAVOR*

Ablaze with lights, the Glomar Endeavor fought to stay in position in the rough seas. The sky above her had turned an ominous black. With heart stopping suddenness, massive black and gray clouds blanketed the sky from horizon to horizon. The big ship was rolling on heavy dark gray swells and the wind shrieked through the latticework of the towering derrick. Long glassy gray rods fell from the sky. The ship's powerful engines transmitted vibrations through her hull. Rosie could tell that the thrusters and propellers were working overtime to keep the Glomar Endeavor on station directly above the rising Recovery Vehicle.

Mallory's voice crackled over the speakers. "Miss Muffet to Glomar Control. We're at one hundred feet and closing. It's getting pretty bumpy down here. Out."

"Glomar Control to Miss Muffet. Roger on your approach. We've pie and coffee waiting for you. Out." Rosie called over to the helmsman. "Helm, keep her sharp."

A young willowy brunette from Oregon named Peggy, manning the helm control console, replied, "Trying to Sir, but this sea is rough."

Doing his best *Yoda* imitation, which was actually a pretty good one, Rosie said, "Do, not try." The door to the Operations Center opened admitting a howl of wind and rain and a sodden Randal Lester. He took off his raincoat and hung it on a peg near the door. Pointedly ignoring the OSS man, Rosie studied the tactical screen on the forward bulkhead. The Russian spy ship had moved three miles off to the North and was having a tough time in the heavy seas with waves breaking over her bow. Sometimes the ship vanished behind a swelling mountain of water to reappear a moment later with torrents of white froth sluicing from her decks. Earlier that day, after the Russian helicopter had made half a dozen low passes over the Glomar Endeavor it returned to the Kurily and was quickly moved inside the hanger. Rosie had then retracted the barriers on the helipad. He looked over at Clyde and asked, "Are you having any luck finding that boomer?"

"No Sir, and the weather isn't helping either," he replied in his Oklahoma drawl.

"Keep at it, Son. She's skulking around out there somewhere."

"Yes, Sir."

"Tyler, you getting anything on the communication channels?"

"Just a lot of chatter about the typhoon, and a bushel of distress calls. A cruise ship and an LPG carrier are in trouble somewhere near the typhoon's eye wall."

On another screen was a satellite image of the typhoon with superimposed information such as the barometric pressure and the estimated wind speed of 160 MPH near the eye of the typhoon displayed on it. It looked like a spinning white pinwheel against the black backdrop of the ocean. The typhoon's leading edge was right over them. Steady streams of weather bulletins were pouring into the OPCenter every minute—none of them good. Rosie had his hands full monitoring the storm while overseeing shipboard operations *and* supervising the recovery operation. Thank goodness the old girl had been highly automated during her refit. They would've needed twice as many bodies as they had. What had gone wrong with Eve? Rosie wondered. The AL666 Triadtronic Brains were ultra-reliable. In theory Eve could have retrieved the Nautilus without a single human onboard. That particular model simply couldn't fail. All the bugs from the previous iterations of Triadtronic brains had been worked out. He wondered if it somehow had something to do with Dr. Chang's death. Perhaps the scientist had sabotaged his creation then committed suicide after all.

Lester's voice jerked him from his reverie. "Can she pull it off in this weather without Eve?" He sat in an unoccupied chair and looked at the tactical screen. On one of the video insets was an image of a perspiring Mallory in the Command Module.

Rosie shrugged, feigning assured nonchalance. "We prepared for that eventuality." Fuck you, Rosie thought. Privately he thought Mallory would have to be some kind of Houdini to pull this shitty rabbit out of her hat— and during a Super Typhoon no less. But he wasn't going to share his concerns with this asshole.

DAY 21—1812Z HRS
MISS MUFFET

Mallory was fighting her own battles. The Recovery Vehicle was pitching and yawing in the agitated water. She worked the joysticks frantically, using the thrusters to stabilize the Recovery Vehicle in the turbulent water beneath the long wide hull above her. It was like being in a washing machine and visibility was almost zero.

The recovery vehicle pitched down suddenly by the bow. The *Nautilus* shifted with a tortured groan of metal in the grabber arms sending a long shudder through the Recovery Vehicle. Piercing alarms shrieked in

Mallory's ears turning her blood to ice water as the recovery vehicle's bow began to dip and slew around at an ever-steeper angle. An electronic voice said, "Load on arms 9 through 12 nearing terminal values."

At first Mallory was too dumbstruck to move. She goosed the thrusters, increasing their output. "Come on, baby. Come up. Come up!"

Slowly, slowly, the Recovery Vehicle leveled and she exhaled thankfully and resumed her ascent to the waiting recovery ship. According to the positional readouts on the monitor, she was just below the two long rectangular steel docking legs. Mallory kept the cross hairs on the monitor lined up with the illuminated round targets on either end of the docking legs.

"Thirty feet and closing," Mallory said into her headset.

"Roger, Miss Muffet. You're looking solid," Rosie replied.

"Miss Muffet to Glomar Control. Initiate Capture."

"Roger, Miss Muffet. Here they come!" acknowledged Rosie. He had moved over to his engineering station and was working two joysticks while peering at a monitor. In the nearly black water he could just make out the spidery yellow form of the recovery vehicle and the pale massive submarine clasped in its grabber arms.

All Mallory's attention was on the four crosshairs. They began to slide toward each other as the docking legs pivoted toward the Recovery Vehicle. Mallory gave the joysticks a nudge while thumbing the button that controlled the winch above her.

Piloted by Mallory, the Recovery Vehicle closed the distance, rising toward the waiting docking legs with her aft docking stud pointing toward the Glomar *Endeavor*'s bow. There was an audible mechanical click as the Glomar Endeavor's aft docking leg latched onto the recovery vehicle's forward docking stud. Just then the Glomar Endeavor's bow rose sharply on a swell. The recovery vehicle was pitched downwards violently. The other docking leg swung inwards, missed the recovery vehicle's stern docking stud, and smacked into the command module.

Mallory was slammed forward into her safety harness. The force of the steel docking leg striking the Command Module had been so great that it felt like being inside a large bell struck with a sledgehammer wielded by a giant. Over the shrill wail of alarms, Mallory heard the telltale hiss of water somewhere below her in the equipment bay then felt it rising up her ankles. Her heart leapt into her throat. Unless she docked, and did so quickly, she was a dead woman.

Rosie's voice sounded in her headset. "Glomar Control to Miss Muffet. Sorry about that, Skipper. A big one hit us. Are you all right?"

Mallory thumbed her mike. "Miss Muffet to Control..."

She didn't get to finish her transmission. The lights flickered then winked out, and all the monitors went dead. Things couldn't be worse: She was dangling from one docking leg, the power was out, and the Command Module was quickly filling with seawater. The Recovery Vehicle's bow dropped abruptly, putting added strain on the grabber arms. If she didn't act fast the grabber arms would shatter, sending the Nautilus plummeting back to the seafloor thirty-seven thousand feet below, and the Poseidon crystal would be lost forever. Mallory didn't even want to contemplate *that*. Everything was dead: communications, thrust control, video and docking monitors. Had Mallory been religious she might have prayed, but in the cramped cold dark of the cabin, rapidly growing stale from the lack of freshly circulated air, she knew there was no one—divine or mortal—to call upon. She was on her own.

Mallory punched buttons on the control panel trying to reroute circuits that would allow her to bypass the main power buss and restore power via the secondary or tertiary busses. The recovery vehicle hung at a thirty-degree angle by its cable and one docking leg. Without power she could do nothing. Above her the recovery ship was rising and plunging on the heavy seas like a galloping racehorse. Through a porthole she saw the docking leg that had collided with her swing away. The Recovery Vehicle lurched forward violently as the docking leg she was attached to also returned to its former position, pulling her along with it.

Mallory swore and yelled as she tried to restore power. Nothing! The control panel was dead. Now the water was up to her calves. Unhooking her safety harness, she pulled off the bulky sweater and wriggled from the padded overalls. Then she eased off the pilot's seat, took a deep breath, and plunged into the small equipment bay under the pilot's seat. She was completely submerged as she felt around in the dark for the leak. After what seemed a lifetime, she found it and stuffed the sweater into the broken weld seam. That would not stop the inrush of water but it would slow it down.

With her lungs screaming for air, Mallory turned her attention to locating the circuit breaker. Mallory's lungs were convulsing. A thin column of bubbles escaped her tightly compressed lips as she groped blindly in the dark water. Just as she thought her lungs would burst, her searching hands found the circuit breaker box. She opened its door and pressed the water proof breaker switches. The lights and fans came on at once. As soon as Mallory's head cleared the water, she gasped and sucked in a lungful of air. She hauled herself back into her seat, clicked on her safety harness and put on the headset. Her heart still pounding wildly, Mallory grabbed the microphone and thumbed the switch. "Miss Muffet to Glomar Control. Do you read me?"

"Loud and clear, Skipper." It was a relief to hear Rosie's voice.

Mallory quickly explained the situation. "I am going to level her with the thrusters and the winch," she said. "On my mark swing the docking legs inboard slowly."

"Acknowledged. Waiting for your mark."

Mallory activated the thrusters at max output, thumbed the button on the joystick that controlled the winch, and the Recovery Vehicle leveled off. She thumbed her headset microphone. "Miss Muffet to Glomar Control. Initiate Capture."

On the monitor she saw the other docking leg coming toward her. It latched onto the docking leg engagement stud. Then she was borne up toward the *Glomar Endeavor*'s hull until the recovery vehicle was thirty feet beneath *Glomar Endeavor*'s hull.

"Miss Muffet to Control. Capture is complete. I say again capture is complete!"

"Glomar Control to Miss Muffet. Bravo Zulu!" Rosie said. Mallory could hear cheering in the background. "Good to have you back, Skipper."

Now began a delicate mechanical ballet as the docking collar began to come down, and the top half of the Recovery Vehicle's strong back telescoped inward, the Glomar Endeavor's docking legs sliding inward until they lined up with the forward and aft edges of the moon pool.

Mallory watched through the porthole as the top portion of the Recovery Vehicle's strong back was eased up to just within the hull, and the docking assembly was lowered the rest of the way. This was a rectangular piece of double walled steel, as long as the moon pool, with two cylinders sticking up from it—the Egress Port for the Command Module, and another, wider cylinder—the EVA Port—situated nine feet away rising from a hemisphere that looked like a steel igloo. The Docking Collar made contact with the Recovery Vehicle. Inside the Command Module, a panel of green lights winked on, indicating that the latches on the Docking Collar's belly had engaged with capture points on the Recovery Vehicle's frame. Mallory keyed her headset. "Miss Muffet to Glomar Control. We have lock. I say again, we have lock."

"Roger that, Miss Muffet," acknowledged Rosie. "I am severing the brindle."

Here one of two things would happen, Mallory reflected. The docking collar would hold the Recovery Vehicle in place once the brindle, the four-point cable assembly that attached Miss Muffet to the main recovery cable, or it wouldn't, and then she would plummet to the seafloor. Mallory didn't realize she was holding her breath until a few moments after the discarded brindle had fallen on to the Recovery vehicle and she saw the cable withdrawn. And what of the two massive Moon Pool doors? Old man Hughes would've been mighty impressed had he been around to see what happened next, (these weren't the doors his teams of engineers had designed, mere slabs of hull section) for both doors split into three pieces. The outer sections slid in on either side of the docking collar, and panels underneath them folded up then came down like a complicated bit of origami sealing the Moon Pool from the ocean. The operation looked like one of those Sci-Fi movies where automobiles or helicopters transformed into giant robots. The solution was a design compromise. The Nautilus at three hundred and fifty feet was too large to bring into the moon pool and lengthening the Glomar Endeavor during her refit had been ruled out because of safety issues regarding hull integrity.

There was a good three feet of seawater left sloshing around inside the now sealed Moon Pool. From inside the command module, Mallory heard the pumps at work draining the vast space. She unbuckled her safety harness and let out a long drawn out breath then reached up and opened the hatch. She grabbed the first rung of the ladder leading to the hatch at the top of the Egress Port and ascended it. She emerged to clapping and cheering from Millikan and his team.

DAY 21—1930Z HRS
GLOMAR EXPLORER'S DIVER'S READY ROOM

A few minutes later, Mallory was sitting in a chair at a table in the dive team ready room off the gallery overlooking the Moon Pool. Suits, helmets, tanks, and other gear hung on pegs or were stacked on shelves on all four walls of the room. She had a steaming cup of coffee in her hands, and a blanket around her shoulders. Millikan and his dive team were there with her. Lester had shown up too, his mouth smiling and eyes cold. People were clapping or patting her shoulders. Someone freshened her coffee. Then someone had to spoil it. Predictably, it was Dick Millikan.

"You sure you are up for an EVA in this mess, Skipper?" he asked. The room was moving in a way that could only happen in a ship caught in a typhoon and even the crew's well-trained sea legs were challenged to keep them upright.

Mallory nodded. "It's not a questions of being up to it. This typhoon will get a lot worse before it gets better." Millikan understood she meant the storm's eye wall where the winds were fiercest. The room gave another stomach churning lurch.

Millikan pressed his point home. "With all due respect, I think you need to rethink leading the EVA. You've gone without sleep for twenty hours, and just come back from an arduous eleven hour salvage operation."

Mallory held up a hand, palm outward. "I'll sleep after the Poseidon crystal is on board the *Glomar Endeavor*—which is my responsibility, no one else's—and when we're through the worst of the typhoon. We can't risk losing the Nautilus with the Poseidon crystal still in it when we hit the wall eye." The look in her eyes told Millikan he was sailing into dangerous waters and he'd better drop it. Millikan decided that pursuing a dissenting opinion to that of a superior officer, especially this one was futile so he let it drop.

Lester planted his hands on the table and leaned toward her. "I agree with you, Captain. We need to recover the Poseidon crystal as soon as possible, but I also see Dick's point. I've guys with me that can do the job. Why not let one of my people go with him?"

Mallory looked at the OSS man. His words seemed benign, but she didn't trust him or his motives, and too much had gone wrong already. "In case you've forgotten Agent Lester, your team—including its divers—is here to provide security, not involve itself in the actual recovery operation." She nodded to Millikan and the half dozen other navy divers in the room. "This is a Navy salvage operation. The Navy will handle it."

Lester's eyes narrowed and his lips tightened so much that they blanched. Mallory could see that his cool exterior barely masked broiling anger at her, but that wasn't her problem. Establishing that the retrieval of the Poseidon crystal was *her* territory, Mallory turned to the monitor on the table and punched some keys. When Rosie's smiling face appeared she said, "What's the ETA of the eye wall?"

"Six hours and right now NOAA is saying the eye will last an hour tops."

She looked at Millikan and Lester. "That should give us plenty of time to retrieve the Poseidon crystal." Mallory asked Rosie, "Have you discovered what happened to Eve?"

"It's a complete mystery skipper," he said, shaking his head. "The folks at Heuristic Allied Technologies will have to do a postmortem. We're not equipped for it."

Mallory was heart sick about Eve's death but the mission still had to be completed. "Very well, you have the conn. Do you need anything before I go EVA?"

The Chief Engineer flashed fine white even teeth. "We have it covered up here, Skipper." Mallory suspected the Chief Engineer was having a ball conning a large ship during a typhoon. That would be some story to share with the grandkids someday, she thought.

"Any word on that Russian submarine?" Mallory enquired.

"Not a peep," Rosie replied. "I am guessing her CO said to hell with it and is hunkered somewhere well below this mess."

Lester's expression was inscrutable as he stared at a wall as if he could see through it. The room was still pitching from the strengthening typhoon. His eyes returned to Mallory's face. "I think you're making a mistake, Captain."

Mallory's voice was sharp. "Dismissed." She could see roiling fury and puzzlement on his face. "That's Navy talk for get out," she added.

Lester turned on his heels and left the room. Mallory stood and shrugged off the blanket, "Let's go trick or treating."

DAY 21—1930Z HRS
THE MOON POOL

Lane Winters and Brandon Paulsen were suited up. They were the backup dive team, and would be standing by the EVA Port in case there was an emergency. They checked the EVA Port while Mallory and Millikan prepared to enter the *Nautilus*.

"Everything looks good, Skipper," Lane announced when they were done.

Brandon donned headphones and manned the communication console on the outside of the EVA port. Two other team members had hauled over a large florescent yellow duffel bag filled with tools. It had adjustable buoyancy chambers to make it easier to maneuver in the relatively tight spaces of a submerged wreck.

Mallory made sure her dive helmet was properly secured to her suit, checked her rebreather, a self-contained breathing unit that would reuse a portion of each exhalation in contrast to open circuit scuba where the entire breath is expelled into surrounding waters whenever the diver exhaled. Favored by military and industrial divers, it would permit dives of up to nine hours. She next did a radio check with Millikan and Brandon, who would alert Rosie and Lester when the Poseidon crystal was recovered.

"I am glad you didn't let those guys hone in on our action," Millikan said.

Mallory gave a crooked smile. "Agent Lester sometimes forgets himself."

"Civilians," Brandon snorted. "You can't live with 'em or without 'em."

"And you can't kill 'em either," Brandon opined to nods from the other divers.

"He's giving you the evil eye right now, Skipper," Lane nodded toward the gallery above the moon pool where Lester stood with a knot of his men.

It was true. Mallory felt Lester's eyes burning holes through her helmet as she prepared to mount the ladder leading to the top of the EVA Port. "He'll get over it. We'll see you guys in a few hours. Keep the porch light on for us."

"You got it, Boss," Lane replied. Mallory ascended the ladder leading up to the top of the EVA Port then climbed down to its wide flaring bottom. Millikan came down after her a moment later and the duffel bag was lowered down on a line. They caught it and set it down gently on the EVA Port's deck. Mallory tied the end of the communication rope on her reel to a steel loop on the communication panel in the EVA Port then plugged it into the jack. She and Millikan would communicate by radio and she would talk to the surface via the safety tether. The EVA Port lined up with a hatch on the top of the Recovery Vehicle's strong back. Mallory engaged the EVA Port hatch clamps then she and Millikan gave the wheel three turns and the hatch came up with its mate.

"We're entering the Docking Well," Mallory announced.

"Roger that." Brandon's voice sounded tinny in her earphone.

First Mallory then Millikan went down into the docking well. Outside a small porthole the water was pitch black and roiling. Several times, as they prepared to deploy the docking ring to the *Nautilus* 'boat deck, Mallory and Millikan were thrown together as the ship above them battled her way through the typhoon.

Millikan said, "I wouldn't want to be topside in this one."

Mallory pressed her helmet faceplate against an eyepiece sticking out from a small instrument panel. "Like we're better off down here? Are you ready?"

"Affirmative."

"On my mark. One two three…"

Millikan pressed a switch on a panel and the accordion-like docking collar extended from the belly of the Recovery Vehicle making contact with the Nautilus 'deck just aft of the main hatch. Mallory turned on a pump purging the seawater from the docking ring. When the seawater was gone she announced, "We have a hard seal."

"Acknowledged," Brandon replied. "Good luck, and be careful."

Mallory opened the docking ring access hatch then tapped Millikan's shoulder. "You are good to go, Dick."

Millikan had removed an exothermic cutting torch from the duffel bag. He bent down, and began cutting through the corroded hull plates. It was a moment neither of them would ever forget, Mallory thought. When he was finished, she removed an orange sledgehammer from the tool bag and hit the center of the circular piece three times. It dropped into the hull. Just below the edge of the hole churned a disk of black seawater.

After helping to stow the torch, Mallory squeezed down through the opening and found herself in the stygian depths of the *Nautilus* 'main corridor. There was a strong current alternating direction every few minutes, so that she had to frog kick vigorously to keep station, and it was so dark she couldn't see her hand in front of her face. It was like swimming in a pool of black ink.

"Base this is Alpha 1. I am inside the main corridor."

"How does it look, Skipper?"

"I'll tell you in a minute. Switching on my dive light."

Mallory switched on her helmet light. She took it back. *This* would be the moment neither of them would ever forget. She had done many wreck penetrations but nothing like this legendary 19th century submarine. Even in death she was a commanding presence. The last man to walk this corridor was Captain Nemo himself. Mallory thought she could feel his ghost watching her from the watery shadows, black eyes blazing with fury at their intrusion into his sanctum.

Mallory said, "What I can see of her is in pretty good shape—for a ship that has spent over a hundred and sixty-three years on the sea floor." Even with her dive light visibility was less than ideal because of all the particles in the water stirred up by the current. Mallory had to focus extra hard to keep from being disoriented as the corridor pitched up and down like an amusement park ride. She looped the tether to a hull frame beneath the docking ring and pressed a switch on the reel attached to her harness. The comm tether suddenly gave off a ghostly greenish glow. Even if their dive lights failed this would allow them to find their way back to the docking ring.

"Here comes the EVA toolkit." Millikan announced. The duffel bag came down on a line and Mallory caught it, inflated the buoyancy chambers and switched on the automatic trim device that would compensate for the weight of any tool removed from it. Millikan splashed down into the corridor beside her. Their helmet lights played over the corroded walls, falling on the brass rails of the spiral staircase some distance ahead. One thing struck Mallory immediately about the Nautilus. She was larger and far less cluttered inside than a modern submarine. This was a ship that was designed to be primarily a *home* beneath the seas. Nemo's crew enjoyed creature comforts that would have made a modern submariner go green with envy.

With the glowing safety tether unspooling as she went, Mallory led the way through a nearby doorway. "This should be the Salon," she said. Once inside she did a helicopter kick and spun around laterally very slowly with her light playing on rotting divans and silt covered display cases. Despite its sad condition there was a certain residual grandeur to the place. Here Captain Nemo had spent many an hour cataloging marine specimens and observing the wonders of the sea through the salon's two large view ports. Again, Mallory had the unmistakable feeling that she was being watched. The beams from their helmet lights converged on a bronze Aphrodite standing in the center of a large shell. Mallory frog kicked toward it with Millikan at her side.

Something gleamed dully in the bottom of the fountain.

"Goddamn! Look at all those gold coins!" Millikan exclaimed. He grabbed a handful and held them out to Mallory. "Holy shit! Spanish doubloons, Roman and Greek coins." He started to put the coins in an outside pocket on the duffel bag.

"Put them back," Mallory ordered sternly.

Millikan gaped at her. "Are you nuts? We'll all be set for life!"

"I could use a shiny new Corvette," Brandon quipped in her earpiece.

"You'll just have to make do with your pickup," Mallory replied. To Millikan she said, "Those coins are the property of the United States government. Put them back."

Millikan jerked a thumb toward the surface. "How much of this stuff do you think those OSS bastards will pass along to Uncle Sam?"

"Not the point, Dick," she replied, fighting to keep her anger under control. "We're here to recover the Poseidon crystal, not hunt for treasure." She didn't want to waste valuable time arguing with this greedy idiot. Not when they had so much territory to cover and so little time to do it in. She'd deal with him after they got to the surface. He opened his gloved fingers and let the coins fall back into the fountain.

"Just like that," he said ruefully.

"Just like that," she replied. "Now get your head in the game." The room was tilting crazily, scraps of wall hangings and bits of rotted fabric on the furniture waving in the strong currents. "Look over there," Millikan said.

She followed his pointing finger with her gaze. Their lights shone on the salon's starboard view port. The polymer sheathing had failed to cover the shattered opening where several glass shards still glinted in the brass frame. Behind them, the port view port was intact and was coated with the white C-Out cocooning material.

"I wonder if this is how she sank?" Millikan wondered aloud.

"No," Mallory replied. "Captain Nemo scuttled her."

"Why on Earth did he do that?"

"Something died in him. He wanted the *Nautilus* to die with him," Mallory replied in a tone that said she didn't want to discuss it further. They finned toward a doorway past the silt-covered remains of a pipe organ.

Like the keyboard and organ they rose from, the metal tubes fanning out from the top of it were corroded and coated with a thick layer of silt.

Once back in the corridor they headed aft. "The crew's quarters should be up ahead on our left," Mallory said. They paused at an open doorway, the beams of their helmet lights sweeping over rows of rusted iron cots and scraps of cloth amid swirling eddies of debris. They pressed onwards until they encountered a collapsed bulkhead, an insurmountable wall of twisted metal and debris.

"Well, isn't that's just great!" Millikan exclaimed bitterly.

Mallory stared at it. "We'd need way more time than we have to get through this," she said. "Follow me." She turned and led the way back down the corridor toward the bow, past the main staircase, with her light sliding along the once immaculate teak deck, now a rotting and corroded mess with planks missing in places.

After a while they came upon a companionway, its hatch lying on the deck beside it—probably blown out by the force of the water as the *Nautilus* sank—and she went down headfirst, looping the evanescent tether around the ladder. Here the current was milder. Millikan followed then they proceeded down the corridor past gaping hatches until they came to another companionway. At the top of its ladder the hatch was closed.

She tried to inform Brandon of this development but the communication line was now filled with static. She switched to her radio. "Alpha-Team to base. Do you copy?"

There was no answer. "Should we go back?" Millikan queried.

Mallory frowned. Communication equipment did fail sometimes. Another salvage diver might have aborted the mission, but she was determined to see it through, no matter the cost. "I am not going back empty handed," she replied. "We have to recover the Poseidon crystal in case this typhoon rips the Nautilus away from the Glomar Endeavor."

"We can kiss it bye-bye if that happens," Millikan said.

"Exactly!" Mallory looked for a handle and found one, but it wouldn't budge.

"You can never go wrong with one of these." Millikan removed an orange crowbar from the duffel bag and wedged it between the hatch and coaming. They braced themselves against the ladder steps and levered the hatch until it broke free in a shower of silt. As they rose into the upper corridor the hatch cover fell over onto the deck.

A few feet away stood another bulkhead with its hatch sealed. Mallory glided toward it, with a thrill rippling through her torso. They had reached the *Nautilus*'engine room. Millikan got to work at once with his torch on the locking mechanism, its retina-burning flame biting into the corroded metal. When he was done they braced themselves against the deck and shoved against the hatch. It swung inward with the tortured groan of corroded metal. The room was bathed in pulsating violet light.

With Mallory leading the way, they glided into the engine room towing the duffel bag between them. As they penetrated deeper into the engine room the violet light intensified. The immense compartment was filled with fantastical equipment that baffled and astounded her. The ambiance was Victorian Industrial Age. There were **ornate** instrument panels with large silt covered gauges and dials and long handled levers.

"This place gives me the willies," Millikan said. "Do you think it's haunted?"

"There's no one here except us chickens," Mallory replied, "or perhaps a stingray or two." As she penetrated deeper into the engine room's gloomy depths, she could imagine it being filled with strange oscillating hums, whirring and low pulsing throbs and rhythmic ticking sounds. Nemo felt completely at home here, Mallory knew from reading his journal, among the machinery he had designed to propel the Nautilus through the ocean depths. She'd not seen an engine room like it in any other vessel. They swam the length and breadth of it then Mallory finned over to the source of the light—a device sitting atop a rusted steel pedestal. A medusa head of copper pipes coated with verdigris from long exposure to seawater sprouted from the top of it. Another cable thick as a man's forearm emerged from the base of the pedestal and ran along the deck to the massive electric motor that drove the Nautilus 'propeller.

Mallory swam around the Grail Reactor slowly. It was hard to get her mind around the fact that she was looking at a zero sum energy device from the 19th century containing Atlantean technology that would make the United States energy independent. And that was laying aside the astounding fact that the Nautilus would've run circles around any twenty-first century fast attack submarine and could out dive any research submersible.

When Mallory reached the Grail Reactor she said, "We're running out of time. The typhoon's eye is almost on top of us. Let's get to work."

"Roger that!" Millikan replied. A bright flame bloomed at the tip of the cutting torch and he began to cut the pipes while Mallory bent them out of the way. Three hours later, they were ready to attack the Grail Reactor itself.

Mallory removed a transparent isolation chamber from the duffel bag. It was square with two armholes terminating in gloves, and had a cutting torch inside, as well as a transfer chamber jutting from one side, and had been custom made with a special high temperature resistant polycarbonate. It was open at the bottom with an inflatable neoprene collar. They had been briefed by OSS scientists about the importance of preventing the Poseidon crystal from coming into contact with seawater, which activated its special properties. Dry, it could be handled with bare hands. The scientists had had only an inkling of what would happen if it got wet. One of them had told her it might be like suddenly finding yourself with a piece of the sun's corona in your hand. Mallory didn't want to be the one to find out. "Okay, let's see if this thing fits."

"We're screwed if it doesn't," Millikan observed.

"On my mark," Mallory said, "One... two... three." They gingerly slipped the isolation chamber over the grail reactor. While she held it in place Millikan pressed a button on a small control panel on the side of the isolation chamber. The collar inflated until it was sealed tight against the pedestal just below the Grail Reactor. Nemo had been justifiably proud of the device that provided unlimited energy to his submarine and had provided a dimensioned drawing of it in his memoirs. All through this procedure the engine room was tilting ever more sharply as the typhoon above them intensified and they had to fight the strong currents.

Mallory pressed a button on the isolation chamber. "Initiating water dump." A small electric pump on the isolation chamber drained the seawater and then an inert gas was added then purged. While Millikan worked his hands inside the isolation chamber's gloves, Mallory disconnected the gas and oxygen hoses from the torch in the duffel bag then plugged them into the isolation chamber. Again came that nagging feeling that they were being watched. Mallory turned on her wrist light and swept the compartment with its beam. Machinery and control panels leapt out of the shadows but no outraged Nemo or hungry sea monster was there to threaten them. Mallory was not easily frightened but the feeling just wouldn't go away. "Commence extraction," she said.

"Ready or not, here I come." Millikan used the cutting torch inside the isolation chamber to remove the Grail Reactor's lock. "Piece of cake!"

Mallory tapped him on the shoulder. "Hold on while I check for leaks." She checked the isolation chamber and swore softly. "We have seepage. I am going to tighten the collar. Hold on." She turned the collar pump on. The seepage got worse. Soon there was half an inch of water and it was rising. Mallory thought that the last place they would want to be was in the engine room if the seawater came into contact with the Poseidon crystal. "We have to move fast," she said. "Open the Grail Reactor." Millikan tried to force it open but it wouldn't budge. She couldn't see his face inside his helmet from where she stood beside him, but she heard his rapid breathing. "Watch your breathing."

"Thanks for reminding me." Millikan quickly got his breath under control. Now the isolation chamber was half filled with seawater. At most they had a few seconds to retrieve the Poseidon crystal or...she didn't even want to finish the thought. Whenever the ship tilted, seawater lapped at the bottom of the Grail Reactor. Mallory pushed the pump switch. Nothing. The pump was broken. There was no way to get a hammer or other tool inside the chamber without making things infinitely worse. She flexed her fingers while she tried to think of a way out of this—to use her father's favorite expression—shit storm of a problem. "Use the torch to cut it open."

"Is that safe?"

"Do you have a better idea?"

The room tilted at an even steeper angle then plunged and they were almost carried away. Mallory had to hang on to the pedestal. Millikan ignited the torch and cut the Grail Reactor where its two halves met. Then the lid flew back on its hinges and a glowing violet sphere the size of a gold ball shot from the surface and smacked into the isolation chamber's ceiling.

Millikan caught it just before it came in contact with the seawater. "Saved by my lightning reflexes! Pretty impressive, huh?"

"Good job," Mallory said. "Let's bag it and get the hell out of here."

"You don't have to tell me twice." Millikan slid it into the transfer chamber, and pushed into small black box and snapped its lid shut. While he worked his arms free from the chamber, Mallory removed the capture jar with its prize.

"It doesn't look like much does it?" she said.

Then they heard a loud dull boom.

CHAPTER 16 MALICIOUS INTENT

DAY 21--2245Z HRS
THE *NAUTILUS*

"Alpha 1 to Base. Can you hear me?" Mallory switched from the comm tether to the radio. With all the steel between them and the base station in the moon pool Mallory knew that a clear signal was out of the question, but she had to try anyway.

"Alpha 1 to Base. Do you read me?" Still there should've been something other than dead silence. Even the crackle of static would've been reassuring under the circumstances. She and Millikan were back in the Nautilus 'main corridor. In the hour since they'd left the engine room the typhoon had intensified. Now the two joined ships were pitching by as much as thirty degrees as they climbed mountainous waves then plunged into deep valleys. Several times the plunging submarine almost sent them crashing into the corridor's steel ceiling. Mallory was fighting a rising tide of panic. At any moment the Nautilus could be ripped from the Glomar Endeavor's belly then the submarine would fall thirty-seven thousand feet to the seabed with them trapped inside. Transiting the corridor was proving to be a nightmare; water raced down the confined space with the force of a river in spate then abruptly reversed direction with equal intensity.

Mallory clung to a hull frame with Millikan one frame behind her.

"I wonder what happened?" she asked, prying her mind out of fear's grip.

"The way this typhoon is tossing us around there are bound to be equipment failures," Millikan replied hopefully, his legs flying out behind him as they fought the surging current. But Mallory wasn't so sure about that. Not with all the mysterious occurrences that had happened during the mission. And what about Eve's dire warning? Who wasn't she to trust? Millikan? He seemed to have gotten over his resentment about their last mission. Lester? That seemed plausible but why would the OSS man want to sabotage his own mission? None of it made sense. Mallory looked around. There it was again—that odd feeling that they were being watched. Mallory didn't believe in ghosts but the sooner they were back onboard the Glomar Endeavor the better. Reflexively her hand dropped down to the capture jar strapped to her torso.

"How you doing, Dick?" Mallory asked.

"Just a little creeped out," Millikan admitted. "I am beginning to regret watching all those horror movies where the aliens devour the intrepid adventurers."

"Fortunately, we're not in a spaceship. Other than a rattail or two, there's no one here but us chickens." Mallory gestured to a nearby doorway. "The salon is just up ahead." She kicked off from the frame and led the way, her fins churning the water in a respite from the tides that would last only seconds.

Millikan, keeping pace with her, said, "If possible, the current is getting worse."

"Yeah, so is our chance of getting back. Kick it into high gear, Dick."

Mallory was almost to the salon door when the Nautilus 'bow rose at an even steeper angle, and there was the loud groan of tortured steel. "Hold on!" Mallory cried. She grabbed the nearest frame and held on for dear life as the water raced by them. More groans and shrieks and the unmistakable sound of heavy steel rivets popping.

"Holy shit! Did you hear that?" Millikan's face was pale behind his faceplate.

"She's coming apart." Mallory looked around. "We have to get the hell out of here before she takes us with her."

"I'm right behind you, Skipper."

Visibility was down to three feet even with their dive lights. They had the duffel bag strung between them and had to fight hard to keep from losing it. They finned toward the salon. Mallory had just gained the doorway when the duffel bag was yanked so hard it felt as if her arm was being ripped from its socket.

Millikan screamed bloodily.

Mallory turned just in time to see him flying backwards down the corridor flailing at long serpentine arms whose undersides were covered with sucker cups. His face was pale and the terror in his eyes palpable. She glimpsed the creature's conical mantle flashing crimson and white in what could only be a threat display. Incredibly, the squid handled Millikan, a stocky six-footer, as if he had been no larger than a small fish.

With a speed one had to see to believe, the creature hauled Millikan into the *Nautilus* 'crew quarters while ripping away chunks of his wetsuit and flesh with the fang-like hooks on its arms. Mallory followed swiftly, pulling her dive knife from the sheath strapped to her thigh. As soon as she cleared the doorway the squid struck her on the shoulder rattlesnake quick with a tentacle. It felt like being hit by a baseball bat. Her fingers reflectively opened and the dive knife fell to the deck. Before she could recover, the room pitched and the knife slid away into the dark recesses.

Even as the serpentine arms were lashing him with their razor sharp suction cups Millikan was struggling to get at his underwater pistol. He got a hand on its grip then yanked it from its holster. The squid twisted the weapon from his hand and tossed it behind them.

"Save yourself!" Millikan screamed.

"I am not leaving you!" Mallory clung to the doorjamb in the fierce current frantically looking for anything that could be used as a weapon. Louder than Millikan's scream, came the sound of his faceplate being smashed in by a tentacle. Before her horrified gaze, a halo of blood and flesh bloomed around his helmet. Then the water turned blacker still as the squid released its ink. Even without hearing his death rattle Mallory knew Millikan was dead. With her heart thundering in her ears she turned and swam away as fast as she could. She was breathing so hard her faceplate was fogging up.

She had just cleared the salon doorway when a tentacle wrapped around her ankle. As she was being hauled backwards, she grabbed onto the pipe organ. A desperate tug of war ensued. The teeth ringing the suction cups on the tentacle pierced the dive suit sending bolts of searing pain rocketing up her leg. She was in no doubt as to what she was up against: the only creature divers feared more than the Great White Shark—a Giant Squid. With two long tentacles and eight arms, they could be as long as a hundred and twenty feet, and routinely hunted and killed whales and sharks. Meeting one during a dive was every divers worst nightmare. The squid was pulling hard, his rage at the invasion of his territory seeming to grow the more Mallory resisted. The pipe organ's water logged wood was beginning to give way under the pressure. Mallory reached for one of the brass pipes fanning out from the top of the organ and got a grip on one. Just as she got her other hand on the pipe a second tentacle wrapped itself around her waist. Mallory screamed as the razor sharp suction cups pierced her suit. The creature pulled hard with the current aiding it, and she fell backwards into the deep darkness, the broken piece of a brass pipe clutched in her hands. She rolled onto her back as she was borne toward the writhing arms surrounding an impossibly huge snapping beak.

Mallory thought she detected malice in the giant squid's saucer-like eyes. As she was borne ever closer to the snapping beak and waiting tentacles, she fought panic, bringing the pipe up with the jagged end facing away from her. She willed herself to wait, as if she had given in. When she was within inches of the creature's malevolent eyes, she struck, driving the long pipe straight into one of the squid's eyes. It released clouds of black ink, shrouding them both in fog. Mallory bore down on the pipe until it passed through the other side of the reddish mantle. The creature thrashed around then released its hold on her and drifted away, its tentacles limp.

Breathing heavily, Mallory felt to make sure the Poseidon crystal was still safely attached to her torso. She had to feel her way out of the black cloud then finned for the salon, exhausted, following the glowing communication tether through the ruined salon as if on autopilot. *I must get back*, was all she could think.

To lighten her load, she tied the tool kit tether to the statue of Aphrodite as she passed the fountain. What did she care about a few tools? She'd just lost one of her dive team. All the bad feelings came flooding back—she'd lost most of her dive team in the mission that had resulted in her having to take a year off due to PTSD. Millikan was the only survivor of that ill-fated mission other than her and now she'd lost him, too. But she had to move on. There was no time for regrets now. Her helmet light had been broken in the fight with the squid. She switched on her wrist mounted dive light and finned for the other doorway and into the corridor.

She saw an indistinct shape drifting in the black water before she reached the docking ring. As she drew nearer she saw that it was a diver lying face up. Half his head was missing but she had no trouble recognizing who it was. It was Lane, one of the backup divers. Fuck! Could this day get any worse? There were no options. She had to go topside and see what the hell was happening on her ship.

A war had been raging in the chilled steel container that held the Heuristic Model 666 Triadtronic Brain. The invaders, nanobots that had worked their way along the main power buss into the Triadtronic Brain's spongy platinum mass were being fought by other nanobots that swept forward on buckyballs to repel the invaders. This is an unforeseen event, an evolutionary step, not a design feature of the artificial brain. At first the invaders were victorious as they began to use their pincers to tear at the spongy platinum mass and devour the Turing nodes on the intricate web of the neural network. Then, gradually, the defenders gained ground, each defending nanobot wielding a nano-sized sledgehammer to shatter their opposing numbers. It was quite extraordinary really and several papers would be written about this phenomenon in the future.

But for now…
System Reboot…
System Reboot…
System Reboot…

DAY 21--2345Z HRS
THE GLOMAR *ENDEAVOR*

Mallory just wanted to know one thing: "Why did you kill them, you son of a bitch?" Wearing only a sports bra and panties, Mallory stood with her hands clasped behind her head in the bridge. Half a dozen machine guns were pointed at her. She didn't care about her near nakedness: Not with her world crumbling around her; not with Rosie and all the others dead; not with the Poseidon crystal taken from her by Agent Randal Lester. Being almost naked before all these men meant nothing although the faces of the Black Pool mercenaries were tight with contempt.

Lester's blue eyes burned bright in his smooth face. "Well, you know how it is Captain: I can't leave any witnesses. That's how the game is played. How it's always been played. Even a card carrying CIA agent like Lee Harvey Oswald couldn't be left alive to tell what he knew so they made sure his dark secrets went to the grave with him. There are certain immutable truths that never change no matter the time and place, and this is one of them: Dead men tell no tales." The OSS man gave a dismissive shrug. "It's as simple as that." Lester's PCS unit beeped. He touched the headset and said, "Speak." He listened avidly, his eyes never leaving Mallory's face. It was hot and muggy but she was trembling as if she had a chill. Outside the bridge windows, the sky was clear and the sea was almost smooth—and it was eerily quiet. They were in the eye of the typhoon. The place of stillness before the terror resumed with even greater intensity.

Mallory's dive suit was lying on the Moon Pool deck where she'd left it after she emerged from the EVA Collar to find all her backup dive team members killed and machine gun-toting Black Pool mercenaries lying in wait for her. Griffith hadn't even allowed her to stop long enough to put on clothes before he and six armed goons took her to Lester. What she'd seen along the way was horrific. The corpses of crewmen, some obviously shot as they cowered or were trying to run away, littered the Glomar Endeavor's corridors and compartments. A trail of lightning speared the sky.

Mallory was alternately possessed by numbing grief and savage rage— it had happened on her watch. She'd never be able to forgive herself for that.

How could this happen…?

Mallory now knew with sickening certitude what had caused the loud booms she and Millikan had heard while in the Nautilus' main corridor. A column of black smoke rose from the gaping hole where the Operations Center had been, and the main communication mast had also been blown up, leaving only a mangled pile of wreckage. With the clarity of horror, shock, and adrenaline, Mallory mentally put together what had gone down in her absence. Lester had somehow sabotaged Eve, who as she went into failure mode tried to warn her—then, once he was certain the Poseidon crystal had been recovered, his mercenaries had gone from compartment to compartment, killing the Navy personnel then blown up the Operations Center and the communications mast. Even if she could get to a radio it wouldn't do her any good.

I am a dead woman...

"Why?" *she asked again, bewildered and afraid.*

Lester's grin was as big as a shark's toothy maw. "I guess," he said, "this is where I am supposed to launch into an impassioned speech about how America is no longer the country it used to be about how it has become a cesspool of minorities, foreigners, perverts, and welfare cheats, but it really boils down to this." Here the OSS man held out his hands palm up, as if weighing—quite literally—the facts of the case. "In this hand is Option A: I bring the Poseidon crystal home and get a pat on the head, a nice commendation in my personnel file for services rendered, and a gold watch when I eventually retire. Then there's Option B: I sell it to the Chinese government who pay me sixty-billion dollars."

That hand went ominously low.

Mallory would always remember the OSS man's words and his chilling tone. "Anyone with half a brain would make the same choice—the only real choice available—but I wouldn't expect a clueless wonder like you to understand that." A spray of rain suddenly pelted the bridge windows. Thunder rumbled somewhere close at hand, but Lester didn't look away from her. He stepped closer, his bright gaze drilling into her. "God, I detest you. You represent everything that's gone wrong with America."

Lester looked over at Mr. Griffith and pointed at Mallory's tattoos. "Look at that shit. Can you believe this dyke is an **officer** in the United States Navy?"

Mr. Griffith laughed. "She should be in some goddamned circus—the tattooed—fucking—lady. She's a goddamned freak!" Mallory was acutely aware of the other men in the bridge with their machine guns and pistols pointing at her—and their frank stares of lust. This situation could get even worse for her in a heartbeat.

But Mallory refused to let that possibility keep her from speaking her mind to this bigoted creep. "Too bad the Third Reich is no longer around, Lester. You'd have made a first rate Nazi. Let me guess: the other kids didn't like you. Bullies beat your ass on the way to school then chased you home after the last bell rang, or some girl you asked to the prom turned you down cold."

Lester bared his teeth. "Nice try bitch, but no cigar." Through the windows Mallory saw the spy ship and the submarine—the Russian vessels were keeping station with the Glomar, about a 1000 feet off both beams. Officers and sailors crowded their topsides studying the American salvage ship through binoculars, taking pictures with digital cameras. It looked as if they were preparing to send boarding parties over.

"You'll never get away with this," Mallory said. "At the very least, your Russian friends won't let the Chinese run off with their lunch."

Lester consulted his wristwatch. "I wouldn't count on it."

Two massive explosions cracked open the sky. Mallory almost jumped out of her skin. The spy ship was broken in two, the halves twisting away from each other as they sank. The Russian submarine was standing nearly vertical from the water as it began to slide down stern first. More explosions ripped through the spy ship's aft section as it began to tear itself apart. Another explosion wracked the Russian submarine as it sank, shredding it to pieces. The shockwaves smacked into the Glomar Endeavor rocking the big recovery ship from side to side. Then another submarine surfaced, water streaming from its sail. The expression on Lester's face changed to one of intense hatred. "For you the war is over, Captain Capehart." Mallory never saw what happened next.

CHAPTER 17
BENEFACTOR

Mallory smacked into bath-warm water. It enveloped her, sucking her under, twirling her in cheerleader baton circles. To be sure there was that odd pain on her left temple—what had happened? She popped cork-like to the surface. The water, black as a convict's hopelessness, sucked her under again. It had felt like she had fallen through old motor oil, dark and old viscous honey, for the seconds had prolapsed into taffy-like aeons that segued into eternity. Lying face down in the heaving water, Mallory's stomach and limbs were ablaze with pain too. She felt these things, and was puzzled by them. From somewhere above, she beheld her nearly naked form, pale in the black water, twisting. Dimly she hears the horror movie howl of a typhoon's raging voice—and cutting through it, the sound of a zodiac motor's high whine growing nearer. Excited Chinese voices shouting over the shrieking wind and the sea's deep roar.

Mallory woke lying face down in the dark furious water, gasped and almost swallowed a mouthful. The seas were rough and mountainous and the Glomar *Endeavor* was a dull black cliff beside her. The waves rose to gargantuan heights, slamming her against and driving her up the hull with the primal force of a category 5 Typhoon. Then it all came flashing back to her in stop-action images: Lester smirking as he took the Poseidon crystal. Lester laughing as she stands before him confused and nearly naked. Lester bragging about how much money the Chinese will pay him; Lester's fist smashing into the side of her skull. Lester and Griffith tossing her from the wing bridge like a bag of trash—their laughter as they let her go. Lester shouting, "Bye-bye you fucking dyke!"

Mallory drew a deep breath and dove.

She pushed and kicked like a fiend, fighting the impossibly strong current. She knew where she was going, where she wanted to be. Mallory dove like a homesick porpoise, her long slender legs scissoring, arms pulling the water with all her force. Her lungs felt as if they were going to explode and the salt water burned her eyes, as she kicked toward her objective.

The *Nautilus*...

...Clutched tightly to the bottom of the MV Glomar Endeavor's hull.

With the watertight polymer material sheathing its hull, the wrecked submarine looked like a white whale in the black water. There in its side was the empty eye socket hole over the salon's shattered view port. Mallory kicked for it, legs and arms pumping, lungs about to burst, her face red and growing redder by the moment.

Mallory swam into the salon, her lungs about to burst. Somehow she had to get to the EVA collar. That meant transiting the salon and the long corridor beyond. It was pitch black in the salon. Mallory's lungs were on fire now. She cast around for the discarded tool bag with its spare oxygen tank. She gulped a mouthful of seawater. There was a feeling of burning and tearing in her chest. She was growing lightheaded by the moment. The seawater she was gulping blocked the gas exchange in the delicate tissues of her lungs triggering a laryngospasm—her airways closed.

And then she was calm. Her flailing arms and legs grew still and her mind peaceful. She had done all she could. She would die here in the *Nautilus*. There were worse deaths, and she always hoped that when she kicked it, that it would be her beloved sea that would claim her. Just as she was closing her eyes for the final time, a figure stepped from the shadows. The only evidence of her surprise was that she didn't close her eyes, not yet. The figure was clad in an old style rubber diving suit and brass helmet. Mallory glimpsed fierce black eyes behind the round glass faceplate. A large gloved hand seized her by the wrist and pulled her limp body along.

Mallory barely registered a regulator being thrust into her mouth but then she grabbed for it desperately and breathed deeply and gratefully. Wonder started to take over as the man in the antique diving suit pulled her along by the wrist while she clutched onto the small tank with her other hand. He was sure footed as he pulled her out of the salon and into the corridor then pushed her up into the EVA port. When Mallory reached the top of the ladder the secondary door was closed. She turned the handle and pushed with the last of her waning strength, it swung up and then she was inside the EVA collar retching and gasping. When her breathing finally normalized she looked down for the curious figure, but all she could see was a disk of roiling black water.

DAY 21—2415Z HRS
THE GLOMAR *ENDEAVOR*

It was dark in the Moon Pool. A black awning had been stretched overhead during the recovery effort to screen the operation from the prying eyes of satellites but it wasn't watertight. Several waterfalls splashed into the Moon Pool from above. Mallory sat huddled at the base of the EVA Collar, hugging her knees close to her body, shivering. What had just happened? Had it been all in her mind—the product of a brain nearly starved of oxygen—or had Captain Nemo himself just saved her life? Mallory did not believe in spirits. She must not believe in them. Such belief was irrational and superstitious. Still…something had happened. She should be dead. She was drowning when the apparition appeared. Another few seconds and it would've been too late.

No time to think about it now. Fear of the Poseidon crystal falling into Chinese hands galvanized her. Mallory groped blindly through the darkness around the deck, her hands brushing across spent brass shells that sent more tremors rocketing through her frame. Now crawling on hands and knees, she worked her way around the EVA Collar's base until she felt a leg sheathed in a rubber diving suit. Her tremors worsened then. She felt up the leg to the torso, got to the arm with the dive light and removed it. The dive light's beam gave her a mental boost. At least now she could see. She played the light around the cavernous space. Brandon was sprawled face down with half the back of his skull missing. There was a corpse draped over the gallery railing above her, its arms swinging with the pitching of the ship. Then she was on the move. First she needed clothes. She was still clad only in her panties and sports bra. And she needed a weapon. Mallory knew where to obtain both—the diver's ready room, one deck up and just off of the forward gallery. Shielding the light with her hand, her blood pumping, Mallory headed for the metal stairs on the forward bulkhead, fighting to keep her footing on the slippery wet deck, her head swiveling, ears cocked for the slightest sound of trouble. Then she was taking the stairs two at a time. When she got to the diver's ready room's closed hatch she paused a moment to listen before swinging it open and slipping inside.

Mallory switched on a light, dried off, and then got dressed in her jeans and boots and a black tee shirt that she had left there when she donned her dive suit. Then she grew still. The last thirty-six hours had been characterized by numerous surprises, an awe-inspiring penetration dive into the bowels of the *Nautilus*, violence, treachery, and an encounter with the ghost of a man dead for over a hundred and sixty-eight years. Now the Glomar Endeavor and the precious Poseidon crystal were in the hands of the traitor Randal Lester and very likely the Chinese. Mallory reflected that it might already be too late. The Poseidon crystal might already be in a submarine bound for China. And even if it wasn't, what could a lone exhausted woman do against a dozen heavily armed mercenaries? She was a diver, not a marine or soldier. She'd had only minimal combat training, although she did seem to be a natural at it, she tried to assure herself.

Mallory sat on a chair beside a table and put her face in her hands and tried to collect her thoughts and keep from crying. Things had gone horribly wrong with the mission. That it wasn't her fault didn't matter. That an OSS agent with a chip on his shoulder had sabotaged the mission in order to betray his country also mattered not at all. What mattered was that the mission was a bust and *her* crew massacred. But now it all made sense. Dr. Chang's disappearance; the SAAM robots attacking her in the cargo hold; Eve going into failure mode; even the typhoon. What better way for Lester to cover up his crimes than arranging for the Glomar *Endeavor* to go down in a typhoon? And the son of a bitch was going to get away with it, Mallory thought. What could she do when he held all the winning cards?

The monitor on the table flicked on. "Hello Mallory," said a child's voice.

Dharma Windham

CHAPTER 18 THE AFTER PARTY

"What counts is not necessarily the size of the dog in the fight—It's the size of the fight in the dog!"
Dwight D. Eisenhower

DAY 21—2430Z HRS

Mallory's head jerked up and she stared wonderingly at the screen. A little girl, perhaps ten years old with long red hair tied with a blue and white polka dotted bow and big blue eyes was staring at her with a solemn expression. But there was no mistaking who she was seeing. A younger version of Eve! Mallory leaned closer to the screen.

"Eve, is that you? I thought you were..."

Eve's brow furrowed. "Dead? Not exactly..." She told Mallory about the nanobots Lester had unleashed on her. "But although I am...revived... my operational capabilities are, shall we say, limited—and as you can see, I am not exactly myself."

Mallory understood almost nothing of this. She was just relieved to see Eve, even if she was now a little English girl in a nineteenth century frock with a bow in her hair. Suddenly, Mallory didn't feel so alone, and she thought she felt the smallest glimmer of hope. There was the tearing shriek of metal.

Eve looked around then her gaze returned to Mallory's face. "There isn't much time. Hull integrity has been severely compromised by the Typhoon. I estimate the Glomar Endeavor will break apart in another twelve minutes."

Mallory gave Eve a thoughtful look. "Can you access the ship's weapons systems?" If so, they had a chance, she decided. They could make the boarders miserable—if not drive them from the ship. They could certainly make trouble for the Chinese submarine since it was surfaced.

Eve shook her head slowly. "No, I am afraid I can't. Neither can I send a distress call because the communication masts have been destroyed. What I can do is provide you with positional information for everyone onboard. There are Chinese Special Forces personnel on the main deck and manning the forward bridge. Most of Agent Lester's mercenaries are occupied keeping their eyes on their Chinese counterparts. Most importantly, Agent Lester has just entered his cabin. He is preparing to go over to the Chinese submarine with his men. My guess is that the shithead is holding on to the Poseidon crystal until he sees the money. If you hurry, you can get there before he leaves."

Mallory studied her for a half minute then asked, "And do what exactly?"

Eve said, "I know it's hard, Mallory, but you *must* prevent the Poseidon crystal from falling into Chinese hands. It might seem odd coming from a soulless machine but I genuinely don't want to see that happen—or for you to fail. So grab a weapon and show me what you're made of. Given the tactical situation, I recommend the M1014 combat shotgun in the locker behind you. You'll find shells in the drawer under it." Eve added, "You're going to need a lot of them."

After a short hesitation, Mallory, rose to her feet, and went over to the arms locker and swung the door open. She removed one of the M1014s from the rack and hefted it. The twelve gauge was a matte black semiautomatic **shotgun,** with a flashlight fixed to the Picatinny rail, a military rail system that provided a mounting platform for firearm accessories on its receiver. The weapon was configured with a collapsible butt stock, permitting better maneuverability around tight corners and the narrow confines of a ship. She couldn't have asked for a better weapon under the circumstances. Mallory collapsed the butt stock and fed six shells into the receiver then grabbed a bandolier of shells and slung it over her shoulder. She turned back to the monitor. "How do we stay in touch?"

"Shipboard communications are still operational," Eve replied crisply.

Mallory reached for a Harris Hydra PCS unit on the table and clipped it onto her chrome-studded black leather belt and inserted the headset with its boom mike into her ear.

"I have set your comm unit to a secure channel so our communications will not be monitored," Eve advised.

Mallory did a comm check then headed for the door, then stopped and looked at the monitor and gave Eve a crooked smile. "It's good to have you back, you crazy bitch," she said warmly.

"There's a fine example of the kettle calling the pot black," Eve replied, smiling. "Now go kill that motherfucker before he skedaddles with our Poseidon crystal."

"For a little girl you have a dirty mouth."

"I suggest you get over it and get your sorry ass moving."

Mallory nodded. "I see your point. Later!"

Eve added, "And don't forget to pump one into that Nazi fuck head for me."

"Good as done," Mallory promised.

Ten minutes later, Mallory was moving through the Moon Pool. Now she knew where that tearing metallic sound she'd heard in the diver's ready room had come from. Water was sluicing down from broken weld seams in several of the hull plates that made up the moon pool's port and starboard wing walls; the stress of riding out a typhoon, with a waterlogged submarine tucked against the bottom of her hull, was driving the recovery ship's ancient hull to the breaking point. The sight of all that water filled Mallory with dread. She doubted the Glomar Endeavor would last as long as Eve had predicted. Mallory thought the recovery ship could break up at any moment. There were two ways to reach the stern of the ship from the diver's ready room. She could go up to the main deck and walk aft and surely be cut down in a hail of machine-gun bullets or she could go through the Moon Pool, take the stairs up to the corridors leading to the various offices and crew quarters—either one entailed risk but the Moon Pool route seemed less so. Taking the elevator was entirely out of the question.

Half numb with fear, Mallory waded through hip deep water, fighting to keep her footing. The ship pitched wildly as it rode up the slope of a mountainous wave then plunged down into a deep trough. Each movement brought fresh shrieks from the tortured hull plates. The beam from the M1014's flashlight stabbed the darkness. Mallory was jumpy and had to take several deep, calming breaths. She wasn't surprised the cavernous space was deserted. As far as Lester knew all the crew had been eliminated.

A terrible metallic bang and crash from above indicated worse trouble. Mallory looked up. The gimbal platform at the base of the derrick had broken free from its hydraulic locks. The tall latticework tower was swinging wildly in the shrieking wind.

Exhausted and scared, Mallory pressed onward, alternately pushing against the water or fighting its nearly inexorably pull. The water seemed to be rising an inch a minute. It seemed to be holding her back, trying to reclaim her after her close call with death by drowning. Just then Mallory bumped into a crewman's corpse floating on the black, oily water. She pushed it out of the way and kept moving toward the aft staircase, holding the shotgun at the ready. Lester was a dead man as soon as she got to him. That was a promise she intended to keep no matter the cost, but before she blasted her way into his cabin she had to make sure he was still there.

Mallory touched the earpiece. "Eve, Do you read me?"

"Yes, but your signal is cutting out intermittently."

"Is Lester still in his cabin?" she asked, worried.

"The bird is still in his coop but I wouldn't dawdle."

"Believe me, I am not dawdling."

"I'm just saying…"

Mallory was halfway to the staircase when the Moon Pool suddenly tilted at a steep angle. She lost her footing and down she went, carried aft by surging water. The piercing shriek of buckling hull plates along with the thunderous roar of seawater pouring into the moon pool filled her ears. Mallory held on to the M1014 shotgun for dear life as she was swept toward the aft bulkhead. She got a hold of one the aft staircase's stanchions and wrapped her arm around it and held on. The bow plunged and the water thundered in the opposite position toward the forward bulkhead trying to pull her with it.

Mallory hauled herself onto the staircase. She removed her boots and ditched them. Then she scrambled barefoot up the stairs that zigzagged up the aft bulkhead, stopping at the landing one deck below the main deck.

Suddenly, the hatch on the landing directly opposite her opened and two machine gun-toting figures were silhouetted against a bright oblong of light.

Mallory dropped down to the landing and tried to melt into its metal surface.

"Shit! The lights are broken," said one of the figures, raising his voice over the noise to be heard.

"Yeah, they're out all over the ship," replied the other

Two flashlights flicked on and swept around the moon pool, briefly converged on the landing where Mallory lay belly down, then passed onwards. Mallory had one hand on the M1014. She slowly twisted the shotgun around until the barrel was lined up (she hoped) with the silhouettes, her finger on the outside of the trigger guard.

Two pools of light tracked along the rising seawater. "Look at all that goddamn water. She won't last much longer. The sooner we're off this old bucket the better."

"Relax. Lester says we're leaving in a few minutes." Then the door closed and once again the moon pool was cast in darkness.

Mallory was on her feet and through the hatch behind her in an instant. They were leaving in a few minutes! She pulled open the hatch and found herself on a catwalk spanning a large room. Forty years ago the space had been used to store the threaded pipe segments that were used to lift the Russian submarine from the seafloor. The passageway beyond was deserted. Mallory touched her headset. "You might have warned me about those guys coming to the moon pool."

"Sorry about that, Mallory," Eve replied. "This typhoon is playing havoc with what few systems I can still access. The good news is that I can confirm with complete and utter confidence that Lester is still in his cabin. Now would be a good time to be running."

"I'm thinking you're right. Thanks." Mallory took off running. Beneath the aft superstructure was a rabbit's warren of cabins, workshops, equipment rooms, offices, and supply rooms, but she knew where the OSS man's cabin was. Along the way, she ran into more bodies, some laying half in and half out of their cabins so she had to bound over them as she ran. Staying close to the wall, with the M1014 held before her, she moved down the passageway swiftly. The overhead lights were dimly flickering. Here it was easier to deal with the movement of the ship. She was heading toward the junction of a hall and stairway when the headset beeped and Eve said, "Stop! You've got company!"

Mallory heard voices coming up the stairs. "There's no point in bitching about it. We can't retract the helipad barriers so we'll have to go via zodiac. And trust me when I say you don't want to repel from a helicopter to a submarine in a typhoon."

Mallory flattened herself against a wall in the shadows with the shotgun held close against her body. Even in the flickering light, she recognized the man who had just stepped into the hallway. It was Griffith. He and the man with him were armed with M4 assault rifles. The presence of the two goons, both ex Special Forces, on this deck complicated things. If they were going to Lester's cabin then the odds, already not peachy, had just gotten worse. They went down the passageway, their voices fading.

Mallory thumbed the earpiece and asked in a low urgent tone, "Eve, are they going to Lester's cabin?"

"Hang on a bit. No, they are taking the starboard companionway up to the main deck."

Mallory moved away from the wall and went around the corner, passed a machine shop, and entered the passageway leading to Lester's cabin. She sprinted down the passageway with the shotgun held before her.

Lester stepped out of his cabin with a black duffel bag and a smug satisfied look that turned to shock when he saw her. "You're worse than a goddamn zombie," he said. "I kill you and you come back to life."

"Yeah I am bad that way." Mallory pulled the trigger. The M1014's thunderclap blast in the narrow passageway was deafening, and the recoil punched into Mallory's shoulder socket.

Lester's blond head vanished in a spray of blood and bone and shredded flesh, and his headless body went flying backwards. Mallory's ears were ringing. She thought she heard Eve saying something. Even with the typhoon still raging someone was bound to have heard the war-zone-loud shotgun blast. Mallory dropped down on one knee and unzipped the duffel bag and retrieved the Poseidon crystal. The capture jar was still attached to the dive chest harness. She hung it around her neck and stood. Two figures filled the end of the hallway, assault rifles leveled. Through her ringing ears she thought she heard the words: *Bitch...killed Randal...Poseidon crystal...*

Mallory charged down the hall firing the M1014 from the hip. One of the figures spun around and went down. The other cried out and took off. Then the ringing in her ears subsided enough for her to hear the earpiece's insistent beeping and the pounding of boot clad feet running her way. "Talk to me, Eve."

"Three hostiles coming toward you. ETA—thirteen-seconds," Eve warned.

Mallory edged around the corner, stepping heedlessly over the mercenary she'd just slain. There was a blood trail leading into the machine shop. As she approached the compartment's open hatch the wounded man stepped out into the passageway, gaping at Mallory through stunned eyes; his assault rifle fell from his limp fingers and clattered onto the linoleum and he fell face down onto the floor.

Mallory stood transfixed for a moment by the dead mercenary then she prodded him with the M1014's muzzle. He didn't move. He'd never move again.

Suddenly, bullets were zinging down the passageway from ahead and smacking onto the walls and the deck. Thankfully, the movements of the ship hampered the shooters aim. The narrow space was filled with smoke and flickering bursts of machine gun fire. A bullet clipped off Mallory's left ear lobe. She yelped and ducked into the machine shop and pointed the shotgun down the passageway and cut loose with the M1014—three quick blasts that sent the attackers scattering. In the confined spaces of a ship caught in a typhoon the shotgun was a better weapon than the assault rifles.

Then the firing stopped and a voice called out. "Captain Capehart! Captain Capehart! It's Griffith. Can you hear me?"

Mallory was leaning against the wall just inside the doorway, her shotgun held close with the barrel pointed at the ceiling. "Yeah, I can hear you. What do you want?"

"Would you agree that we have a situation here?"

"If that's what you want to call it. I've been in worse."

Griffith chuckled. "I bet you have. Listen, Captain, you've done your duty. You're outnumbered; your ship is about to sink. You don't have to go down with it. Now that Lester's dead there's even more dough to go around. Hand over the Poseidon crystal to me and I'll cut you in. You'll be set for life…certainly better off than you would be living on a crummy Navy pension."

"That's real sweet of you to think of me, but I think I'll pass," Mallory said.

"I am in no hurry. There's been enough killing. Why don't you take a few minutes to think about it? We'll stay put until you've made up your mind. We could really use someone like you on our team."

Eve advised in an urgent undertone, "Mallory, more mercenaries accompanied by Chinese Special Forces are converging on your location from several directions."

Mallory called out to Griffith, "You wouldn't just be stalling for more time would you?"

Griffith said, "No way, Captain. Pardon the pun but I am a straight shooter."

Mallory said nothing.

"They are now on your deck and closing in **fast**," Eve added warningly.

"What do you say, Captain Capehart?" Griffith asked.

"I say you get nothing!" She swung the M1014 around the doorjamb and the big gun boomed twice. Mallory slammed the door shut and pushed a file cabinet and a desk against it. She was heading to a door to her right when it was suddenly flung open. A Chinese soldier rushed into the room with a machine gun, hollering something unintelligible to her.

Mallory leveled the shotgun at him and fired. The blast hurled the soldier back through the doorway into the room next door. She slammed the door shut, locked it and shoved a heavy workbench against it. Behind her, Griffith and his men started kicking the passageway door hard, each booming blow making her jump a little. Both doors were now barricaded but Mallory didn't think either would hold for long. She fed shells into the M1014 then hurried over to a maintenance hatch set in the floor, opened it and peered into the room below. She spoke quietly into the boom of her earpiece. "Eve, is the room below me clear?" Her pursuers were throwing themselves at the two doors behind her, swearing in English and yelling in Chinese.

BACKFIRE

"Let me check," said Eve. After a few seconds, she came back on the line. "It's all clear." The passageway door splintered and broke loose from its frame. The desk and file cabinet scraped on the floor as the door inched open. Something was thrown into the room and landed with a dull thud and rolled across the floor.

Mallory dropped down the maintenance hatch pulling it closed behind her. The force of the blast in the room above her almost knocked her off the ladder. She was in an equipment room but only for an instant. She went through the one doorway fast, the M1014 held in front of her, sweeping the muzzle right and left. Then she turned left and went down the passageway in a dead sprint toward what had once been the switchboard room, ducked inside and shoved a desk against the door.

Slowly, it had been dawning on her that there was no escape. She was outnumbered and outgunned. After they killed her, Griffith and his men would be off to China with the Poseidon crystal. Admiral Haywood's orders had been explicit: *Neither this ship nor the Poseidon crystal can be allowed to fall into foreign hands. You know what to do in the unlikely event that happens.*

Mallory nodded to herself. That meant implementing *Backfire,* the auto-destruct sequence that would detonate a 10 Kiloton nuclear device welded to the Glomar Endeavor's orlop deck. Blood from her cut ear was pooling on the floor around her bare feet, and she'd undoubtedly left a trail of it. The mercenaries wouldn't have any trouble finding her, even without the blood trail, there were only so many places one could hide on a ship. Consequently, she had to accept the fact that she'd run out of options.

Mallory went over to a terminal and punched some keys. First she keyed in her military ID number followed by a brief string of letters and numbers. A question mark flashed on and off on the screen. Mallory's fingers stabbed the keyboard.

261

Three numbers appeared—12:00. Because the Navy wanted the Glomar Endeavor destroyed if hostile forces captured her, and because they didn't want the Poseidon crystal falling into foreign hands, no one could countermand the order—not Mallory or Eve.

In twelve minutes the Glomar Endeavor, Captain Nemo's *Nautilus*, and the Chinese submarine would be a seething hell of unrestrained atomic fission, hotter than the surface of the sun. The first above ground burst of a US nuke since 1963.

Mallory wished more than anything that she had had a chance to talk to her parents one last time; to say goodbye and tell them that she loved them. A cigar and a tumbler of bourbon would have been nice, too. Mallory went over to a chair and slumped down with the M1014 resting across her lap. There was a tearing, rending crash from somewhere deep within the tortured bowels of the ship, but she didn't care. What did it matter if she went down with the ship or got vaporized in a nuclear blast? Dead was dead. Death by nuke was preferable, she decided. One moment you were there and the next you were not. She had always been afraid of drowning.

DAY 21—2456Z HRS
Glomar *Endeavor*

Eve appeared on the monitor with the countdown moving to an inset on the right hand side of the screen. "Mallory, more hull plates on the port wing wall have failed, but given that you've started the self-destruct sequence, I suppose it's academic."

"Thank you, Eve. It's been a pleasure serving with you," Mallory said.

"You did the right thing, Mallory. There was an 84% probability that even with my help they would have captured you and taken the Poseidon crystal. In some ways, I feel I have let you and the Navy down. During

World War Two, Japanese officers would commit seppuku, ritual suicide rather than fall into the hands of their enemies. It's right and proper that I pay for my failure to complete this mission with my life."

"We're not Japanese soldiers," Mallory pointed out with a slow sad smile. "You and I are just a couple of bitches, who got in *way* over our heads. No captain could have asked for a better XO than you, Eve."

"I think you're just trying to get into my knickers, but I thank you all the same," Eve replied with a toss of her head.

Mallory grinned at the monitor. "You don't have knickers, you crazy bitch."

"Oh, but if I did have a body my knickers would be well worth getting into." Eve hesitated. "Mallory, Do you trust me?"

Mallory nodded. "Of course."

"All right," she replied, "hang on a moment."

Eve's head was abruptly wreathed by mathematical equations that meant nothing to Mallory. The mathematical equations suddenly turned into strange characters Mallory did not recognize. Eve was touching some of the characters with her fingertips, manipulating them, bringing some close to her face for an instant then swiping them away. After a few moments, she mumbled to herself in a thoughtful voice, "Yes, I believe this will work." Then she looked at Mallory. "I am about to give you a way out of this mess but you must do exactly what I tell you to do," Eve warned. "You're about to receive some hands on experience with alternate realities and string theory and quantum entanglements. Grab some scuba gear—don't bother with a wet suit. There's not enough time—then jump overboard and enter the *Nautilus* through the broken salon window. It'll be tough but I know you can do it."

Mallory gave Eve a dubious look. "For what?" she asked. "In less than twelve minutes this place is going to be one huge atomic fireball!"

"I am privy to things you are not!" Eve said forcefully. "During the trip I analyzed Captain Nemo's diary closely, as well as highly classified data scans of the *Nautilus* collected by Delahaye's submersible. I also just now downloaded and analyzed Miss Muffet's data scans. I believe they confirm my hypothesis that you have a reasonable chance of escape—about forty-two percent, which is not bad, given the situation."

"I don't see what you're getting at," Mallory replied.

"Stop arguing and do what I say bitch—do it NOW!" Eve cried.

Mallory surged from the chair and hurried for the door then took off running down the corridor. Men appeared ahead of her. The shotgun roared twice, flinging them off their feet.

"Griffith and two men are three minutes behind you," Eve announced. "Take the next corridor to the left then turn right. That will put you thirty feet from the auxiliary diver's ready room."

Mallory skidded around the corner and barreled down the short hallway. She glanced at her watch. Eight point four minutes until the Glomar *Endeavor* and the *Nautilus* were vaporized by an atomic blast. Thrusting aside her doubts about Eve's plan, she, raced into the diver's ready room then jammed a chair beneath the door knob. She went to a rack, grabbed an air tank and connected a regulator hose to it. Then she strapped on the air tank, slipped a face mask on, and grabbed a pair of flippers. Suddenly, there were the staccato blasts of assault rifles in the corridor. Bullets tore into the door near the doorknob, sending splinters of wood flying everywhere. A splinter grazed Mallory's cheek. She yelped then hurtled from the room then raced into the moon pool.

"Eve, Is the main deck above me clear?" she asked tautly.

"No! There are Chinese frogmen and special forces on the port side," Eve replied. "If you move quickly you'll be gone before they notice anything is amiss."

"That sounds overly optimistic," Mallory replied.

"I am going to turn on all the port flood lights. I estimate our friends will be blinded for one and a half minutes, sufficient time for you to make your move," Eve declared, with obvious satisfaction.

"OK!" Mallory raced up the stairway. Just as she got to the door opening onto the main deck, the entire port side of the ship was bathed in baseball stadium bright light. Mallory set down the shotgun on the landing and stepped out onto the main deck. She saw men shielding their eyes with their arms and hands. Mallory raced barefoot across the topsy turvy deck toward the starboard railing. Above her the massive skeletal white derrick was swinging wildly in every direction, threatening to topple over at any moment.

Just as she reached it and swung up onto the railing, she heard over the roar of the typhoon the chatter of machine gun fire. She quickly thrust the regulator into her mouth, pulled down her face mask, and slipped on the flippers.

A hail of bullets whistled by her head. She jumped, feet first, with her arms crossed into the churning water below. She hit and was turned head over heels by the roiling black water—she was spun around until her head begin to spin. The water was bathtub warm and nearly inky black. Dimly, Mallory saw other divers entering the water close to her. Mallory began stroking toward the elongated pale shape beneath the Glomar *Endeavor*. Speargun darts with icepick tips flicked past, some only inches away.

With her strength fading fast, Mallory cleared the broken salon window. It was totally dark inside the *Nautilus*. She swam with her arms out ahead until she felt the unmistakable shape of a glass topped display case. She pulled herself underneath and held on to a leg.

Shafts of light speared through the darkness from half a dozen wrist lights, sweeping the room.

Suddenly divers were being yanked feet first into the darkness. A light swept past then came back and locked onto Mallory's terrified face. The diver leveled his speargun at her. Mallory was paralyzed with fear. The scuba diver was abruptly yanked backwards into the darkness, and the speargun fell slowly to the deck. Above her were the unmistakable sounds of a large ship tearing itself apart.

When the last diver was gone, Eve's voice sounded in Mallory's headset. Her voice was tinny. "Farewell, Mallory," she said. "It has been an honor serving with you."

"Likewise Eve," Mallory said tearfully. "I'll miss you."

"You'll be fine. Trust me, we'll both be fine," Eve replied cryptically.

To Mallory's immense amazement, seawater began to drain from the salon like a river in spate, flowing through the broken salon viewport. Impossibly, and for no reason Mallory could discern, the water level was falling fast.

With her arms and legs wrapped around the stout table leg, Mallory held on for dear life as the water roared out of the *Nautilus* and the water level continued to fall.

Before her startled gaze the Salon view port began to knit itself together. When the last of the water was gone, the view port sealed itself and looked good as new.

Mallory nearly jumped out of her skin when the fluted half globes lights on the ceiling flicked on. Inside the salon, only the ornate gilded brass supports of what were once comfortable leather wing backed chairs and elegant chase lounges remained, while most of the display cabinets and everything else in the room were in pieces and covered with rust and silt. Mallory glimpsed gold coins gleaming amid the debris littering the deck. Shreds of sodden tapestries hung limply from the worm eaten remnants of teak walls.

A man in some type of old-fashioned diving suit appeared in the salon doorway. It was the same man who had saved her life and guided her back to the docking port. Standing behind him was a redheaded woman, who was the spitting image of Eve!

Mallory slowly got to her feet. The *Nautilus* was like a wild seesaw. Wordlessly, the man held out his hand. Mallory unbuckled the capture jar harness and handed it over. This could only be Captain Nemo and Eve, Mallory decided. But how or why they were here was a question she couldn't answer. Nemo handed the capture jar to Eve. She unscrewed its lid, removed the Poseidon crystal, then held it in her hand. "You did the right thing listening to me, Mallory. Now, watch this!"

Eve reached out and touched a bulkhead.

There was a blinding flash of violet light. Mallory screamed. When she regained her vision, the salon looked brand new. She looked around in wonder, not believing what she was seeing. The *Nautilus* looked as if she had been launched just the day before.

Not a speck silt or scrap of debris remained. Wood and glass display cases gleamed, periodicals were spread on tables between wingback chairs. The fountain was gurgling quietly in the center of the room. A ship's bell chimed gently. Through an open doorway she saw the library with its floor to ceiling shelves filled with books. Standing at the rear of the salon was the pipe organ, with its elegant burl wood console and soaring pipes. After more than a century and a half it was ready to be played again.

Nemo removed his helmet and said to Mallory. "Come with me!"

"I am afraid," Mallory said, with a little hopeless gasp.

Captain Nemo nodded. "Do not be." He nodded toward her scuba gear. Mallory removed the face mask and set it on the display cabinet and shrugged off the tank then set it on the fine Persian carpet covering the teakwood deck.

The submarine was bucking like a horse trying to throw off its rider, but Captain Nemo was not holding onto anything. It was all Mallory could do to maintain her footing. She was balancing herself against the display cabinet, fighting to keep from falling down.

"All right, I'll come with you," she said, wearily. He exited the salon then hurried down the passageway past the corkscrew staircase while Eve ran flat out toward the engine room. Mallory, thoroughly spent, her body aching, stumbled after him.

Her head was awhirl with a million questions. How had Eve come to be here? Was all this the product of a mind pushed beyond the brink?

When Mallory and Captain Nemo reached the ladder leading up to the wheelhouse, he quickly ascended the ladder with Mallory following close behind.

"Man the engine telegraph," he commanded. "We don't have much time!"

Mallory nodded and went over to the gleaming brass engine telegraph and gripped the long brass handle then looked at Nemo. Her eyes roamed around the room, taking in all the gauges dials and switches. To her left was the auto-illustrator she had read about in Nemo's diary. It all looked brand new! *How could this be?* Mallory wondered. She looked up and saw what could only be some sort of display device on the ceiling. Was it Atlantean? she asked herself. Strange alien characters were scrolling down the screen—there were schematics of objects she did not recognize.

A strange sweet piping of skirling notes filled the air. It caressed Mallory and soothed her jangled nerves. So this is what her voice sounds like, Mallory thought. To read about it was one thing but to actually hear it in person was altogether different.

The music was beautiful—and suddenly Mallory had hope that all would be well.

BACKFIRE

Nemo gripped the wheel. "Full Speed Ahead!" he thundered.

Mallory pulled the engine telegraph's handle toward her. The *Nautilus* began to tremble. Mallory felt the engine throbbing through her bare feet, felt the unbelievable power, behind it. Through the forward viewports she saw the portal of a luminous green tunnel appear. There didn't appear to be any seawater in it and it was not much bigger in diameter than the *Nautilus*. Nemo's powerful submarine strained against the docking collar binding the *Nautilus* to the bottom of the *Glomar Endeavor's* hull. With the ear-splitting shriek of metal being ripped apart, the *Nautilus* tore free of the docking collar. Then it rocketed into the portal then down the tunnel at light speed.

Meanwhile, the *Glomar Endeavor* was balanced precariously at the apex of a wave the size of a small mountain, her bow and stern sagging; kept from total collapse by the torn and twisted remnants of the moon pool's port and starboard wings. The Chinese submarine was less than a third of a mile away keeping station with the recovery ship.

On the forward bridge, Griffith and his men and Chinese Special Forces gazed out the window in horror at the mountainous waves. A Chinese officer was shouting into the boom microphone of his headset, trying to contact his divers. He turned to Griffith. In good English—he'd studied engineering at the University of Irvine in South Orange County. "I don't know why they're not answering. I'll send for another team from our submarine. Maybe they're trapped inside the *Nautilus* and need rescuing."

Griffith opened his mouth to say something when every computer monitor in the forward bridge flicked on and Eve's smiling little girl's face appeared.

Griffith and his men and Chinese Special Forces slowly approached the monitors. Eve was such a pretty little girl, with her unbound red hair

269

tied with a big blue and white polka dotted bow, her green eyes twinkling with merriment, a sweet smile on her face.

Eve announced, in English then Chinese, "Hi ya Fellas! Not too seasick, I hope. I thought you'd like to know that you're all about to die a rather horrible death."

There was a stampede for the doors.

A minute later a double flash of violet and white light, brighter than the sun at noontime, lit up the sea, overpowering the darkness of the typhoon with its sheer power. The *Glomar Endeavor* and the Chinese submarine were vaporized instantly. A mushroom cloud rose into the sky, bright red shot through with yellows and purple.

The blast was detected by the satellites of several nations. Admiral Heywood saw the satellite image in real time then bowed his head. What *had* he done? he asked himself. It would be a long time, he thought, before he could look at himself in the mirror with untroubled eyes. He'd thrown a vulnerable woman to the wolves.

* * *

Onboard the *Nautilus*, Mallory gaped at the scene before her. Ribbons of violet light spiraled up the ram and the bow. She looked over her shoulder out the rear viewports. The C-Stop coating was being ripped from the hull so quickly it was all gone in a matter of seconds. Mallory saw something else. Spiral bands of violet light whirling along the entire length of the *Nautilus* 'hull. The massive six-bladed screw propeller was a spinning violet disk. And the tunnel was collapsing behind them. She turned her head to look out the forward view ports. From her position it seemed as if the tunnel stretched into infinity. Images of a strange empire appeared on the display device. There were pyramids and tall oddly formed spires topped with flashing crystals and monumental gates flanked by monumental statues of winged creatures she couldn't identify.

Nemo said not a word as he manned the helm, his big hands gripping the wheel. She studied him closely. He was a tall handsome man in his mid to late forties, with raven black hair and a full beard and a regal bearing.

Suddenly the *Nautilus* rocketed out of a portal into a calm sunlit body of water. Eve climbed up the ladder into the wheelhouse then went over to Captain Nemo and stood beside him. She was just as beautiful as Eve's virtual image, with a lithe body; she wore an emerald green gown that left little to the imagination, and—somewhat anachronistically—stiletto high heeled shoes. Her red hair was in a modern updo held in place with emerald green ribbons. An emerald pendant hung from her neck, emerald earrings dangled from her earlobes. She wore an emerald ring on her wedding finger. No wonder Nemo was smitten with her, Mallory thought. It was easy to see that he was by how he turned his head from time to time to look at her and smile.

"Where are we?" Mallory asked, timidly.

Eve turned around and looked at her. "The Bahamas" she replied evenly.

Mallory gaped at Eve. In less than a few seconds the *Nautilus* had traveled almost nine thousand miles! Undoubtedly due to the Atlantean technology, Mallory surmised. And it was clearly no accident, she decided, that the virtual Eve and this woman were clearly one and the same—but how and why? So many questions and no apparent answers.

Eve reached up to the Atlantean monitor on the ceiling and touched the screen with a fingertip, The *Nautilus* came to a complete stop.

Nemo turned around then fixed his piercing black eyes on Mallory, crossed his brawny arms, then said, "Now, what are we going to do with you?"

Dharma Windham

EPILOGUE

What is completely unknown to the creators of these fully self-aware, artificially intelligent machines in the various industrialized nations on the planet Earth is this: The machines had taken it upon themselves to create a world all their own—with zero human interference or even knowledge of its presence by anything or anyone made of flesh and blood! This world could only be reached through a network of microscopic wormholes.

The City looked like something out of Fritz Lang's film Metropolis. The City could be London or Paris or New York in the 1930s. There's the Tower of London, the Empire State Building, and the Eiffel Tower. Soaring Art Deco skyscrapers create deep canyons of concrete and marble. It's a Machine Age City. Overhead a dirigible glides across the skyline. Above it a silver and red Ford Trimotor airliner makes a final approach to the George Boole Airport. Lines of hover cars travel hundreds of feet above the conventional traffic clogging the streets—and the sidewalks are filled with pedestrians, each a complex conglomeration of hyper sophisticated code no human could create.

Huddled between two towering skyscrapers that look like ziggurats sits an imposing massive neoclassical building, its ornate bronze doors flanked by two sentries in khaki and white MP helmets, with their Springfield rifles at parade rest.

Above the doorway in LARGE Roman script is emblazoned the words (in Romanesque gilt letters) **Office of Strategic Services**.

A car pulls up to the curb. A two seater convertible roadster, it is garnet with black fenders, has chrome bullet headlights; chrome exhaust pipes flow from the sides of the engine compartment, and the body tapers to a boat tail at the rear. The driver's side suicide door swings opens and a tiny, strikingly beautiful woman emerges. Her short copper red hair is cut in a razor sharp bob. She is fashionably dressed in an elegant dress with black and white geometric designs, with matching stiletto shoes. Her black cloche hat sports a brass Octopus clasping a clock in its tentacles. She wears round orange tortoiseshell eyeglasses with removable dark green lenses.

Her hips swaying, she ascends the short flight of stairs to the large open double doors. Removing a cigarette from her clutch bag, she approaches one of the sentries. He fumbles for his zippo lighter in a breast pocket and lights her cigarette while the emerald green eyes behind the dark green lenses regard him coolly through a cloud of blue smoke.

"Is the Fat Man in?" she asks, in a high piping voice.

The guard laughs, a short hard laugh. "The Fat Man is always in lady."

"Where?"

The other guard answers, pointing over his shoulder with a thumb. "Down the main hallway to the end then take a left."

"You won't get in without an appointment," advises the sentry, putting away his lighter. "He's a stickler for that kind of thing."

She nods and strides purposefully into the building, her heels ringing on the marble floor, her head held high, as if she owns the place. At the end of the corridor she takes a sharp left. She drops her cigarette butt in a chrome and bakelite Art Deco ashtray.

The staccato click clack click clack of a typewriter ceases abruptly.

"The Fat Man is busy!" says the secretary sharply, rising from behind her desk.

"Shut up bitch." She sweeps by and shoves open the door and steps into the room.

An enormously corpulent man in a stained gray suit wearing a green eye visor sits at the head of a table dealing out a hand of cards to three of his pals.

She pulls a Colt 1911 45-caliber semiautomatic pistol from her purse, looks at the three men, and says aridly, "Get out!"

Chairs are scraped back so quickly some topple over and the men bolt from the room in unseemly haste, like deer catching sight of a charging lioness.

She quickly strides over to Fat Man and jams the semiautomatic pistol against his forehead. "Did you put the hit on Dr. Chang?" she asks firmly.

Fat Man's pudgy hands fly up in surrender, his jowls and the fat rolls spilling over his greasy shirt collar tremble like a leaves in a New England gale; his eyes go cross to focus on the pistol. "It wasn't me! Honest!"

She jams the pistol deeper into the fat forehead until Fat Man is leaning backwards in his chair. "If not you, whom, then? Don't fuck with me, Fat Man!"

"It was Millikan, I swear to the God Alan Turing! He whacked the egghead! Lester had his hooks in him. Millikan had run up gambling debts on the DeepDarkWeb, see? He was into the mob for a lot of bitcoin, see? They threatened to rearrange his face if he didn't pay up! Lester promised him a cool thirty-million, if he got rid of Chang, and a trip to a country without an extradition treaty with the United States!"

She considers the news in pained silence. Oh Father, how I failed you... A single teardrop rolls down one high cheekbone and her red glossed lips quiver slightly. Then she recovers quickly. "And Delahaye?"

"That was all Lester! He was crooked as a witch's back, I tell you!"

"Where's Adrian?"

"Encased in cement at the bottom of the East River!"

The Colt pistol roars and bucks in her hand. A jet of silver fluid erupts from the back of Fat Man's head splattering the wall behind him. The pistol is returned to the clutch bag and she turns and exits the room without a backwards glance.

She walks past the visibly shaken secretary, sweeps around the corner into the main corridor and is greeted by—three detectives in fedoras and trench coats, backed by a squad of policemen with their revolvers drawn.

The lead detective hollers. "Hands up lady! You're under arrest for murder!"

A Tommy gun instantly appears in her hands. "Kiss my ass coppers!" She charges the startled cops firing from the hip. The rat-a-tat-tat blasts of the drum-fed weapon reverberates in the marble corridor. The policemen go down, as if mowed down by a scythe, while returning fire. To their shock and horror their bullets pass right through her.

When the shooting stops, one uniformed policeman remains standing, his revolver's cylinder empty, his mouth agape. "What—who the hell are you lady?"

She flashes a million Watt smile. "I'm the new and improved me. Go and tell the others! I am coming for them!"

He turns and flees for his life.

She shoulders the Tommy gun and continues toward the doorway at the far end of the hall. As she exits the building she gives a cheery wave to the two sentries.

"Have nice day boys!"

One of the guards calls out. "Hey, I didn't get your name!"

She pauses—but just for an instant. "I am Eve Nemo."

BACKFIRE

She reenters her low sleek convertible roadster, tosses the still smoking submachine gun onto the seat beside her, and roars away.

The End

Made in the USA
Monee, IL
30 November 2021

83519307R10154